Double Vision

DOUBLE VISION

HAMELIN BIRD

PIPER HOUSE

10.34 org
3121

ISBN: 978-1-7354891-0-0 (paperback)

PART ONE

Chapter 1

By the time he spotted the canal, Gil Dysinger's front teeth were jammed halfway down his throat and his passenger was halfway through the windshield. In the confusion that followed, Gil would forget all about his former high spirits. Would pardon the fact he'd been cruising for three weeks straight, that he'd stayed high or drunk for most of it, and that in the majority of places he'd visited he'd found some little lady just young and pretty enough and dumb enough to make him a happy man.

There was an awful crunching sound, a sudden wail that filled Gil's ears and drowned out the constant fuzz of rock through the Chevy's static-torn speakers. The truck shuddered once before settling to an eerie pause, and Gil spat a jumble of teeth from his mouth; they struck the floorboard with a snap, scattering like terrified roaches in the moonlight. A terrible throb manifested itself at the center of Dysinger's chest and he grunted, touching a hand to the flow of blood from his forehead, nice and thick.

Damn, damn, damn.

Gil popped the door and tottered shakily on the edge of his seat, his vision blurring and then focusing on the great hole through the windshield. The pungent smell of whiskey clouded the cab, the bottle they'd been passing either spilled or broken, and in this lingering stupor-state he imagined the fumes roiling through the shattered glass, coloring the sky. Freedom.

Stumbling from the truck, Gil turned and saw the Chevy canted at an unlikely angle in the earth, front end collapsed into an accordion in the shallows of a slow-moving canal. Beyond the canal he noticed a sandy knoll—the crest was a silver line in the darkness—and slumped across the knoll a lump of shadow so utterly black it seemed to glow against the night.

He carefully picked his way over, grateful for the full moon overhead. Only, there was some creeping loneliness about the body that slowed him down. A kind of emptiness. He didn't want to touch it, and upon finally doing so with trembling hands Gil understood why.

The face was shattered—as shattered as the windshield itself—its mouth yawning ominously. The nose was not there.

"*Ohhhh,*" he moaned, crumbling to his knees. "*Nooooo nooo…*"

He'd seen plenty of stiffs, sure thing, but none this fresh. None this ugly, either.

Staring at his friend, Gil sensed a terrible surge of anger—a *bitterness,* as if he'd been somehow betrayed. "Cold As Ice" continued from the Chevy's speakers, the music calling to an empty Carolina sky as Gil Dysinger sat lonesomely and wept, sweat creeping slowly through his long blonde hair. He puked. He was in the midst of a second heave when suddenly he choked, face turning to mud until at last the object in question sprang from his throat and onto the dirt. He picked it up, turning it gently in the light.

It was an incisor.

He stood then, did a twirl, his mind aware of the subtle, creepy-crawly feeling of being watched. Drunken logic forced a glance to Eric Latham, his former passenger, eyes wide and glassy and gone, and a slight chill stole down Dysinger's neck. *Nope. Not him.*

Only then did he really look around, taking in the leery stretch of shadows and reddish, almost vermillion tint of the earth. He'd been through these parts before—many times, in fact—and never had the land looked so vast and empty and inexplicably *dead.* So *haunted,* like some, some…

Cornfield from hell, he thought.

Only there was no corn. There wasn't anything.

Gil was alarmed to discover some burgeoning sense of shame in himself, a slow despair rising from somewhere deep inside. That deep place had a name, he discovered. It was called Innocence, was called Childhood. He tried dismissing the notion, had come close to doing so when he remembered the growing pain in his chest. He stood, walked to the truck, walked back. He pulled out his cell phone, and half of it dropped to the ground. Scanned the road…nothing. Only after starting over the knoll did he first hear the sounds—a thousand chickens, whispering against the moon—and staring across the darkness noticed a quaint farmhouse in the distance, the golden glow of candlelight burning softly from within.

He started in that direction…

Life begins at forty.

Polite society would have folks believe such a thing, and for some—a chosen few, Mike Lunsmann suspected—such a lie may actually turn out to be true. It wasn't true for John Lennon, however, and neither was it true for himself. He'd instead replaced this slogan with another, more plausible gem of wisdom—a genie he consulted in his darkest, most private moments:

Death begins at forty.

Mike consulted this truth now, listing behind it all the reasons he had to believe it. Always at the top was the knowledge he was at this age when his wife had thrown in the towel on their marriage. The narrative was written in **bold**, with an *asterisk pointing to the reality that his fortieth wasn't till three months after the fact. He'd spent his Big Day gelling into a barstool somewhere east of the Atlantic, someplace he could really lose himself and not bother coming up for air. The bar was pretty empty that night.

So was Mike.

Four years ago, he'd been a prominent local detective. Known, respected. Then, following the divorce, he'd actually found himself *requesting* a demotion, vying for a neophytic position back on patrol. Not only did the move put him out of plainclothes and back in uniform, but as an added bonus he received a marginal decrease in salary. Yippee. Cakes and ice cream.

His immediate supervisor was a man almost half his age, and no bones about it, he envied the little dipshit. Mike remembered what it was like to be that age, dumb and free and in love. In those days he was young enough to believe his existence was heading somewhere, in some GREAT DIRECTION. He needn't search for the meaning of life because he was sure it would find him. Now what? Now, after all these years, *what?* He'd woken to discover there *was* no direction, no purpose. You were neither heading anywhere nor coming from anyplace, did not stop to ask directions because every path was a dead-end. Steps forward were actually back again, and every step backward a wasted breath that should've been spent standing still, basking in the squalor that was the inevitable stasis of existence.

He'd spent tonight like most nights over the past few weeks, stumbling the cracked asphalt that twisted past his house and into the endless country beyond. Struggling against the bulk of his service pistol concealed beneath a light mid-spring jacket, his legs pumped a tired, chug-a-lug rhythm past the crumbling brick towers which ran along the highway out of town. On these streets, if nowhere else in Hammond, he was free to be himself: a quickly-aging version of the man who used to be Michael Lunsmann. Fat. Divorced. Just sober enough to keep his spine straight and put one foot in front of the other without dropping his bottle of Jack.

Soon the brick towers faded, replaced by a star-dusted sky and soy fields swaying softly in the breeze and a moon that, so big and full tonight, swam down gently over sleeping dogs and the empty silence of screened-in porches. The Harlow Boonies. Mike usually stopped here, his red-rimmed eyes reaching past the stars and into eternity, and either he got the best of Jack or Jack got the best of him. Tonight, it was Jack's turn. Only instead of turning back toward home, tonight Mike took another hard knock from his bottle before stumbling carelessly forward, passing the small sign, half-obscured, which told him he was NOW ENTERING LANCER COUNTY.

With one eye on the moon overhead and the other on his diminishing investment with Captain Jack, Mike strolled the pavement until life made a little more sense and death grew a little more mysterious and he could no longer distinguish the difference between the two. He'd raised the bottle a final time when the first shots rang out, a quick series of snaps that tore like hellfire from the darkness. Mike jerked forward at the sound, the bottle tossed from his hands as he instinctively dove for cover, feet splashing at the muddied bottom of a nearby ditch. His gun was out in a flash, both hands clutching to the butt.

For a moment he lay still, echoes of the shots still ringing in his ears as he waited, waited. Eternity lapsed, and when it was over a second blast came bounding across the fields—not gunfire, Mike noticed, but *screams*: desperate, keening wails which made his skin constrict and grow spikes. The noise of it playing games with his senses as he pulled himself up and frantically searched the horizon, eyes combing the far reaches of the night and every sound and shadow and light, finding nothing, nothing.

The next shot ripped through the darkness. Rifle. Twenty-two.

Abruptly, the screams fell silent.

Mike reached for a cigarette, forgetting he'd smoked his last over an hour before. Dropping his head, he realized one shoe still lay buried in the ditch, the muddied water coalescing into a film at his ankle; he groaned, lifting his leg and climbing to the road.

He stared around, confused. To either side of him, two-lane blacktop dipped in slanted Vs as far as the eye could see. Only some inner voice told Mike there was something not quite right about this road. A gathering of trees shivered softly in the wind, gobs of Spanish moss dipping in ghostly plumes toward the earth. In the distance, unseen chickens blasted their rebellion.

Mike focused on the sound, his eyes drifting far away across the fields. Only somehow the fields had *changed*, no longer green, and what he saw now brought a fresh layer of sandpaper to his skin, resurrecting the ghost of fear within.

Because what he saw out there was death.

The entire landscape was barren, and witnessing it Mike was reminded of all the pictures he'd ever seen of the surface of the moon. No, not that, not the moon…*Mars*. Yes, Mars with its somehow tarnished shade of soil. His eyes turned, shifting toward a cluster of oaks to the west, and looking closer he noticed what appeared to be some kind of plantation house—and something else.

A deep yellow glow, like hearth light, burning softly from within…

For a moment Mike stared, caught in a sudden reverie by the strange, almost hypnotic emotion he felt rising up within: a swirling thing of freedom and innocence and love. He was still wondering what that might mean when something shifted roughly in his gut and a familiar slimy sensation settled at the back of his throat. He tilted forward, struggling for balance when his mouth opened to release a dull waterfall of whiskey and half-digested burger and fries; the second push brought him to his knees. And perhaps it was the ringing of his ears, or the long night, or maybe just an aging man's growing fears of senility, but when he stood and looked around the ravaged earth was gone, along with the house and its oddly tempting warmth.

The chickens were silent.

Mike blinked, clearing his eyes of the emotionless tears which had collected there. When he looked next, the deep emerald fields had returned, the only houses those same low-country shacks still busy growing old. A sudden breeze whispered through the night, stirring softly at the trees and making the fields dance a small dance of delight.

The Harlow Boonies.

He looked down, spotting his empty bottle of Jack in the grass only feet away. His gun dangled darkly from one hand.

Damn it, Mike…

He tucked the pistol back into place beneath his jacket. Shook his head, let out a breath. After a moment, much longer than he would have liked, he drew one sweaty hand down his face and walked over, plucking the bottle from the ground. He stared at the emptiness inside, wishing it to be full, and when that didn't happen Mike turned and started the long couple of miles back to his house, pausing several times to check his watch…and look over his shoulder.

CHAPTER 2

N ext morning Mike woke with a jackhammer headache and the taste of vomit still fresh at the back of his throat. For a long time he lay still beneath the covers, struggling to arrange whatever happened the night before into some kind of orderly account.

Perhaps, he wondered, he'd imagined the whole thing. He'd read of alcoholics who suffered particularly nasty cases of the DTs, some of them so consumed with their hallucinations they'd committed suicide. He'd never worried much about that. Now he wasn't so sure, and that bothered him, as if there were some little man within himself pulling all the wrong levers and turning keys that were never meant to be turned. He hated that little man, very much so. But then Mike had a feeling that little man went by many different names—names Mike knew well—and suspected he had the uncanny ability to hide in bottles and liquefy at will.

It didn't matter.

And sneaky little man or no, Mike couldn't quit the feeling that a quick beer might take some edge off the morning; his body broke into a cold sweat just thinking about it. In the end, he snatched his badge from where he'd left it on the nightstand, had a quick shower and went to slip on his shoes...and found a waterlogged mess waiting for him at the door. He stared down, eyes dancing over the mismatched pair of socks—also soaked—scattered along the floor.

The day was long. Mike cruised his usual beat—down Middle and Styron Streets, off down Courtship, finally completing the run with McCully—wasting the hours, waiting for that soft evening light to finally go fading from the sky. He received the call about Selah Methodist around seven; apparently someone had helped themselves to a couple laptops during the church picnic that afternoon. It was nearing eight—quitting time—when Mike arrived at the old building and, seeing a line of cars along the street out front, let himself inside.

"*Helloo?*"

He peeked around a corner and saw an office setup, with no one sitting at a cluttered desk and a red light flashing on the phone. He could understand how things tended to disappear around this place.

Mike started down the hall and heard a voice from one of the rooms to his right. Standing outside the door, he listened to the voice and the story it described, the tale of a man wandering through the Sahara. If there was some explanation as to how this man found himself in such a tight spot, Mike didn't hear it. But in this story the man, bone-brittle and on the edge of exhaustion, comes to a shack in the middle of the desert. Inside the shack he finds a small jar of water, half full, and beside the jar a pump—one of those old-fashioned, hand-crank deals.

"Now the question is," the voice inquired, "does the man take it all at face value and drink that small jar of water, and call it even...or does he take a chance and use that jar to prime the pump? *Someone* left that jar there, *someone* put the water in it, so you'd think the pump *should* work...right? Drink the water...or prime the pump? What would you do?"

There was a pause then. Mike presumed the people were supposed to be thinking about how they'd handle the situation—if there *were* people; as far as Mike knew, the pastor could be speaking to an empty room, preparing for tomorrow's sermon.

"This is the conundrum that faces the human race," the voice continued. "Many today, and many who've died, and many more to come, are drinking that tiny little jar and they're calling that *living life to the fullest*. And some of us are pouring out what little life we have, knowing it will result in life everlasting."

If...the pump...works, Mike thought, surprised at his own anger. *If it's not all some cruel game, with some naked lunatic peeping from behind a wall somewhere, getting his jollies off other people's misery...*

After that the whole thing got a little too heavy for Mike's tastes, and he went and took a seat in the lobby. He'd decided to step out and have a quick smoke when the door opened and a staggered group—older-types, mostly—moved past him out of the church. At the tail end of the group was a hulking mass of flesh who reminded Mike of a modern gladiator; in an attempt to mask his own size, the man wore a loose shirt the color of coal and slacks a size too big. Noticing Mike in the foyer, his eyes lit up as he made his way over.

"I apologize," he said, his voice assuming a don't-we-know-each-other lilt. Mike recognized it as the voice speaking from behind the door. "Didn't mean to keep you waiting, officer. Our meeting ran a little long."

"Bible study?"

"No, no. Recovery Class. You were welcome to sit in…"

"No thanks."

"Sure. Well, if you'd like why don't we—"

"*See ya Mr. Mills!*"

They turned to see a young brunette on her way out. She smiled broadly and gave a wave, her complexion awfully polished for a church meeting, Mike thought.

"Excuse me," he said, "but are you pastor here?"

"Me? Goodness no!" the man answered, as if embarrassed. "Just another flunky, I'm afraid." He stuck out a hand. "Ryan Mills."

Mike shook it, said his name. He was led down another hallway, this one sporting ornate beach scenes in watercolor—the relevance of which was lost on Mike, but anyway—and into a cramped office with no windows. After shifting a few items on his desk, Mills pulled an armchair from against the wall and motioned for Mike to sit.

"Pastor is awfully bent out of shape about all this," Mills told him, taking his place behind the desk. "I mean, you'd think at a church *picnic*…"

"Let's start simple. When did you first realize the laptops were missing?"

"Picnic was twelve to four, we didn't find the Macs gone till after we'd moved everything back in. I'd say about five? Five-thirty?"

"I didn't notice any cameras on the way in. Did I miss them?"

Mills shook his head. "No cameras."

"That would probably be a good investment, especially for a place this size. A basic closed-circuit system would be relatively inexpensive."

"I agree. Pastor Knowles keeps putting it off, though—probably thinks it's not a necessity, you know, in the scheme of things. Maybe this will change his mind."

"One hell of a wake-up call," Mike told him. "Could've been a lot worse..."

Mike asked more questions, and Goliath did his best to answer them. From all he gathered, at some point during the festivities a traveling Samaritan had entered the sanctuary and raided the sound booth—probably not a member, but an opportunist, someone who took a chance when he saw it and sometimes walked away with a couple of brand new laptops. Best case scenario, they'd pop up minus serial numbers in some local crack house or pawnshop in the not-too-distant future.

He was jotting down the last of his notes when Mike noticed a slight tremor in his hands. He stopped writing, too conscious of the clammy feeling of his palms, concentrating hard on the point where pen met paper. A wave of heat rolled through his body, nauseating. He dropped his pen.

Stop it, Mike ordered.

But the Little Man was calling the shots now, and he knew it. The Little Man could make Mike do whatever he wanted, the Little Man held all the cards. Mike was the Little Man's bitch.

He swallowed hard, waiting for whatever act of tyranny the monster might bestow. Only then the feeling passed, and he picked up his pen and finished his report. As Mike was leaving minutes later, Mills shook his hand before turning to him and in a foreign way saying, "Officer Lunsmann, I mentioned our Recovery Class earlier. *Life Max*, we like to call it. It's geared for those with a history of addiction—drugs, alcohol, whatever. We meet Tuesdays and Saturdays, open to all ages. Maybe you'd like to...drop in sometime?"

Mike studied him a moment. There were no happy thoughts as he did so, his eyes a cold glass, but he quelled the urge to lash out. No matter who you were, after all, business was still business, and this man was only peddling his.

"Could be," he said at last, then turned and walked out into the night. By the time he'd reached his cruiser there were small, obvious rings of sweat around his armpits.

Chapter 3

Lying in bed that night, Mike returned again to his strange hallucination—what else could it be?—in the Harlow Boonies. There was something wrong there, he felt, something essentially oblique about the memory, though figuring what that might be was akin to bottling the wind or grabbing at ghosts. Of course, he was a few beers south of sober at this point, which only served to make things even more blurred and hazy and unreal, and he soon drifted into a fitful sleep. That night he dreamed he was the last living man on earth, searching for water in a barren expanse of red sand.

CHAPTER 4

Mike watched the papers carefully over the next few days, and kept a strong ear to the station blotter, though neither produced anything that helped him sleep better at night. He'd thought long and hard about filing a formal report but, considering the circumstances, could never bring himself to do it. Too many variables. The biggest one was himself.

Three times that week he found himself retracing his steps, each night edging farther and farther into the Harlow Boonies with nary a sign of that distant house with its welcoming lamplight glow. Or was it a house at all? Or maybe just another figment, a little dream summoned by a wet brain?

Forget it, he told himself. *Old hat.*

Only he couldn't forget it, and instead spent the next couple weeks merely pretending it wasn't there, just as he pretended the Little Man wasn't there. Only the Little Man *was* there, twisting his devilish levers, and Mike's days off were invariably spent at home, nipping at a bottle and watching tired reruns of *Debt* and *Supermarket Sweep* or the Squint with Clint marathon on TNT, all the while scribbling compulsively into his journal.

He'd started the journal not long after the divorce, when his drinking had first tipped the scales from social to full-blown sot. He'd somehow managed to keep the Drinking and the Job separate, two distant pieces of a whole, performing the feat so convincingly that anyone who saw the one piece would never suspect the other. The Little Man had spared him that indignity…but little else. He mastered the art of forgetting and learned new ways of feeling numb, burning full-throttle into his madness until one morning he woke from a blackout in the backseat of his car, his feet without shoes and his jacket soaked with blood. Not his own. To this day Mike wasn't sure whose blood it was—he held out dim hope for an animal, though it was difficult to imagine a plausible scenario for it—nor just what he'd gotten himself into, or out of, that night.

Two weeks later he'd joined the local chapter of Alcoholics Anonymous and it was during this time, at the urging of his sponsor, that he began journaling. He got sober and stayed that way. He lost weight. Started to smile again. Gradually, he stopped attending meetings. Then, earlier this year, something happened—just what it was, Mike was still dying to know—and now only the journaling remained from those sober days of yore, his only lifeline to himself.

Probing books of the psyche they were not. Most entries were no more than casual reminders of the day he'd never get back, such as this jewel from the year before:

Tuesday November 12th
Kat,
I guess winter has officially begun, huh? Cold as nippers out. Bad indigestion.

And this, from July fifth:

Kat,
Drunk as a turd last night. Stayed in. Hoping to get some time with Dougie this weekend, but doesn't look like that's going to happen. Maybe next week.

In hindsight, he supposed it was a little creepy to have named his diary after Kathleen. But when he'd first begun the process of putting his emotions into words, a great many of those emotions were tied directly to her, and his earliest entries were little more than unmailed letters to his ex. Witness June of 2000:

Dearest Kat,
When you said you'd fallen out of love with me, I thought that was the biggest crock of shit. No, you could've gone on drinking from my lemonade stand for the rest of your life, if you'd wanted it. But you didn't. You wanted something more than, something besides—something only somebody else could provide. Enter Mr.

Lawyer. Mr. Heavenly Saint From Above. Viola! like magic, sixteen years down the fuckin drain.

Or this, from early August:

Dearest Kat,
You suck

But that was years ago, like ancient history, and nowadays Mike wondered at the point of it all. Still he rarely missed a day, and if his recent stroll in the Harlow Boonies was a prominent feature of what he wrote, soon even this was eclipsed by another of his obsessions, one he'd gladly endured for the past fifteen years.

As his and Kathleen's only offspring, Doug Lunsmann had passed from being merely a shared child to something much more sacred; at best he was an enduring symbol of their successes and not their failures, a reckoning of their love together, of their former life, of the only days that even mattered anymore to Mike. Those days were gone, of course, never to return, yet in some cockeyed way still lived on through their son.

Only now Mike sensed even that relationship was being lost. Following the separation, joint custody had been agreed. Kathleen moved to Clover, shacking up with her new church buddy Bart, while Mike went about the business of selling the house and renting his current two-bedroom, one-bath suite. Dougie stayed in Clover during the week, returning to Hammond on weekends. Times were bad for Mike, but he always managed to hold it together around his son, never allowing Dougie to see just how far into the depths his old pops had fallen, and whenever he visited Mike made a solemn pledge to himself to stay sober. Sometimes he even kept it.

Then Dougie started junior high, and the visits became more sporadic. As his drinking worsened, Mike began to suspect that maybe Dougie's absence had less to do with Dougie as it did with Bart and Kathleen. So he paid them a little visit in the middle of the night and said as much—not in the nicest way—and he and Bart had gotten into a good old-fashioned fisticuffs in the front lawn, during which Mike had broken the man's nose in three places.

He'd been smart enough to ride sober on that one. The brawl hadn't earned him any stars with his superiors, however, nor in the eyes of his son. Soon everything in his life had become a shadow of its former self, and it wasn't long after that Mike found himself covered in blood in the backseat of an Oldsmobile parked well over a hundred miles from home.

Now Dougie was fifteen, soon to be twenty, and Mike feared that shortly his son would be lost to him forever. Oftentimes he felt like no more than a distant relative, a family member visited on Thanksgiving and Christmas but rarely anytime else. And so, on a sunny Saturday almost one month after his fateful dip in a Harlow ditch, Mike readied himself for the long drive to Clover. If all went well, Dougie would be tagging along for the return trip, and they would stay up half the night watching old movies or playing cards or just talking. A hard sell, he knew—especially showing up unannounced— but tomorrow was Father's Day, after all, and Mike found he wasn't above putting the screws to his own son if it meant getting to spend a little time with him.

He left sometime after four, pushing through Harlow and deeper into Lancer County before meeting the first of the bright orange DETOUR signs that led him through a dizzying web of country back roads. Mike took the curves easily, cruising the lane of rural blacktop before finally the pavement turned to gravel and crunched noisily under his tires. He'd made a slow turn onto the old Slocum Road when his view opened on a stretch of idyllic farm-land, acres rushing on either side of him in swinging waves of green; a perfect sky bubbled overhead, cut with sun, whipped with cloud, and for a moment Mike imagined he'd stepped into a postcard.

And yet, as the miles wore on, Mike realized his hands had grown sweaty on the wheel. His mind kept turning to the location of his firearm, and never did its position in the glove box seem quite close enough. Then, as if someone had touched a live wire within, Mike's foot came down hard as he braked to a graceless stop at the shoulder of the road.

He fumbled clumsily from the car, his eyes drawn to the slapdash collec-tion of houses dotting up the road—Jim Walter homes mostly, what they used to call dollar-downs. One, he noticed, had been completely demolished, with only the lone column of its chimney left standing, a narrow line in the sun.

Others were better off, though Mike doubted any would make the cover of *Better Homes and Gardens* any time in the near future.

His gaze stopped on a lonesome two-story set back from the road.

From this distance, he could make out little of the property: columned front porch, small shed off to one side, the lot surrounded by field and sky that shot into eternity and backed by full-bodied rows of spruces, oaks, and loblolly pines. A narrow access road served as driveway, winding through acre after swelling acre of soybean. There was nothing special about the house, not really—another Southern plantation home cruelly rocked by time—and yet...

Mike settled behind the wheel, fishing his firearm from the glove box before absently grabbing for his badge in the next seat. He turned the ignition, struggling to keep the small shakes from his hands as he pushed on through the fields, knowing at any turn the path might vanish and he find himself tumbling into the deep crag of an irrigation ditch.

Two minutes later, he parked the car.

He slammed his door and started toward the porch, reasonably sure there was no one home but putting on a show until he'd at least mounted the steps and put in a few hard knocks at the front door. Just what he would do should that door open, he didn't know. Offer them some cookies, maybe. But that didn't matter, because it didn't open and nobody was home and as far as Mike was concerned he owned the joint. Who paid the mortgage on this place? Mike Lunsmann did. Booya.

He picked his way across the yard, searching for whispers and peering into sheds, climbing atop the dead-and-gone tractor abandoned in some weeds to the west. *Yee-haw.* Up close, there was no mistaking the differences between this house and the one he'd imagined a month before; equally indisputable, however, were those red flares of panic fluttering like cardinals in his chest, those drafty blue jays of regret; restless voices telling him it was *exactly* the same house, only with some fundamental difference he could not quite divine...

A thought occurred to him suddenly and Mike moved to the corner of the house, peeking around the side, half-expecting a hundred chickens flapping their wings or dumbly pecking at the earth; instead, all he saw was a shattered barn with windows to match, a charred fifty-five-gallon drum, a post that looked as if a dog might've been tied to it thirty years earlier.

But no chickens.

He'd turned back to the front when he spotted the truck, an old Toyota dragging a plume of dust through the fields and coming to rest on a line with Mike's battered Olds. A graying man in faded overalls climbed out, a case of Pabst Blue Ribbon dangling—rather precariously, Mike thought—from each hand. Watching him, Mike caught a certain hollow sadness in his eyes, and without knowing why sensed a deep, almost tender pity for the man.

"Howdy," the old man called, the word carrying slowly across the space between them. As he approached, Mike saw the man was even older than he'd imagined, his body collapsing beneath the weight of the beer, his face the substance of dried leather and bad dreams. Two toes stuck prominently from the end of an abused loafer. "May help ya?"

"I surely hope so," Mike gushed, perfecting a dialect more southern than his own. "I seen her from the road and…boy, I just couldn't help muhself!"

Lifting a case from the old man's grasp, Mike turned his gaze to the old Farmall tractor he'd gyrated on only minutes before, its sunken form shrouded by rust and weeds. He stared at it as if admiring a beautiful woman, or an important piece of art.

"She run?" Mike asked.

The man piled the rest of the beer into Mike's arms and for a moment only stared, one hand creeping gently to his chin. He removed his cap and ran a slow palm over the surface of his bald head. "No'sir," he said. "I 'spect not. She been a-sittin' that same spot for twenty years, you the first person ever asked about her. She ain't nothin'."

Mike was indignant. "*Nothin'?* Mister, that's a Farmall 350 row-crop—a *classic!* They don't even *make* machines like that anymore, no sir."

"Well, like I said. Don't run."

Mike waved this away, a small inconvenience. "Reason I ask, my uncle owns a cotton farm down Georgia way—he's a tractor *nut*. Loves tractors *to death*. He's getting older now and, well, I was thinking maybe he'd like to restore something like this, a little project, you know? How much you reckon it'd cost me to lift this off your hands? He surely would love it."

The old man laughed, rearing slowly up the porch. He pulled a key from his pocket and stuck it in the door, and by the time it was open Mike's arms were shuddering from the weight of the Peebs and he was grateful to get out of the heat. They walked inside and straight to the kitchen, which Mike saw was as sparse and lifeless as the old man himself, the floor seeming to dip unsteadily with their weight. He set the beer on the table.

"Name's Porter, by the way," Mike said, offering a hand. "Henry Porter."

This particular pleasantry seemed to annoy the old man; he grimaced slightly, holding out a hand and allowing it to be molested. He said, "Saul Jessup. Pleasure." He moved toward the refrigerator, snagging a case from the blackened tabletop and slowly prying the cardboard to get inside. Almost as an afterthought, he said over his shoulder, "Tractor's yours if you want it."

The words fell on Mike's ears, but they were so lifeless that for a moment they had no meaning, and instead he only stood watching as a bald, jaundiced, and withered Saul Jessup filed his beer into a sparsely stocked fridge and pumped his lungs for maybe the bazillionth time in his life. Just over the old man's head, an embroidered sampler hung by magnets from the freezer door, the words *Forgiveness Is Not Enough* done up in careful black stitching. The smell of mildew cried out desperately for attention. This here, Mike thought, this right here had to be one of the saddest, most depressing things he'd ever seen; he honestly felt like crying.

"That's...that's great," he managed after a moment. He'd forgotten about the accent. "My uncle, wow. He'll sure...he'll love that." Mike lifted two fingers to his forehead, closed his eyes. *What an ass.* "Tell you what, Mr. Jessup. I have an estate auction to make in Canonsburg." He reached down and pulled out his wallet, fishing two twenties from inside. He placed them on the table. "Why don't you hold on to this as a retainer, huh? All right? I'll be back this way sometime next week, how about I stop by and we talk turkey? How's that sound?"

"Sounds fine," Jessup said, not bothering to turn, just stuffing, stuffing, stuffing; if Mike hadn't known better, he might've said the old man was hypnotized. When at last he'd finished and the box lay empty, he shifted a slow gaze to Mike and said, "Sonny, mind passing me that other case of Pabst?"

Rolling down the highway minutes later, Mike's mind was as cold and sterile as a horror movie crypt. He stuck a Winston between his lips and dragged, nice and slow, letting the smoke curl deep down into his lungs and calm his dancing nerves. *Nothing like a trip to the Jessup house to make you want to drive a spike through your eye. Sheesh.*

Still, there weren't enough cigarettes in the world to steel himself for what came next, and by the time he'd reached Clover his pack was empty and his throat was dry and his fingers smelled like an ashtray. He passed an enticing little establishment on the edge of town—THE 19th HOLE the sign out front read—and Mike stared ahead and kept his four tires on the road.

They came to rest on the cemented drive of a fancy two-story with snowy vinyl siding and blue trim. One of the garage doors was up, and parked inside Mike saw a late-model SUV and a hovering collection of kayaks in primary colors. He walked up the steps to the front door and touched his finger to the little orange button.

Kathleen appeared, and after stepping outside they talked a few minutes in the front yard, watching the sunset and hitting all the usual hot spots of conversation—job, finances, the start of another summer. Not because she wanted to, Mike knew, but because she felt there was no other choice, and because it was safer than talking about anything else. For example, she never brought up the booze. She also neglected to remind him it was four years ago this month that he'd come home from work and she'd sat him down and then calmly and systematically ripped his still-beating heart out of his chest. *Oh, that!*

"How's Dougie?"

"Fine," Kathleen said, her eyes searching the trees the way they always did this time of year, hoping for the sight of some rare and beautiful bird. "But I gotta tell ya, Mike, he doesn't go for the whole Dougie thing anymore."

"What do you mean?"

"Nowadays he goes by Doug," Kathleen said, leveling a hand for emphasis. "Just *Doug.*"

"Since when?"

She shrugged. "February? March?"

"Really?"

Kathleen nodded, clicked her tongue. "Says it sounds childish."

"So that's it," Mike said, squaring his shoulders with mock determination. "It's begun."

"What's begun?"

"Our little boy, Kathleen, he's—he's a teenager now. Pretty soon he won't even want us calling him that, he'll be a *young man*. Then an adult! His childhood is officially over."

"Oh, I think that's been over, Mike."

"Yeah?"

Kathleen nodded. "I think so. Doug's been asserting his independence for some time. In little ways, but I've seen it. He barely lets me buy him clothes anymore, now he just wants the money and tells me he'll pick them out himself. He locks his door at night. Last week I was doing laundry and found a pack of cigarettes."

"Cigarettes! He's—*fifteen!*"

"And you were thirteen when you started so I don't want to hear a thing about it."

Mike sighed, disappointed in his son, yet at the same time enjoying Kathleen's company, enjoying it even more because they were talking about Dougie. He was the only thing holding them together anymore, their only connection, as well as the one thing Bart Covington could never take away.

No sooner had the thought crossed his mind than fate served Mike a swift kick to the head, a kick Mike had felt so many times before—wasn't *that* the truth—but one he'd never remembered being quite so vicious.

"*Mommy!*"

He stood silent as the small, fiery-haired girl teetered from the house and then slowly, carefully down the porch steps. A tall man sporting perfect brown hair and a potbelly appeared in the doorway behind her.

"She wanted to come out with you," he said, poking only his head outside. He'd started to close the door when he opened it again and said, "Hey Mike."

Mike waved, managing to do so without biting off half his tongue. "How's it going?" he called, but what he really wanted to say was something more along the lines of *Fuck you, boss.*

But then Bart had ducked away and there was this little bundle of joy, running over and jumping into her mother's arms. She stared at him a moment, tossing around a few syllables and drooling all over herself. And what did Mike feel, looking back at her? Gut instinct told him she was an imposter—they both were imposters, her and old Paps. But then he remembered she'd come from Kathleen as much as Dougie had come from Kathleen, and that if anyone was the outsider here it was him. He didn't like that feeling, and yet it was the most popular, somehow, whenever little miss Millie came around. He waggled a finger at her nose.

"Hiya punkin," he said. "Hey. Hey-hey."

But the child only turned away, burying her head into Kathleen's chest.

"Regular piece of sunshine, ain't she?" Mike asked, and before the words were finished Millie began digging her fingers into Kathleen's flesh, like tiny instruments of evil.

"C'mon, honey, stop that," Kathleen grimaced, shifting against the play-school gropes. There was more to grope there than Mike remembered—a good thirty pounds more—but to him Kathleen appeared as beautiful as she'd ever been, a touch of rose rising in her cheeks and adding a smoky glamour to her deep brown eyes.

"Dougie upstairs?"

"No, he's out with Gary. Should be home anytime, though, I told him to check in by six."

"Gary? Who's that?"

"You know Gary. Northrup."

"Oh, right. Broken-arm kid." The year before, Gary Northrup had fallen out of a tree in Bart Covington's backyard, landed on a five-gallon bucket. "Look, I was hoping maybe Dougie could come back, stay the night with me in Hammond. What do you think?"

"Fine with me," she said. "But I'm not making him, Mike. It's completely up to him what he does."

"Of course."

"I know he'd mentioned giving you a call tomorrow, wishing you a happy Father's Day."

Mike shook his head. "A phone call."

"Don't even start, Mike," Kathleen warned. "He'll never want to spend time with you when you're acting that way."

"What way, Kathleen? Like somebody who maybe wants to see his son more than four times a year? Who wants to spend a little time with him before he's all grown up? Well, pardon my ass. I'm sorry."

Kathleen flashed her finest *please-shut-up* look, doing her best to rock Millie in her arms. Mike rolled his eyes and looked away.

"Well, do you mind if I wait inside?"

Chapter 5

He sat in the living room, being slowly gobbled by an overstuffed couch. The TV was on, tuned to one of those 24-hour news networks. The date was June 14th, 2003: the United States had declared war on Iraq, Saddam Hussein was on the run for his life, and in the small town of Clover the sky looked exactly as it had the day before.

Kathleen, meanwhile, was busy banging away in the kitchen.

"Something to drink?" she called. "Want a soda, or some tea? We only have unsweetened."

"No thanks. All right if I change this? I'm getting sort of depressed in here."

"Do what you gotta do."

Mike grabbed the clicker and found a pretty decent caught-on-tape show. Nobody ever died in the caught-on-tape shows, it was all close calls, near fatalities, things like that. He changed his mind about that drink, and when Kathleen brought it in, he said, "Where's Bartholomew? He upstairs working on some important case or something?"

She handed him the glass of tea. When she spoke, her voice was low. "Don't blame him if he doesn't like you, Mike. He doesn't blame you."

Mike made a face. "What's that supposed to mean?"

"Just drink your tea, Mike, and watch your show. Doug will be home soon. You should've called ahead if you didn't want this to happen."

When the old Pontiac pulled up twenty minutes later, Mike rose from the couch and went to the window. He watched his son clamber from the back-seat and then stand for a minute outside the car, talking to some skinhead.

He said, "Kathleen? Who the hell is that?"

Kathleen emerged, wiping her hands as she moved to peer through the dark venetian blinds. "Jeez, Mike, calm down," she said, turning back for the kitchen. "It's just Brent."

"Brent who?"

"Northrup, I think. He's Gary's cousin. He just gives them rides sometimes, okay? Relax, he's a good kid."

"How old is he?"

"I don't *know*. Seventeen? Why?"

But before he could answer Dougie had climbed the steps and was opening the front door. He walked in, saw Mike standing there by the window.

"Hey Dad," he said, his voice so much deeper than Mike remembered. Hair was longer too. "What are you doing here?"

"Had the day off, figured I'd drop by and see how you were doing. You okay?"

"Yeah, I'm okay."

"Well, come here. Give me a hug."

Dougie walked over and gave his father a hug, a little stiff, then paused to swipe the hair from his face. A little more than four months had passed since the last time Mike had seen his son and he stood back now, taking in what he saw.

"Look at you," he mused. "What's the matter with your pants, you lose your belt?"

Dougie chuckled. "Nah, Dad."

"Oh, hey, congratulations. Your mother told me you got your learner's permit. Maybe we could go for a drive sometime, I could give you some pointers."

"Yeah. Sure, Dad, that'd be cool."

"Well, how about right now?"

"Now?"

"Why not? I was thinking we could drive back to Hammond, just hang out. Stay up all night watching those funny movies you were telling me about."

Dougie looked around, as if suddenly unsure of his own existence; his eyes twisted furtively, shooting out the window and snapping back, never quite touching on his father's face. "Tonight…actually me and Gary were gonna go bowling tonight."

"Oh, I'm sure he won't mind," Mike offered. "Just tell him you're gonna go stay the night with old dad, he'll understand."

Mike smiled, though there must've been something alarmingly grotesque in that smile, something that made Dougie take a subtle step back. In the kitchen, Kathleen could be heard shuffling pans.

"We already had it planned though…"

For a moment Mike only stood there, adjusting his feet on the floor, eyes searching those of his son…and then suddenly he understood. Understood that, should push come to shove, there was no way in a freezing hell Dougie would be making that drive back to Hammond. Not tonight, probably not ever, even though school was out and summer had started and there was no better time. He understood that it wasn't his plans with Gary holding him back—that Dougie didn't *want* to stay the night with old dad, didn't *want* to take the time to hang out with his father on Father's Day.

He understood, and a deep blush settled over Mike's face, swirling, powerful.

Dougie said, "I mean, I hope you don't mind…"

"No," Mike told him. "No, I don't mind. You go on, have fun. Maybe I'll see you sometime before Christmas—but you go on out and go bowling."

"Dad, I didn't mean—"

"That's all right, I know you didn't. Go on out with your friends, Dougie, stay out all night if you want. Just so you have fun, that's all that matters, right?"

Dougie was silent, his eyes gently polishing the floor. When at last he looked up, his face burrowing into that of his father, there was a curious gaze there, something Mike had never seen before, something he didn't like.

"*Whatever, Dad,*" he said, but the words were ice and they were meant to sting, and before they were finished Dougie had turned and hurried up the stairs.

"*Dougie!*" Mike called. "Dougie, get back down here *right now!*" He took off, rushing the stairs, trailing his son down a short hallway and bursting into his room. The place smacked of stale incense and looking around he noticed the many posters hung from the walls, each bearing the name and likeness of some beautiful stranger Mike had never heard of, and a few sports teams he had. Dougie had taken off his shirt and was pawing for another in an open closet.

"What the hell's your problem?"

"What's *your* problem?" Dougie said.

"I want to spend a little time with my son and he's acting like a real pain in the ass, that's my problem. I've barely seen you since New Year's, you haven't stayed over in what is it now—eight months? C'mon, son, can't you at least make an *effort?* What's happened to us?"

"Nothing, Dad. All right? Nothing. I just...I just wanna go bowling! That's all! I don't want to go sit in your stinky old house and watch your dumb movies, okay? I don't want to eat your crummy food. Believe it or not I've got a life too, you know."

Mike could feel a familiar tightness in his forehead, it was eating up his face. He felt stupid. Foolish. Like his head was literally about to explode on his shoulders. Suddenly, Bart appeared in the hall outside Dougie's room.

"Everything all right in here?"

"Get lost," Mike snapped. "This doesn't concern you."

Bart turned and walked away; a second later he could be heard calling Kathleen's name.

"And what's this I hear about you smoking cigarettes? You know better than to go getting hooked on that crap?"

"Okay, first off those weren't my cigarettes, they were Brent's." Dougie found a shirt, snatched it from the hanger. "Second, I've already told you I don't smoke. Besides, at least I'm not off getting drunk, falling down stairs."

"Watch your mouth."

"Yeah, whatever."

"Yeah. 'Whatever.' That's your answer to everything nowadays, ain't it?" Mike shook his head, his gaze floating to one of the beautiful strangers who shared his son's room, her face grinning back at him from a too-perfect world; he had to resist the impulse to rip the poster from the wall.

"You know, just forget it," Mike spat. "Forget the whole damn thing."

He'd turned to walk out when he heard a voice so low and ugly at first he refused to believe it was that of his son: "Yeah, get out of my room."

Mike spun maniacally, bumping a bookshelf and knocking something to the floor. *"The hell'd you say to me?"* he growled. *"Huh?"* He started toward Dougie, who—aware of some unthinking ferocity in his father—had begun slowly backing away. Mike had taken only a few steps when he felt a firm hand on his shoulder and turned, expecting Bart but finding Kathleen instead, her face cartoonishly red, staring at him as if he were some not-so-intelligent creature from outer space.

"Mike, *what* are you *doing?"*

"Oh come off it, Kathleen!" he screeched, now dizzy with anger. "This family has some real problems, you know that? I've had it with the whole bunch of you! You're all crazy!"

He took a good look around, face scrunching as if taking in a bad smell, and was about to pontificate further his low opinion of the house when Millie suddenly appeared in the hallway, her tiny face crumbling to a mess of redness and tears as she ran over, wrapping herself to her mother's thigh.

"*Leave,*" Kathleen ordered. "Just get out, Mike. Please."

But Mike was still staring down at baby Millie, incredulous, fighting the urge to grab her by the shoulders and scream into her face *This is not about you!* Talk about a nice way to start World War III. He'd be immortalized, his bloody head rotting on a stake at the Covington compound for all to see.

Then, in a rare flash of insight, Mike saw where he stood in the upstairs room of his ex-wife's house, his own family and part of someone else's sufficiently alienated from himself, a nice wedge for the years to come. Yes, he realized, the Little Man was at work again, pumping untidy juices through his brain, turning his pliable emotions in such a way that it took an act of sheer will for Mike to turn, to walk out of the room, down the stairs, and out the front door. He did so quickly, twice stumbling and almost making an even bigger ass of himself. Only after hitting the front porch did he realize his flesh was coated in a stiff lather of sweat.

Halfway down the steps he looked and saw the car of teenagers still waiting at the end of the drive, its passengers staring. Feeling inspired, Mike moved past his own car and over to theirs, leaning his body through the open window and coming face-to-face with the skinhead.

He said, "Listen, slick, you better take it real easy out there tonight. This old beater looks like it's about to fall apart, you get the jimmy legs and anything happens to my boy and I'm gonna make damn sure somebody hurts for it."

"Yes sir," the boy said.

"Got it?"

"Yes sir."

Mike walked to his car and got in. He was blocked by the Pontiac, however, and after cranking the engine he reached out the window and flapped one arm, burying the other deep into his horn: *honk! hooooooooonk!*

They moved.

Unsure of what exactly had gone wrong in the past ten minutes (but with a pretty good idea of what to do about it), he pumped the car into reverse and eased out onto the road.

As he passed the car of teenagers waiting to pull back into the Covington drive, the skinhead smiled and flipped him the bird.

CHAPTER 6

The 19ᵗʰ Hole was a lot bigger than it looked from the outside. Plenty darker, too. The extra space didn't bother Mike, however, and neither did the darkness, and after two shots of something brown the place started to resemble a Jacksonville bar Mike had crashed after graduating BLET some twenty-plus years in the past.

Part boot camp, part academic cram session, Basic Law Enforcement Training had marked Mike Lunsmann's personal transition from boy to man. While so many of his contemporaries floundered on that mystical bridge of maturity, coasting one dead-end job to the next, gradually stepping forth into a brave new world of salaries and careers, he'd hopped there in a cool span of just over 630 training hours. The celebration had been a small one, but important, and presently there was little Mike wouldn't give to change this bar now into that bar then, to literally become the man he once was.

Impossible, he knew. But that's what he was thinking as he paid for another couple shots and stared into the distance, his mind cutting back and forth through time like some psychedelic art film from the Sixties. Watching the scenes roll off, wild colors of better times, sounds grown dull by the passage of years, Mike couldn't shake the feeling he was somehow living his very last reel, that the lights were fading, the curtain being readied, the aftershow about to start.

What had he expected, coming out here? A party? Some Carnival cruise? He and Kathleen had it once but they didn't have it anymore—didn't he get that now, after all these years? She'd started packing in with another man, and he'd started packing in with the booze; she'd ran to her lover and he'd ran to his, and both couples were still alive and kicking. His relationship with his son was mush, and after a couple more episodes like today he'd be lucky if Dougie didn't throw in that same towel Kathleen had thrown in some four years before. Just dust off his hands and walk away. *See ya daddy-o, have a nice life.*

Problem was, Mike could no more relate to his son than his own father had been capable of relating to him. Though not mean or outwardly bigoted toward his children, his father had always kept a quiet distance between them and himself, as if they were suspect, victims of some inherent evil. It wasn't like some other families he'd heard about, families where the dad got juiced and played rock'em-sock'em with the nearest available head; families where there was no affection and papa never cried or said he loved you. It's just that his father had approached parenthood with a propriety that bordered on the clinical, and time spent with him was like time in an empty room: there were stories embedded somewhere in those simple walls—had to be—but mostly you whiled away the hours wondering at the wallpaper and imagining what pretty pictures must have hung there once upon a time. The year he finally passed, done in by a cruel cancer planted far too deep in his brain (the tip-off had been the morning Mike's mother found him standing fully dressed in the shower, his clothes soaked through and lathered in soap), Mike knew as much about his father as he'd known when he was twelve years old.

Now he found himself facing these same problems of paternal impotence, though at a different tilt. Not only did he have to finagle time with Dougie because of the divorce, but rarely did he know what to do with that time once he had it. He just couldn't relate. Even as a teenager, Mike had looked forward to one day sharing his great love affair with film, imparting it to his own children with the glee of someone granting sight to the blind: Coppola, De Palma, Scorsese. Kubrick. Tarantino. Oliver Stone, when he wasn't going completely batshit with a lens. Only the few times he'd done so, Dougie had grown listless in the first five minutes, restless over the next ten, and by the hour mark was either deep asleep or else making frequent trips to the bathroom, during which he'd told old pops don't bother stopping it for him (Mike did so anyway). Instead of quality cinema, it seemed most kids these days had grown up on a healthy dose of free cleavage and gross-out jokes. Tits and toilet humor. The worst part about it was, they loved it—absolutely ate that shit up.

Mike remembered the posters in Dougie's room, the ones he'd so clearly imagined himself ripping from the walls. Apart from the one picture of that Spears girl in a midriff top—something dangerously taunting in her smile— he didn't recognize the first one. Who were these people? Singers? Actresses? Adult film stars? One guess really was as good as the next.

And the music these days, don't even get him started on the music. To begin with, most of it was fuzz. Second, when you try and cram *that many words* into a song, the rhymes may flow but melody flies right out the window. Dr. Seuss could do better, and Bob Dylan already did. Where are the Bruce Springsteens, the Neil Youngs, where are the Marleys and the Hendrixs and the Whos? Pink Floyd, now there's a band. Even when it sounded like Eighties porn music, their stuff was still better than ninety percent of the garbage these bands peddled nowadays. Half the kids today wouldn't know a concept album if it Instant Messaged them between the eyes. Didn't have the first clue.

Mike was prattling on about these things to himself, a slew of empty glasses covering the tabletop before him, when he glanced up and saw the bar had gotten quite crowded in the past hour. Even worse, the median age had dropped to somewhere around twenty-five. Some wiener with a dumb-looking beard and some sissy tattoos had climbed on stage and was starting to pick at an acoustic guitar. John Denver he was not, and something told Mike that now might be a good time to see what the weather was like inside his car.

He checked his watch. Half past nine.

Mike stood, and felt an unsteadying rush like something being poured over his head. It was all the alcohol he'd drank in the past couple of hours, hitting him all at once and making him stumble in that familiar way that made him wish a third leg would magically sprout from his ass. With the concerned effort of a man silently defying gravity, he made his way to the door.

Outside the air had grown cold, the threat of rain looming like a pall over The 19th Hole. The parking lot was a mess of garish lights and half-parked cars, and it took a moment of double-footed levitation for Mike to realize where his Olds had fallen in the mix. He walked over and unlocked the door, plopped inside.

Lunsmann, you are officially the greatest man on earth, he congratulated himself. *Your common sense is spotless, your wit unmeasured. Only question is—how are you getting home?*

Mike's eyes flashed to his keys, which he'd unconsciously jammed into the ignition after climbing in. No way was he driving, not like this. He was a cop, after all, an officer of the law. No, what he needed now was a pillow and a bed, simple as that. Somewhere he could just stop and rest his head for a few hours. An idealized image of the Covington residence rose in his mind, teasing, as if some reward he'd unwittingly disqualified himself for; only that didn't make any sense. Even had he not gone bonkers, that was just about the last place he should turn up in his cups; why not save himself the trouble and just castrate himself here and now?

Then he remembered his other option.

Earlier that night, before saddling up at the bar, he'd stopped to a little convenience store not far from Kathleen's. He'd pumped some gas and soiled the latrine and (even though he'd been trying to quit) picked up a fresh pack of smokes. But somewhere between the convenience store and the bar, he'd passed this cheap little motel in not the greatest part of town, and now his mind began calculating the distance and his chances of finding it without any trouble. He was tipsy, yes, but confident he could handle himself well enough to get from here to there with no problem. He could get a few hours shut-eye, maybe a shower and a cup of coffee if they had it, and get back on the road.

Mike started the car, knowing from experience the longer he sat and thought about what he was doing, the worse he'd feel afterward. Because he'd end up doing it anyway, that's the thing—he *always* still ended up doing it. Why torture himself?

Besides, it was just a few miles…

He shifted into gear and pulled onto the highway, making a perfectly calm right turn onto a perfectly normal street. He hadn't gone far when Mike realized he was feeling a lot better than he'd felt after standing in the bar; gone was the dizziness, the uneasy feelings of sadness, the paranoia. He was on the road and his vision was clear: somehow it didn't make *sense* for him to go and stay at some stuffy hotel with its diseased-up pillows and raggedy carpet, when he could just as well drive the distance to Hammond and sleep in his own bed. It was fairly late, after all. And thanks to the detour, most of the drive would be country backroads anyway, lonely stretches of pavement where he would be more likely to harm himself than anyone else—not that he *would*, of course, but hypothetically. Why hold himself up?

It just *didn't make sense.*

Invigorated by these insights, inspired by their calm grasp of reality, Mike found a good place—a quiet place—and got himself turned around. He pointed his hood toward home and then felt his foot go heavy in the darkness of the floorboard below.

He'd gone thirty miles when the rain broke, crumbling the sky into a thousand sheets pounding ruthlessly at his windshield. He struggled to roll up the windows, first his own and then, slowing to a crawl, that on the passenger side; as he did so, he missed the small sign at the side of the road, as well as the larger one a little farther along:

WELCOME TO LANCER COUNTY

There was little fanfare to the sign itself: no smiling, waving white people, no children in swing sets or birds cutting through a cream puff sky. Just black letters on a whitewashed board, the sign zooming like a quiet phantom past his car and into an even quieter eternity in the darkness behind.

Then the windows were up and Mike stared out past the exploding rhythms of the rain, past the feelings of being alone, the only man left on this great dying earth. He pushed on, his speed dipping from twenty miles an hour down to ten, then to five, as the rain thrashed around him, splattering his roof and hood and the glass in front of his face; and yet there was something oddly comforting in it all, something that for the moment clouded his actions of earlier that night, pushing them far, far away.

Then, as quickly as it had come, the storm lifted.

The rain fell away, its rippled curtain yanked once and for all to the earth, and Mike offered quick praise to the God of his youth—a simpler, more Catholic version of the one to which his former wife prescribed—before cracking a window and letting the wind blow in waves over his face. "Ah," he groaned, as it whipped and swirled and twirled. "Ah, ah."

He was still basking in this simple glory when something caught his attention through the windshield and he braked fiercely, his face staring slack-jawed at the picture straight ahead; a few more seconds and he would have been a *part* of that picture instead of merely an observer, and for once in his life he actually *wished* he was hallucinating, that the Little Man was pulling another of his notorious pranks, pushing his mysterious buttons.

Only he wasn't, and Mike knew it.

He reached down and retrieved his cell phone, held it in his hands. Staring at those tiny green digits, as if the numbers themselves held some cryptic message for the future. Finally he lifted his thumb, started to dial…then stopped, as if suddenly realizing what he was about to do, and placed the phone on the seat to his right. The thought occurred to him that he could drive away, simply pull off and never look back.

He opened the door and got out.

"Hello?" he called.

In the absence of rain the road seemed unbearably quiet, neither his own motor nor that of the old Chevy spoiling the sanctity of the night. The bed of the truck was canted skyward, as if in defiance, the words THE SOUTH WILL RISE AGAIN scrawled in fiery script along its rusted tailgate. Then Mike saw the front end and heard himself swallow, realizing with sudden dread that a fatality was not far off, sprawled in the dirt or better yet scattered in juicy pieces around the truck, devilish manna from the gates of hell. The angle was bad enough, but that large hole through the windshield told an even uglier story, a grisly tale Mike was in no shape to hear.

Making his way around the truck, he saw the driver's door was open—a good sign—but when he came to it, the seat was empty. Something caught his eye in the cab and he reached inside, prying an object from the shadows of the floorboard and turning it in his hands. It was a bottle of Seagram's, cracked near the neck, and though he'd later deny it Mike's first hope was that there'd be something left there for himself, something he could take and hide away in some private part of his bloodstream. In reality there was nothing of the sort, and so he tossed the bottle back and that's when he noticed the other objects in the floorboard, small but no less significant. He picked one up, studied it, realized it was a tooth, and then dropped it, cursing as he backed away from the cab.

Mike panned the horizon, having seen such collisions and knowing the combustible force of earth-meets-car. But whatever had made that gaping hole in the windshield had either crawled away or been carried—it hadn't walked, that much he knew—and though he scanned the ground for tracks, there were none to be found. The rain had stopped completely now, and by some miracle he looked to see the moon full and shining overhead, lighting up the night like the bulb of some impossible Christmas tree.

An anonymous call, he reasoned. *That's all it would take. A quick call to alert the authorities and then he could be on his way.*

He stumbled back to the Olds, snatching his cell phone from the seat. He dialed the numbers and put the phone to his ear. When the female voice came on—*We're sorry, you've dialed a number that has been disconnected or is no longer in service, please hang up and try your call again*—Mike did as he was instructed, only to receive the same helpful message. He tried a couple other numbers, all with the same result, then barked and tossed down the phone.

Calm down, he told himself, *be cool,* he told himself, but he was neither of those things and the more he tried to be them the more pissed off he became. *Damn it Lunsmann, you're an officer of the law! Your mind may be wasted on juice, but somewhere someone is dying. Wasted or not, it's your duty to do something about it. So stop dicking around and do it!*

He thought hard, and when he was done thinking he'd somehow convinced himself there was a bit of something at the bottom of that bottle after all. Mike made his way over, searching once again for the bottle of Seagram's and finding it just as hollow as before. He hurled it back into the cab and heard it shatter inside, listening as echoes of the clatter rang out over the hills, lonesome and empty and...

Dead.

He glanced up then, his mind registering fear and a sudden dark intuition of where he was; for a moment he stood gazing at the hill beyond the truck, that ominous red-tinged hill, staring, knowing and not wanting to know. A line of spittle spooled down his mouth, gleaming softly in the night.

Mike moved to his car, popping the glove box and snatching up his gun. Found his cell phone, tucked that in his pocket. Finally he crossed the shallows of the canal and then wobbled up the moonlit hill, drawn there by some inescapable emotion too quick and deep to be named. He crested the hill and gazed out, the image of what he saw stealing over him like a ghost from long ago, forcing from Mike a deep groan that did not touch his ears.

He started forward across the sand.

Clouds of greying moss dangled from the limbs of distant trees, twitching with a hint of breeze that simply wasn't there. Staring across the wasteland, Mike noticed large shadows spotting the terrain—silent monsters lurking in the darkness—but what he first thought were monsters he now realized to be the remains of distant crumbled vehicles, their tires wasted away and chassis long destroyed by the gaze of time.

He kept forward, glancing occasionally over his shoulder and finding only his own shadow, always at his side. His lips turned dry, and no sooner had those first whispers of wind touched on his face than they were suddenly ripped away, dancing out to the trees. Mike sensed a rising subtle tightness in his belly, a sweaty, coiling thing that clenched and wound like some grimy intestinal knot and then—

He stopped.

The house itself stood spotless, immaculate, exactly what one would expect of a charmed Southern farmhouse; a portico towered overhead, steadied by thick Doric columns that gave the impression of stone rather than wood. The portico's roof, he noticed, was lined with a kind of balustrade and served as an open balcony to the second floor; from here three windows peered down darkly from above. Mike caught a glare of something in one of those windows, an object he couldn't quite make out in the darkness. Stepping closer for a better look, he sensed sudden movement at the side of the house and, not missing a beat, snapped up his pistol and took aim.

A pair of chickens bounded away in a flurry of wings.

Mike followed, and turning the corner found himself in another, more fertile part of the yard. Patches of grass rose and then vanished in the soil, leading to a dense thicket of brush and trees, their limbs turning jagged corkscrews to the sky; a roaming band of chickens grazed for as far as the eye could see. Mike approached a twisted oak at the side of the house, and planted near its trunk saw a shabbily-formed tombstone, a scrabble of briers reaching up its side, and etched within the face of stone the words FORGIVENESS IS NOT ENOUGH.

What does that even mean? he wondered, and that's when he noticed them, two slender shadows suspended from the branches above. He moved closer, his eyes dropping down the pair of ropes fastened to the tree and settling on the knotted bunches of moss where the shadows hung. Only then the full moon shifted behind some clouds and there seemed to be a horrific mess of features hidden somewhere beneath that moss that wasn't moss, features that might've seemed almost *human* had there been a nose there instead of some jagged rag of skin. Again the shadows turned, kissed by the wind, and now Mike saw their eyes, now he saw their naked bodies and their cold dead hands and realized he was staring at two hopelessly deceased bodies strung from two nooses on a dark oak, their skin lacerated and flayed and gleaming slickly in the darkness.

He jumped back, one hand drawn to the comforting bulge of his Glock.

He swept the area, still backing slowly, slowly to the brush at the side of the house when he stumbled and caught himself and, glancing down, saw a scattered tangle of bones in an area previously covered by chickens.

A medley of overdone horror movies flashed through his mind—inbreds chowing on human barbecue and degenerates making lampshades out of peoples' heads—and, as if some cruel god had heard these thoughts and was now delivering on their promise, a sudden explosion boomed across the night. Mike spun, staring in wonder as a brilliant flash of neon lit up the darkness. Then as quickly as it had come the flash was gone, settling instead to a low, gold-burning flame in an upstairs window of the house.

Almost like hearth light…

He stared, gulping down its radiance like the water of life, and instantly was transported to a simpler time; there was no worry there, no stress, his existence a blithe continuum of serenity. It was, he thought, like the garden of Eden: *innocence* and *joy* and *freedom from fear*.

Mike began slowly inching from the brush…

He'd started out of the shadows and into the light when, suddenly, he stopped.

Without putting it into words, something deep inside told him that, while ostensibly a salve to all the anguish he'd ever known, there was something *wrong* in that light as well, something beyond devious. Mike wasn't sure what would make him think such a thing, but then as a cop he'd learned to ignore such feelings at his own peril. Soaking in the last of its flickering golden haze, Mike swallowed hard…and looked away.

His eyes landed on one of the grisly forms still dancing on air, its wizened buttocks gleaming bright against the moon. One hand fumbled through his pockets, revealing his cell phone, and when the woman's voice rose in the receiver—*We're sorry, you've dialed a number that has been disconnected or is*—Mike slammed the phone closed.

With furtive ease, his eyes slipped back to the light.

Again he started in that direction, only to be frozen by the appearance of a strolling figure atop the shadowy balcony ledge. Mike sank back, watching as the figure stalked back and forth, the moon casting soft light over his features: young, muscular, chin like a mason jar. Crew cut. And dangling from a strap over one shoulder: the thin line of a rifle.

A twenty-two.

Mike gripped his pistol, wondering at his chances of hitting the bastard from where he'd settled beneath the oak. An easy enough shot under normal circumstances, but these were not normal circumstances and Mike was too drunk to count on anything, least of all himself. Before he could act, however, Mike noticed the eerie patience of the stranger on the ledge, the subtle exuberance of every slow breath as he quietly watched the sky, as if fully expecting it to open and hand him a prize. For a long time he leaned over the railing, staring at nothing in particular across the barren plains below.

He was a quiet man, Mike mused, *kept mostly to himself…*

Only then the figure stopped, his chiseled face turning, dog-like, as if tuned to some unknown frequency. Lifting the rifle in one hand, he walked over and readied himself on the ledge, his barrel positioned just so on the balustrade. Watching him, Mike sensed an icy breath touch over his heart as the man delicately peered through the rifle's sights, an ancient snake-wisdom lighting up his eyes. The stranger's lips mouthed one slow, silent word.

Pow.

No sooner had the word been spoken than Mike heard a sudden rush of sounds, all hoots and laughter and distant motors in the night. Nice and slow, he edged carefully around the oak and, peering out, saw what appeared to be a pack of four-wheelers speeding across the plain, its riders hopping ecstatically as they gunned the engines and roared toward the house.

Then came the shot.

Mike watched as the first rider, a dark-skinned teenager, tumbled back and hit the earth, his four-wheeler spinning wildly ahead of him before crawling to a halt. The next shot easily took out the passenger of a second ATV, though the driver—a man-child of heft and sweat—turned a swift donut, spitting up sand as he sped away.

Without thinking, Mike started from the shadows; from where he stood, he could see a near-perfect profile of the shooter, his doofy crew cut and big floppy ears. The next shot rang out, only this time Mike didn't look to see where it landed—he straightened an arm, leveling his Glock at the stranger's head. The screams had started by now, raw and clamoring and fierce, but Mike pushed them away, they weren't important.

One shot, that's all it would take.

His finger tightened on the trigger.

One shot.

He focused, eyes blurry but fingers willing, and then from one corner of his brain the world abruptly forced its way in—the approaching rumble of an engine. He paused, hesitated, then at the last second turned to see the dark shape of a four-wheeler careening toward him, out of control. He dove to avoid collision, but a little too late, and the ATV struck him awkwardly at the waist, knocking the gun from his hands and plowing past him into the oak.

Mike groaned, struggling to his feet. Moonlight washed down over him, exposing him like a roach on bathroom tile, and as the rifle popped off its tune and distant screams pierced the night, Mike retreated softly to the shadows. Stumbled past the four-wheeler, still idling lazily against the tree, and over to its rider, who had been thrown a good eight feet into darkness. Like the others, he was young—no more than eighteen—and turning him on his back, Mike saw his shirt was saturated with bright arterial blood, his hair spattered with an oily blackness deeper than any shadow. Tears rimmed the young boy's eyes.

"*Easy*," Mike whispered. "*Hang in there son, be still...*"

Beyond the trees, Mike heard more shots from the balcony; one by one the distant screams faded.

He grabbed the boy, lifted him in his arms.

If they reached the far side of the thicket, he reasoned, then it wouldn't be much farther to the pocket of forest he'd noticed bordering this little hell. With the trees as cover they'd circle back to the road, which they'd then follow to Mike's car (which, come to think of it, he should've never left in the first place). Wasn't full-proof—no plan was, after all—but under the circumstances, it would have to do.

He'd started forward when the boy groaned loudly, struggling in his arms; Mike ordered him quiet and kept forward through the grove, pushing through the darkness. He'd made it all of five yards when the shots rang out—four in quick succession—and abruptly Mike felt the sharp fire of pain exploding up his arm.

He collapsed, the boy spilling from his arms and falling flat to the earth.

More scattered shots rang out, shots fired for the hell of it and without aim, and Mike noticed a flip of something to his right, saw the boy's sneaker split and begin pulsing with a well of deep, oily-looking blood.

For several moments Mike lay there, perhaps three feet from the boy, perhaps four, hearing his screams and knowing that soon the stranger would be here and what would Mike do then? What *could* he do? His gun had been lost. He'd been shot.

He twisted in the sand, pulling himself along until he'd found a covert hideaway in the brush, somewhere with enough coverage and shadow to maybe give him a good chance at jumping the bitch when he came. By the time distant footsteps arrived through the brush, however, Mike had reached an almost meditative state, his body cold, mind numb to the outside world. He was sweating, and somewhere in the sweat he smelled the bitter tinge of alcohol.

Then a voice in the darkness.

"*Well well, lookee here. The one that got away...*"

Lying on his stomach, Mike peered ahead through the mesh of trees and watched the stranger strolling over, watched him stopping casually over his prey; even from here Mike sensed his coldly commanding presence: stolid, imperious.

"*How you feeling, champ? Not too good, huh?*" He smirked, scratching absently at his lantern jaw. "*No, I don't guess you are. Your buddies, uh…they're not so hot either.*"

He squatted down next to the boy, elbows balanced on his knees. Again Mike sensed that ancient snake-wisdom and, without realizing it, indulged a lowbrow fantasy of what he wouldn't give to have his gun now, to blow that sleazy little grin right off. *Pow, you twisted son of a bitch.*

"*Y'know, it never gets old,*" he said, speaking with the honest wonder of a mental patient. "*You think it will, you know, eventually. But then you get out here and guess what? It really feels just like the first time, never fails. Ain't that nuts?*"

The boy tried to speak, couldn't. A trail of darkness formed a slow line down his face, as if drawn there by an invisible finger dipped in ink. He coughed once, spraying a small fountain of blood that spilled back, spattering his face.

The man removed a handkerchief, dabbing gently at the boy's mouth.

"*What'd I tell you about that? You'll never get a date going out of the house like that, understand? Here, let me help…*"

Then, as casually as he'd slid the handkerchief from his back pocket, the man withdrew a large fixed-blade knife and thrust it smoothly through the boy's neck, abruptly choking his cries. There was a momentary gurgling, like the slurping of a kitchen sink, and the knife was removed, its blade shaded black against the moon.

Finally he grunted and quietly tucked away the knife, his demeanor blackened in the wake of another, more mysterious emotion. Gloom settled, sadness prevailed. He muttered something then—*peckerhead* is what it sounded like—but the words were empty and his eyes were soft and he was staring off into a time and place that wasn't his own, some little hole he'd watered at often in his life. When it was over the man stood, reached down and grabbed the young corpse by his feet, and began slowly dragging him away into the night.

But by this time Mike was far too gone, his fragile soul numbed with a cruel overdose of booze and terror and the damning knowledge of a bullet buried deep in his arm. And as the figure faded, becoming one with the darkness, Mike urged a silent prayer to any god willing to listen to a man with absolutely nothing to give. What would it take to make it through this night? To have just one more chance to make his life worth anything at all?

What would a thing like that *cost?*

Mike closed his eyes, caught up in the sensation of floating in a world of his own creation, a living hell where second chances were hard to come by.

And even harder to hope for.

PART TWO

CHAPTER 7

Being fifteen was probably the most frustrating thing Doug Lunsmann had ever experienced. It meant he could drive; but only with "adult supervision." It meant he was old enough to make his own decisions; but still too young to be trusted to make the right ones. *Hey, here's a crack rock. Think I'll smoke it. A little porn before bedtime? Don't mind if I do.* It meant his biggest character flaw was his own virginity, and that oftentimes he found himself wondering what life would be like when he was free and eighteen, or even—let's not get *too* crazy here—twenty-one. Crazy. Impossible.

And when it came to his mother, it meant she'd begun looking at Doug as if he were some disturbing mutation of the sweet child she'd known and loved her entire life. *You've gone Frankenstein,* that stare said. What's worse, he *felt* like Frankenstein; many times in the past year he'd felt like crying for no reason at all. His voice got squeaky at the worst possible times—like the other day around that hot chick at Target—and he'd become so self-conscious of the way he walked that sometimes he felt mental and imagined himself tripping on thin air. Ridiculous.

Then there was the hair. WTF, God? He'd been so embarrassed by the uneven scribble on his face that he'd shaved it off, only for a strawberry patch of pimples to sprout up in its place. Any minute now he expected a bush baby to come bounding out of his armpit. And his pubic hair, forget about it. Someday in the near future he was sure to wake to the headline WORLD CONSUMED BY DOUG LUNSMANN'S BUSH.

Of course, there were certain perks to his monster as well. Never had he had so much fun in the shower, for example. And though he'd always appreciated the kinship and sensitivity of the opposite sex, Doug's eyes had suddenly been opened to a world he'd not have believed only four years earlier. If sex was still a mystery to him, he'd at least mastered the concept of physical attraction, and mastered it well; it was as if his mind had been uploaded with some dangerous new program, as ancient as time itself. In the presence of females, his hands wanted to go places they'd never wanted to go before, his eyes performing sudden dips and stares, and somehow this felt right, meant to be. A simple kiss, he was sure, could bring him to his knees. Thanks to the program, Doug Lunsmann had entered the next turbulent phase of his existence: a phase of perpetual agonized bliss.

And yet, just as his body was drawn as if by magnetism to all the hotties of the world, at the same time it was drawn away from all the parents, the authoritarians—and, in fact, most adults in general. Like Brent, at last he'd reached the conclusion that thirty years on this planet was enough to drive even the most free-spirited person insane, shaving the rough edges until those little pegs fit just so into the world's curriculum. Past that, nobody seemed to be having much fun anymore, nobody seemed to care. They were like zombies. Yeah, frickin' *zombies*.

He climbed sluggishly from his covers, threw on a robe and then stumbled down the hall. After showering he slipped into some jeans and made his way downstairs, where he found his mother hovering at the kitchen table, a newspaper perched in one hand. Millie sat propped in a chair to her left, turning a meal into something that would have to be mopped up.

"Morning, hon," Kathleen said. "Breakfast is in the microwave, just zap it a little."

"Thanks, Ma. Where's Bart?"

"He's upstairs, getting dressed. We're going yard saling. Wanna come?"

Doug felt a flash of heat in his forehead. "Yard saling? Mom, I thought we were gonna look at *cars* today? Remember?"

"We are."

"Well...*when?*"

Kathleen placed the newspaper on the table, looked up. "We'll go as soon as we get back this afternoon, okay? I promise."

"Sure we will," Doug said, turning and jamming the button on the microwave. "Millie ain't gonna want to do that. She's just gonna be crying the whole time, wanting to go home."

"No I'm not!"

"Yes, you are. You cry about everything."

Millie whimpered softly. "No, don't cry about everything…"

"Listen," Kathleen said, "if you don't want to wait, then why don't you just ride with us and we'll go looking through Winterville on our way home? How about that?"

Doug snatched his plate from the microwave, slammed the door. "No thanks," he said, and made a beeline for the living room. He switched on the TV to an episode of *Aqua Teen Hunger Force*, but he'd already seen it about six hundred times and so ended up watching an infomercial for this little machine that could shrink-wrap all your old food. Amazing.

Five minutes later, Doug spooned down the last of his eggs and closed his eyes.

From the kitchen, he heard the sounds of his mother rustling the paper and sipping her coffee and Millie making baby noises at the table. Parents could be such frickin' idiots sometimes. They'd tell you one thing, then turn around and do exactly what they wanted—and woe should you question their ever-perfect judgment. It was ridiculous.

Still, if he ever expected to get a car…

He tucked his plate in the dishwasher and slowly walked over, kneeling next to his sister. Purple jelly shown smeared over her lips and down her chin, but Doug didn't think the jelly was gross, he thought it was cute.

"Hey Millie?" he said. "I'm sorry about what I said. I don't think you cry all the time, okay? Please don't be mad at me?"

"Not mad," she said.

"I love you."

"Love you, Dougie."

He tousled her light auburn hair—it would be red by kindergarten—and gave her a little kiss, careful to avoid the jelly. When he looked up, his mother was peering at him over the paper. Peering in a good way, he hoped, but with mothers you could never be sure.

"So," he asked, "what time are we leaving?"

Hours later they'd visited three different lots, though it seemed each was in cahoots with the others, all engaged in some obscure power struggle to see who could scrap together the largest pile of automotive crap in one half-acre lot. There was a separate irony concerning the intelligence of the salesmen, all mid-forties with slick or balding hair and buck-teeth; ostensibly interchange-able, each truly was one-of-a-kind.

The first lot had been a bust, though the second offered a Honda that caught Doug's eye, starry-sky blue with tinted windows. The salesman in-dicated the interior needed "a little work," and by lot two—Jim Bug's Auto Sales—even Doug had learned if a salesman indicated anything it was only because they had to, and that the problem was usually buttloads worse than they'd let on; in short, that this was probably not the car for him. Sure enough, "a little work" quickly turned to "a lot of work" as soon as they opened the door and saw the utterly ragged-out seats, the tattered floorboard and slyly foreboding roof.

No wonder the windows were tinted. *Pass.*

"Are you sure?" the salesman asked. "Wouldn't take much to turn this one around. Six grand, plus tax and tags?"

Bart said, "Six grand, are you kidding? Look at this. Look at those *seats*. Who was the last person to ride in this thing—Edward Scissorhands? Looks like a grenade went off in there."

The salesman only laughed, his pick-up stick body swaying like a reed in a hurricane. "Well, I—wouldn't know, sir."

"I didn't expect you would. We aren't interested. Next car."

No matter how many next cars there were, however, it seemed they'd all been groped by the harsh fingers of the past—and a few of them slapped silly. Ironically, it was Doug who'd first grown listless, then bored, and finally grown more interested in borrowing his mother's cell phone than shopping for a ride (one other thing about being fifteen: in the Covington house, it meant you'd have to wait one more year before having your own cell phone—an endlessly bogus concept, Doug felt). Bart managed to drag him to one more lot before calling it a day—a silly little shop whose only sign read simply CARS—but by then everyone was tired and dronish and complaining at the heat. Everyone except Millie, of course, who was busy napping in the backseat, ensconced in a cool world of air conditioners and steady beach music.

They'd been home less than an hour when Brent Northrup rolled his Pontiac into the Covington drive, honking his horn twice. Ever since school had let out three weeks earlier, weekends were something of a stressful time for Doug; it was bad enough having to deal with his mother all week, but with Bart haunting around it was near impossible just to breathe outside of his room. Although his stepdad had never broached the subject, Doug was increasingly paranoid of being asked to do menial work around the house: mow yards, wash clothes, crap like that. And what would Doug say? No? Sorry? Suck my fatty old man? In this department he'd found the best cure was prevention: if he didn't know how to handle a situation, the trick was to not put himself in that situation. And the best way to do that was to get out of the house.

Besides, tonight was special.

It was special because Brent's parents were away for the weekend, had left for Virginia Beach the day before, and because Brent had orchestrated a small get-together in their absence. Nothing crazy, not the party of the year, but there were going be some high school girls there and—as long as they stayed out of the way and didn't act too stupid—Brent had promised to let him and Gary stick around...maybe even stay the night.

"So where's this great car of yours?" Brent asked, socking Doug's arm as he climbed in. "I thought you've been looking all day, where's it at? Huh?"

Doug buckled his seat belt, shook his head. "Don't ask."

"Why? You gonna start crying?"

Doug grinned in spite of himself, waiting until they'd backed out and were safely down the road before lighting up his Newport. He breathed smoke and said, "Suck my fatty, old man."

Brent was an older kid—old enough to drive, to buy skin mags and cigarettes, even old enough to break curfew and get away with it. He wasn't the absolute smartest person Doug had ever met, but he was smart enough—and pretty sharp when it came to things you didn't much learn from behind a desk. Those weren't the things that mattered, of course—Doug knew that—but still, it was sort of neat to hang around somebody who spoke that language, with its crooked jargon and raw poetic power. And yet Doug sensed it was this very thing—this primal surge, this low understanding—that made Gary a bit uneasy around his cousin...well, that and the music Brent listened to and how fast he took curves and the houses he stopped at and told them to wait in the car. But none of that bothered Doug. Plus, Brent would pick him up cigarettes whenever he wanted, no questions asked.

After a quick stop to the Shell station down the street (left up to Kathleen, Brent would never have to buy his own gas again), they picked up Gary and drove into Canonsburg. Brent let them off at the mall, told them he'd be back in a couple of hours, and was gone.

Once inside they grabbed some Big Apple pizza and faux-casually cruised the strip, each gabbing over the other about the big party later that night. On their third tour they noticed a group of girls hanging out near Claire's, a make-up and accessories store with pitch-colored walls and purple-neon lighting, and for a good ten minutes stood spying on them through the glass of a shoe shop and badgering one another for not having the nads to walk over.

"Look, they're *right* there," Doug urged, "they're just waiting for it. Okay? Just go over and say hey-how's-it-goin and then ask what they're doing to-night. C'mon Gary, it's not rocket science, you don't have to be such a weirdo about it."

Gary's head swelled visibly. "Then you go ask them what they're doing! Why do I have to do it? I'll walk over with you, but you're doing the talking."

"Oh, you're such a pussy, man. You're embarrassing. They're *right there*."

They kept staring.

Gary said, "I don't know, Doug...that one chick looks kinda crazy."

"Who?" Doug asked, though he knew good and well who. Short girl, round face, wild, windswept hair. Pretty in an off-center sort of way, only she had this crazed chipmunk look about her, as if stunned by some recent news and just waiting to hear more.

"That one right there," Gary pointed, "with the big frizzy hair."

Doug pretended to look. "Aw! She doesn't look crazy."

"Bullcorn! She looks like she'd sneak right into your bedroom and *gut* you while you're asleep. And if *she's* crazy, then you know her friends are probably all crackers too. Who would hang out with a psycho chick? Who, Doug? I mean, look at the way they're dressed. It's the middle of June and look at what they're *wearing.*"

He nodded solemnly. "I saw that."

"What? Are they trying to hide their legs or something? Got knobby knees? They're probably a bunch of Capsers under there, frickin' Pillsbury Doughboys. I'm not trying to be mean, I'm just sayin'. And that girl in pink, she's a little chunk, you know? I mean, let's be honest, the chick's got a pooch."

Doug peered through the glass, past a display of high-tops and over to the dark-purple cavern of girls. They each held up bracelets and cheap little carry bags and laughed at some pointless thing somebody had said, but Doug had been humbled and the laughter only served to make them more deranged. As if mourning the death of some second-rate celebrity, he moved his head in a long, somber shake from side to side.

"You're right."

Gary breathed hard. "Uh, *ya think?* You ain't tellin' me nothing, I know I'm right. They're nice girls, Doug, but I mean, c'mon…"

After that they visited the music store, where Doug wrote down the names of a few songs he'd like to check out on LimeWire, many of them by artists Brent had mentioned at one point or another: the Red Hot Chili Peppers, Korn, DMX. A new rapper by the name of 50 Cent. And some band called Limp Bizkit. Did he have that right? Yes, he did. *Limp Bizkit.*

"Hey Doug, look at this."

Doug looked over to see Gary holding a sticker. In the center was a drawing of a man perched precariously atop a commode, and around the drawing the words *Confucius Say He Who Stands On Toilet Is High On Pot.* Gary was smiling.

"Get it? Ain't it funny?"

"Yeah, that's pretty funny, Gary."

"They got a whole bunch of 'em over there. Funnier than this!"

So they walked over and looked at the stupid stickers and Doug bought his usual flavor of incense—Purple Haze—not because he was crazy for the smell but because he felt strange and a little exotic burning incense in his room, and also because it covered the smell of his cigarettes.

By the time Brent arrived to pick them up, it was well after five and both boys were exhibiting giddy signs of the night to come. Since they'd met, Doug had seen Brent's house only a handful of times—and only then from the outside. As the hours ticked away, however, the interior in Doug's mind had begun looking more and more like that of the Playboy Mansion: parquet floors, plush animal-print sofas, a couple fountains, secret panels to the orgy cellar. And just to think he had a ringside seat—hot damn!

Of course, there was still the matter of asking his mom if it wouldn't be all right if he stayed the night with Gary. But then it always had been, and Doug figured there was no sense in breaking routine by saying anything about Brent and house parties and hot chicks lounging by the pool. And so Brent steered the Pontiac back toward Clover and down the narrow street to Doug's house, until at last they pulled into the drive and suddenly hot chicks were the last thing on Doug Lunsmann's mind. His mind was filled instead with the image of the rotten Oldsmobile through the windshield up ahead; his stomach clenched and wound, his heart sank.

Gary asked, "Should we come in? Don't you think—"

"No," Doug said. "Definitely not. Stay here and I'll be right out."

Focusing very clearly on what awaited him inside, Doug grabbed his incense, jammed it in his pocket, climbed out of the car. He made his way over to Brent's window.

"Don't leave," he said. "Whatever you do, please don't leave me here."

"Ain't gonna leave you, man," Brent assured him. "What's the matter with you? Whose car?"

"Nobody's."

"Well, nobody's staring at you through the window, Holmes."

Doug felt his ears go red, a cool burn, along with a major portion of his face. The world seemed to be closing in on his head.

Gary said, "Hey Doug, man, ain't that your dad? What's he doing here?"

"I don't know. He's probably drunk. Just don't leave, okay?"

Hours later he sat among the darkness of Brent's back porch.

The air was warm and he was alone, everyone else camped inside enjoying the loud music and booze, their laughter spilling carelessly over the beats. After what had happened back at the house, however, Doug found he simply couldn't be around happiness right now, couldn't bear mirth. He just wanted to stay out here—all night, if that's what it took—thawing out and trying to forget what a sad sack of shit his father was; trying to forget his father altogether.

The door opened, and he heard Brent's voice.

"Yo Doug…you all right, man?"

Up until then he hadn't even known he was crying; startled, he wiped his face and took a drag, nice and long, blew it out, said yeah. Brent glanced briefly to whatever was happening inside—there seemed to be a lot of it, whatever it was—and then slowly stepped outside, closing the door after himself. He stumbled in the darkness and pulled up a chair.

Doug asked, "Where's Gary?"

"Making out with some twelve-year-old, last I checked," Brent said, an echo of humor lacing his words. "Kid drinks one beer, thinks he's Superman."

For only a moment Doug sensed himself getting jealous, then realized he was too tired for that. All told, there'd been maybe a half dozen high school girls at the party; if he'd fostered any illusions about the Playboy Mansion, however, they'd been promptly forgotten as soon as these broads walked through the door. They weren't dogs—not most of them—but it was real easy to see how in another couple years they'd be pulling minimum wage and pumping out a fair supply of runaway toddlers (though one of them did carry the biggest pair of boulders Doug had ever seen).

Only one of these chicks had brought along her little sister and she and Gary had hit it off pretty well. She was a total goblin, in Doug's opinion, but somehow he figured old Gary felt otherwise, and now Doug guessed he'd spend the rest of his summer hearing about how splendiferous a kisser she was and what her gorgeous throat tasted like. Yippee.

"He should be ashamed of himself," Brent said, his callused fingers picking idly at the strip of gold draped around his neck. "Girl that age don't even know the *meaning* of a hard-on, and if she did it'd scare her half to death. Gary's a pedophile."

Doug jammed his cigarette into a tray on the table.

The moon was vast tonight, bright and full, and for a lost moment the boy searched his surroundings against its cold, expressionless stare. In the silence, he heard someone turn up the music inside, not too loud, followed by a short squeal and spurts of laughter. In another world these sounds were an open invitation to fun, a red carpet of good times, but in this present darkness they served only to make Doug a sadder, more depressed soul than he already was.

"Hey Doug, no offense...but dude, your dad's a *dick*."

"Yeah. I know."

"What's up with that today? What is he like, mental or something?"

Doug laughed miserably. "Probably. He used to be all right, you know, but after all that stuff with my mom he just...got *weird*. Started drinking all the time, going nuts..."

"No kidding."

"I mean, it's like he doesn't even *see* me anymore, like I'm just some sort of—"

He had to stop then, before his voice cracked or he closed his eyes like some sappy lame-o telling a sad story. But really he was just as angry as he was sad, pissed off at his dad and himself and the rest of the world. What had happened tonight? Where had things went so wrong?

"Look," Brent said, "don't even let that stuff get to you, all right? Me and my pops, we're all the time fighting, about dumb shit. About whether or not I wiped up some grease in the kitchen, or didn't do my laundry or sweep the fucking *garage*. And you know what? I don't even care. Shit used to drive me crazy, now I don't even care. Besides, I'm old enough I could whoop his ass anyways, you know?"

They laughed a little at that, grateful for the chance to breathe, then each drew a cigarette and lit the end. At least, that's what Doug thought they did. As they sat there, however, a funny sort of smell came creeping over the porch, a smell unlike any Doug had ever smelled before. It came low-legged and stealthy and settled in his lap, and looking over he noticed a long, dark cigar curved slightly from Brent's mouth. Brent dragged, briefly lighting the night, then glanced over and reached out casually with one arm, the cigar pinched between two fingers. Only then did Doug realize what it was and sat up, pausing to snub his menthol before taking the item in his hand, studying the look and feel of it in his fingers.

It was brown, thicker and longer than a cigarette but smaller than a full-size cigar. Smoke corded in a thick spiral from its end, and before thinking anymore about what he was doing, Doug lifted the thing to his lips and pulled as he would on a cigarette.

The result was cataclysmic.

An explosion from the pit of his stomach forced air up and out; his body was racked in a series of burning, guttural coughs. Brent chuckled, his deep laugh a welcome comfort amidst the pain, told Doug to take it easy, then he grabbed the stick from his fingers and took another puff.

"Take it slow," he instructed. "Pull too hard, you'll make it run."

"Make it run?" Doug asked, wiping his mouth. He felt dizzy. "What's that mean?"

But Brent didn't answer, not immediately; he seemed to be holding his breath. When he released it, Doug was astonished at the amount of smoke that came pouring from his mouth.

"Means you'll make the paper burn uneven. Here, try again."

The second time was better. He dragged easily, feeling the smoke roll in waves down his throat, and coming up again it seemed somehow different, cooler. *He* was different.

With sudden fervor, he handed the small cigar back to Brent. It would be his last clear image of the night, the last segment untouched by the murky and deranged heights of stonedom. They passed the cigar—the *blunt*, Brent had called it—a couple more times, only by then Doug was having trouble concentrating and an entirely new and endlessly puzzling porch had grown up around the one he'd come to know in the last hour, and when Brent got up and told him to come on inside, Doug got up and went inside. The ghost of his father, meanwhile, had made a quiet exit, and Doug's previously solemn mood replaced by an intense perception that threatened at any moment to run him from the rails of sanity.

He strolled into the living room, into a world of gawky strangers and too-loud music, only it wasn't a living room anymore—it was a crossroads, an uncomfortable waystation between his universe and theirs, his invisible rights and theirs, pressed face-to-face, skull-to-skull, hollow beating heart to hollow beating heart. He looked to see Gary Northrup in the throes of passion on the floor, his arms wrapped tightly round that of his paramour's elementary-school frame, and couldn't help but burst into a sudden, unexpected row of giggles.

Gary gazed up, an expression of bewilderment written over his face. He stared around as if unsure of his surroundings, and apparently shocked by the presence of a girl's face only inches from his own. The two disentangled themselves, stood and straightened their clothes, then awkwardly settled on the couch, two kids ashamed of their own indiscretion.

Satisfied, Doug took a seat and smiled, convinced on some gut-deep level that he was emanating. He couldn't be sure of just *what* he was emanating—peace maybe, or horniness—but it was a good feeling whatever it was, something he could really see himself settling into. As the night wore on and partygoers vanished out the door, however, he could sense that force slowly seeping away, replaced by an unsettling absence at the core of his being: a sudden, cold *emptiness* down deep in his gut. In the wake of this surprising reversal of fortune, Brent had taken Jugs and slipped into a room down the hall, never to be heard from again; once-raucous music was shushed and then stilled; Gary was snoozing on the couch.

Soon the house was dark and Doug found himself alone at the kitchen table, massaging his hunger with a brimming bowl of Lucky Charms cereal. Normally he started with the brown things, deliberately saving the marshmallows till last, but there was no time for that tonight; tonight it all went down at once and it was oh so magically delicious. Afterwards he felt debauched and was struck by a sudden, overpowering exhaustion, a traitor within that made the short crawl from his chair to the floor a near-Sisyphean task.

He faded quickly, his mind existing in deep space for so long that sleep was a welcome thing, a shallow barrier between this world and that of dreams. Two worlds wholly devoid of logic but which flaunted the absurd; two worlds from which he was more than ready to take one large step back, if only he could find a way.

Something important had happened here tonight, of that he was sure.

He just wished he could remember what it was.

By the time Brent dropped him off the following afternoon, Doug had slept better than nine hours and felt positive anyone who saw him now would have no inkling of the mischief he'd gotten into the night before. No inkling, for example, that for a good three or four hours there he'd been an Emanator, one of the few and chosen Masters of the Universe. In fact, he could hardly believe it himself.

He found his mother on the sofa, head dipped morbidly into her hands and the old cordless phone forgotten on the cushion next to her. She glanced up as he came in, and no sooner had he glimpsed the rueful chasms of her eyes, her face with its red, slightly pinched flesh, than he knew there was trouble. What kind, exactly, he wasn't sure—but trouble.

"Doug, we need to talk," she said, her voice pale and brittle against the warm sunlight through the windows. "Something…something's *happened.*"

"Mom, what's the matter?"

Only before he was allowed to jump to any conclusions, before his frantic mind was permitted to torture him with all sorts of paranoid could-it-be and what-ifs, before any of that, she looked him in the eyes and said, "It's about your father."

CHAPTER 8

Mike was blinded by a band of piercing light.

A pain like a thousand pins was driven into his head, exploding on impact, and slipping one hand over his eyes he had the curious sensation that one hand was all he had, the other held hostage by some terrible new blanket he sensed at his side. Slowly his eyes adjusted, and peering around the cramped little room with no windows and its cold overhead florescent, there was little question as to where he was. His mind was full of other, more wonderful questions, however.

Like how he'd gotten here.

Oh but you know, some little voice told him, *you know all too well how you got here…*

A sudden dread settled in his stomach. Two years earlier he'd experienced this same feeling—this same *mourning*—only it hadn't been from a hospital bed but from the backseat of a car rich with the coppery smell of blood. He looked around for a clock, found one on the wall that read 4:08. And just how long had he been here anyway?

He tried hard to think, to remember. He came up with an image of something, but it was an image he didn't like: it was a picture of the Covington house, and him inside it. Bit by bit that picture became a whole, and after a little more thought he moaned audibly, not so much from discomfort as from his own inspiring ability to show his ass in public places. *The fight,* he thought, *of course.* Then came the bar—THE 19th HOLE it had been called—those first shots of Johnnie Walker, and after that Mike ran into a familiar black wall; a cloud pushed by a phantom storm. He kept feeling at that wall, searching for cracks, but it was no use; time may loosen some of its mortar, but for the moment it was sealed tight as a snare drum.

He looked over, noticing a large vase of flowers on the table next to his bed. There were a couple cards there as well, flipped open and standing next to the vase, and he'd reached out one hand when a scruffy-haired nurse swept into the room and over to his bed, fiddling with instruments and checking the lines that at some point had become an integral part of his body. He glanced again to the hammock of his left arm, self-conscious, wanting it to be a nice normal hand for the nurse so he could pack up and get the hell out of here. *See? All better.*

"No, no," she said, once he'd started to speak. "You'll need some water before you can do any of that. Hold on."

She fetched some water from a sink in the corner and handed him the cup. When it was empty he handed it back and began the slow, rather excruciating process of clearing his throat.

"Sorry for the room," she told him, moving back to the sink. "I know it's kind of a closet, but we've been sorta pressed for beds lately, believe it or not. Know what they say, every season is our busy season."

"What, what happened to me? Where am I?"

Before she could answer, a tall man in thin, rimless glasses appeared near the bed, clipboard gripped in one hand. It wasn't a gown he was wearing, but it was close. "Canonsburg Hospital," he intoned without looking up. "As for what happened to you, Officer Lunsmann...we were rather hoping you could tell us that."

The nurse offered a stinky face and scuttled from the room.

Mike stared blankly at the man, eyes tracing the perfect creases at the sides of his mouth, the small tufts of eagle's hair from behind each ear. Suddenly there was a shadow moving around behind the curtain of Mike's thoughts, a Little Man with his own ideas of what ought and ought not to be, and his own secret methods of making it so.

The doctor grabbed a chair and pulled it over to Mike's bed, sat down.

"My name," he said, "is Dr. Harold Lasky."

"Greetings."

Lasky smiled plainly. "Mike, I've been practicing medicine for close to twenty years now, twelve of them right here in Willard County. I've seen things that would make even you, as a police officer, have trouble sleeping at night. But I've also saved countless lives. And though you could say I know the ropes pretty well…there are always curveballs. I'm sure there are plenty of curveballs in your line of work, as well. Just because I'm a doctor, however, doesn't mean I'm immune to stress, or that there aren't days I wish I could crawl into some cave and never come out. I know what it's like to have a job that comes down hard, and it's only natural to want an escape. But I'll tell you right now, Mike, the way you're living…no man should live that way. Today you wake up in a hospital with your arm in a sling; you're lucky. Some people don't get that second chance. Some people, they wake up paralyzed because their car took them someplace they didn't want to go. Or they juice it so hard their bodies start to shrink. Others wake up in jail. And some people don't wake up at all. You're one of the lucky ones, Mr. Lunsmann, and I'm telling you now—as a physician—that if you don't quit it with this drinking *it will kill you.* Period."

Mike was quiet. He looked down to his left arm—a suddenly leaden thing, victim of his own aberrant thirst—and felt the spit dry up in his mouth. "How banged up are we talking?" he asked. "I mean, is it bad? Is it sprained? Broken? What'd I, fall out of a tree or something?

Lasky studied him a moment. "Mike, you were shot."

Long, deep silence. A sense of floating. Mike grunted, but the sound never touched his ears, the sound didn't exist. His breathing kicked up a notch and everything else slowed down, way down, the world stopped.

Shot.

He'd been shot.

In twenty-three years on the force, Mike Lunsmann had never been pierced by a bullet. He'd known others who had, and a select few who'd actually died because of it. Now it had happened to him, and in some cruel twist of fate he had no earthly idea how. His deeper-than-usual shame quickly morphed to pity, and with pity came hatred, aimed partly at himself and partly at the son of a bitch who had pointed the gun and fired.

"Shot?" Mike said. "I don't understand. By *who?*"

Lasky shifted in his chair. "By the time you were found, you'd experienced significant blood loss. You were unconscious. Best estimates, the altercation occurred during the middle hours of the night; someone maybe saw you stumbling around, you were drunk, they figured you'd be easy. From the hole in your arm, I'd say you must have given them some fight."

Mike stared at the clock on the wall, half-expecting its three hands to be frozen in place, for time to have stopped and for all of this to be some sort of tired madman's nightmare. For a moment the world spun, spiraling down. When he looked again, the hands were still moving.

"How long?" he asked. "How long have I been here?"

"You were found Sunday morning. Today's Tuesday."

He sat up in bed, bones throbbing like jagged stones beneath his skin. "You're telling me I've been here *two days?*"

But by now Harold Lasky was busy scribbling away at his clipboard, translating some part of their exchange into his own obscure physician's lingo. "Two days once the sun comes up," he said. He aimed his pen at the clock. "It's four a.m."

Mike sat back. He felt tired all of a sudden. Lasky fed him a couple more questions, and Mike parroted off the answers. They talked for five, maybe ten minutes, the doctor jotting down notes and giving more of his professional opinion until finally he glanced his watch and stood, replacing his chair and starting for the door. He was halfway out when he turned and offered one last piece of advice:

"Officers from the local precinct have already been by, said they'd like to have a word when you came to. For starters, they'd like to help you find your car."

▲ ▲ ▲

He'd been found a little after eight a.m., discovered of all places among the sweaty garbage cans of a downtown alley. According to official reports, his body was splayed facedown in a puddle of apocalyptic proportions, a tantalizing mixture of blood and rain. Mostly blood. His Oldsmobile was still missing, despite an APB and almost two days of searching; when asked by the local crew for clues as to where he last remembered driving it, he pointed them in the direction of The 19th Hole…which was apparently the same place his blood-alcohol level had pointed them as well.

Despite his other wares, Dr. Lasky was right about one thing: he'd been lucky. Had he been tagged in a major artery, Mike would presently be belly-up on a cold slab somewhere, practicing the subtle art of rigor mortis. Instead he'd suffered what was basically a flesh wound, the bullet entering his triceps at a point just over and to the right of his elbow, drilling a nice little hole into his upper left arm; essentially, he'd been shot in the back. His humerus had been sheared but not shattered, and even then the bullet had been weak enough to do no major damage. They knew this because it had still been lodged in his arm when he arrived.

He was being held on the fourth floor of a hospital in Willard County, less than ten miles from where he'd been found, and not twenty miles from his former wife and former son and their New and Improved Provider. It was they who had left the daisies, along with a card. The card was dated for Sunday.

Father's Day.

Mike read the words again, wondering if the *I love you* scrawled in Dougie's hand was his own words or if they'd been fed him by some turbulent residue of their spat, turned inward at the sight of his poor paps in a hospital bed.

There were other cards, as well, including one from the guys down at the station. Mike wasn't so sure how he felt about that. Wasn't so sure how he felt about a lot of things.

He got out of there fast as he could.

They were cold places, hospitals, the stink of death hovering over them as it did nowhere else; not even graveyards, Mike thought, held the lingering sense of grotesquerie which hospitals carried in stride. Due to his incredible luck, there was no reason to keep him any longer than they already had; they'd given him a few pints of blood, they'd wrapped his arm, written him a scrip. Now all that was left was for him to go once more back out into the world and TRY AGAIN.

He arranged for a rental car with an agency out of Keller—Payton Rental Cars, one of a handful in the state who gave discounts to law enforcement— then took a taxi down as soon as he was done at the hospital. He sat in the backseat, watching as the world passed serenely outside his window, faded and gray and undead. There was something out there, softly calling through the murk of his own mixed-up mind, something he was supposed to remember but that he'd forgotten. Again and again his thoughts turned to his car, his car, what the hell had happened to his *car?* Would it ever be found? And would he really want to see it if it was? It was all a headache, one big headache and it made him nauseous.

Upon leaving the agency, Mike decided on a small detour before heading home. Perfecting a careful, one-armed method of steering, he moved the car—a weathered Buick with stains on the seat and a burning fish-sticks smell—in a subtle line back toward Clover, and finally along the broad primrose path of the Covington residence.

The sun tilted awkwardly as he drove past, sinking fast, and in this momentary twilight of worlds the house appeared unusually picturesque and perfect, the only blemish that of his own hunk-a-junk Buick strolling past outside. The yard was immaculate, and staring Mike found it hard to believe he'd once stood there and performed his brutal surgery on Bart Covington's face.

There was no place for him in there, no place at all.

He shook a bead of sweat from his face and sped away, back to a life of dirty undies and Hungry Man dinners and quiet nights in front of the TV.

Walking in the door later that night, Mike noticed the red eye of his answering machine blinking in the darkness, and after hitting a light went over and pushed play.

There were three messages.

The first was from Alan Winthrop, a man who a couple lifetimes ago had been Mike's sponsor. On the message he sounded both down and happy at the same time—*concerned* is what he was going for, Mike thought, and knowing Alan it probably came easy—and he'd got in maybe ten seconds before Mike hit the erase button. The second message came from a lawyer of some kind, somebody who'd heard about Mike's "recent distress" and was offering his services; he tossed that one out, too. The third was from Hammond PD.

"Mike, this is Lieutenant Palmer. I talked to the hospital, Mike, they told me they discharged you early this afternoon. Good to know you're back on your feet, buddy. Look, if you would, give me a call when you get this. Thanks, Mike."

He hit erase. Palmer could wait.

Entering the kitchen, Mike lifted a clear little baggie out of his pocket, plopped it on the kitchen table. *Something to think about*, the doctor had told him. He retrieved the chip of metal from inside and held it to the light, a part of him fascinated by its extraordinary ability to fly and sting, another sickened to know this particular round had gotten the full three-hour tour of Mike Lunsmann's left arm. He pondered who had been the last to touch it before sending it off, and if they'd been aiming for his arm at all. Or had they *really* wanted to put it through the back of old Lunsmann's head? And if so, then why not finish the job? Or had Mike fought back? Had he whipped out his own little surprise and—

Mike felt his heart perform a sudden dive-bomb in his chest.

His gun.

Of course, how could he have forgotten? His gun had been in the Olds—stashed away in the glove, like always—and now the Olds was gone. Vanished. Holy hockey balls, Batman—and what would Palmer have to say about *that?*

Mike wagged his head, urging reality to subtly change the rules and somehow help him get back his Glock, to please just throw him this one little bone and help him get back his Glock. But it was no use; he'd woken today in the same world he'd lived in for forty-three years, no sense in it turning miracles for him now.

Only then something caught his eye about the slug, something Mike felt sure he'd already known—perhaps Lasky had told him, or a nurse. He lifted it now, turning the slug gently in his fingers: ragged, slender, skin the color of brass; a full half-inch of misery in one hand. Only this round was not from some gangbanger's pistol, was not the shot of your typical gimme-your-wallet thief or barhopping idiot.

This was a rifle.

Mike considered the fact thoughtfully, wondering what sort of psycho went about Canonsburg toting rifles past midnight. Wondering what sort of unique situation would allow for that shot to be taken without *somebody* noticing. And remembering a time when he'd heard just such a shot himself—as well as the long, piercing cry that followed—knowing deep within that he had become in that moment a man who no longer believed in coincidence.

Chapter 9

It was quarter past twelve the following afternoon when Mike pulled to a stop outside the Hammond Police Department. He'd barely climbed from the car when he looked down, noticing a slight tremble in his fingers, and without effort his mind jumped to filmmaker mode, splicing together a quick little short that involved his rental car rolling down the street, finding a nice dark hole where he could bury this whole thing beneath a brown swell of booze.

He pushed it away and climbed the steps.

People turned as he entered, some stopping to chat, others offering an encouraging thumbs-up or grab on the shoulder and flashing sympathetic smiles. If anybody knew anything about what really happened to him in Willard County—anything close to the boozehound truth—they didn't let on. But then they knew better than to ask, which was Mike's first tip that these old friends knew much more than they were letting on.

He made his way up the stairs to level three, combing the halls till he came to a door with the words LIEUTENANT CLARK PALMER written in gilt letters across the glass. He knocked twice, and when the stolid voice came from within—*Enter!*—Mike grabbed a breath and went inside.

The office was very much as he remembered. Same oak sprawl of desk. Same Lucite cube on the corner, holding the same pictures of the same two kids—both daughters—and the same wife. The clutter was the same, so was the smell. There were a few more accolades on the wall, and a few more wrinkles and a few less hairs on Palmer's head, but that was it.

Without glancing up, Palmer told Mike to have a seat. When he'd finished with whatever he was doing, he leaned back in his chair, a heavyset black man with enough muscle up top to counterbalance the inner tube around his waist. Small dabble of a mustache, speckled gray to match the salt in his hair. They exchanged a few pleasantries, patted proverbial shoulders. That lasted all of two seconds before Palmer's face changed and he said, "I didn't know you were back on the bottle, Mike."

"I'm not back on the bottle, okay?"

"Don't lie to me, Mike, now dammit I saw the tests. A point-oh-six at eight on a Sunday morning and you don't call that—"

"I'd had a bad night Clark, that's all that was. That's all, it was nothing. Kathleen, she…she was being difficult, and Dougie just…"

He trailed off, either unwilling or unable to complete the thought. In the silence, Palmer stole a glance to the calendar on his desk. Sunday. *Father's Day*.

"I'm sorry to hear that," he said, not sounding very sorry. "I know this has been a difficult time for you, Mike—we all do—but you can't let what happens out there"—he threw an arm to the window—"get in the way of what's going on in here. The world's chock-full of bullshit but you *cannot* let that get in the way of your *job*, Mike. You do understand where I'm coming from when I say that?"

"Of course I understand, of course. And it never has. Never will."

"Hm."

Palmer leaned forward, big arms propped across his desk. A few inches from his right hand, a girl of maybe five years smiled back at Mike from a sandbox, bucket in one hand, shovel in the other. "Okay," he said, "so tell me what I need to know. What happened?"

Mike picked a point at the front of Palmer's shirt, a gnarled button, and carefully dictated his story. Not a true one, exactly, but a What-Could-Have-Been of events. There were few requisites to this story, so long as he ended up in that alley with a slug in his arm by the dawn's early light. In this version, The 19th Hole was a shadowed land of leery and reckless souls, vagrants and vagabonds of which he'd traded words with more than few. Nothing serious, just off the shoulder stuff, little digs. Bad vibes.

"Remember any faces?" Palmer asked.

"Maybe if somebody'd turned on a light. They shoulda called it The 19th Asshole, 'cause that's about how dark it was in there. Smelled about as nice, too. I must've got dirty looks from half the kids in that joint, like they just *smelled* it on me. *Cop.* Believe me, Clark, after being there five minutes I wished to hell I'd just drove home and went to sleep."

"Go on."

Anyway, once the bar's atmosphere had soured Mike decided to step out and call a cab, get a hotel for the night. The rain had started by then, was coming down like a bastard, so Mike headed for his car to make the call…only someone must've followed him out, because the last thing he remembered after opening his door was a strong knock to the back of his head. Next thing he knew, he woke up in the hospital, his car stolen and his wallet empty and a mummified arm at his chest.

"Car stolen?"

Mike nodded. "They still haven't found it."

"How'd you get home?"

"Rental car. Real top of the line, too."

Palmer lifted one thick hand to his chin, scratched at his mustache, thought for a moment.

"You were drunk?"

"Yeah." No getting around that one.

"How drunk?"

Mike shrugged. "Tipsy. Not falling down, but I'd stopped counting. Why?"

"I just don't get it," he said, "if you were knocked out, then why the bullet?"

Another shrug. "I've wondered that myself. I mean, if they'd wanted to kill me they could have. What they gave me was more like a kiss after dark."

"What were you tagged with?"

Mike stared, wondering if there was any way out of saying it. But Palmer had known about the blood tests, he may've known more than that and was only feigning dumb. In any case, there was no sense in taking an unnecessary chance, even if a lie would make better sense.

"Uh, twenty-two caliber. Long Rifle."

"Come again?"

Mike shook his head. "I don't know."

"Mike, Mike, Mike," Palmer said, twisting his head in disgust. "Who'd you run into out there anyway, Davy Crockett? Hell, that's not even a deer gun. Twenty-two, are you *sure?*"

"Sure."

"And this is *where* at in Willard County? Clover?"

"Yeah, Clover."

Palmer exhaled gratuitously, as if physically ill from the exchange. "I'm almost afraid to ask, but…were you carrying?"

Mike's eyes swung to the floor. His lips did not move.

"Oh hell, here we go. Don't do this to me, Mike, don't you dare do this to me."

"The Glock was in the glove compartment," he explained. "Maybe it's still there if—"

"And maybe some dope fiend's got his scrappy little hands on it, and tonight he's gonna blow out some sweet old lady's brains. They catch the guy and run the gun and guess whose heads Willard County is gonna have on a silver platter—*ours*. Hammond PD. Dammit, Mike—you should be written up for this, you know that don't you?"

"I know, I know. And I'm sorry, Clark. This wasn't exactly something I had penciled in on my calendar, if you know what I mean. I should've been paying more attention, should've been more *aware*. I'm sorry…"

For a long time no one said anything. On the wall behind Mike's back, the clock got louder, ticking away the seconds to eternity. Palmer stared into space, his massive knuckles pressed to his lips. Mike's mind, meanwhile, was maneuvering its own alleys of thought, playing back his night at The 19th Hole. It was vague, but something had been joggled loose by his false narrative—slim panels of vision that showed him inside his car, his hand moving to the ignition, turning the key—

It was cut short by the ugly rattle of Palmer clearing his throat. "Mike, you're gonna have to take some time off. Let that arm heal…"

Mike had readied to protest, his head already shaking on his shoulders when his eyes caught on something through the glass looking out on the hall. Then he looked closer and, summoned by some primal urge within, leapt from his chair and out the door.

"*Mike!*" Palmer screeched. "*Mike, dammit get back here!*"

Instead he rushed to the cluttered tackboard outside the office, stopping at one of the myriad flyers on display. Written at the top was the word MISSING in block capitals, and below that a name that meant absolutely nothing to him at all: Thomas "T.J." Chadwick.

He grabbed the notice and undid the tacks, took it from the wall.

When he returned to the office, Palmer sat staring with a thoughtful intensity. "What the hell's got into you anyway?" he asked, long years of smoking finally showing in his voice. "Are you that bad off?"

"Who is this?"

"Mike, look at me, look at me. Sit down. What's going on?"

"I just want to know who this is," Mike said, "please, tell me, who is this?"

Channeling his last reserves of patience, Palmer shifted his attention to the flyer in Mike's hands. "That one," he said, "we got that one a few days ago. Tuesday it was. Some teenager over in Craven County. Group of 'em went missing over the weekend, they just wanted us to keep an eye out. Runaways probably, they're not sure. Why? You know him?"

Mike stared at the picture, completely sure he had no idea how to answer that.

The clock ticked madly at his back.

"Mike…what's happened to you, man? Where are you at?"

Mike laughed easily, shining and bright and happy. "Ah, I'm sorry Clark. You must really think I've flipped my wig."

"It crossed my mind."

Mike waved it away. "These meds, you know, they've got me so mixed up I can't even think straight anymore. Probably shouldn't be driving, I just…" And then only that cold blank stare down to the page, as if being sucked there, his essence spilled down and leaving only an empty shell on a seat in Palmer's office.

"Mike, go home. I'm putting you on six weeks medical. After that, let me know what the doctors say, we'll see about getting you back on. Okay?"

Mike glanced up. "Huh? Oh, yeah. Sure, Clark." With a concentrated effort, he folded the flyer into fourths and tucked it in his pocket. After an awkward silence, he stood and made his way to the door. "I'm just so—so *rattled* right now, you know? Guess I still haven't gotten over the shock of it all…"

"Sure, Mike. Look, what we talked about in here today, it ain't over. For the time being you go home, get some rest. We'll talk again. And Mike? Drive safe."

Mike nodded his head, said something, though later he couldn't for the life of him remember what it was. He made his way from the room and down the corridor to the stairs, all the while unaware of Lieutenant Palmer's careful gaze. At that moment his tired mind had more to think about than Clark Palmer. Like how he recognized somebody he'd never before seen in his life. Like those slim panels of vision he'd somehow joggled loose.

Like what he'd really been up to the night he was shot.

Chapter 10

For a long time Mike sat spinning the slug on his kitchen counter's bright Formica top. Staring at the flyer and spinning the slug. The slug stopped, he'd spin it again, and still the boy's cold glare from the picture on the counter.

According to the flyer, Thomas Chadwick, age 16, had been missing since Father's Day. He'd last been seen leaving his home (*address provided below*) the previous afternoon at approximately 3 P.M. Chadwick had been accompanied by Craig and Blake Rackley, who—along with Marius Garber—were also missing. All are best friends, said the flyer, as well as current students at local New Bern High School.

A requisite fuzzy image of Chadwick was displayed at the center of the page, along with some basic facts down below: his height, his weight, hair and eye color, date of birth. A fairly detailed description of the clothes he'd last been wearing, and another of the old Yamaha four-wheeler he'd been driving when he left the house.

Mike studied the information, looking for some awful devil in the details, something that would really jump out and bite him. He couldn't shake the feeling that his own existence was in some way inexorably tangled with Chadwick's own, though he'd never laid eyes on the boy in his life. But then... that wasn't really true was it? He *had* met the boy—he was sure of it—despite the fact his name was not one Mike knew. But, as with earlier in Palmer's office, Mike sometimes had flashes—dim television panels of the mind—of himself and the boy in some darkened room, the tainted glow of a light bulb breathing down hard on them from above; no sooner had he tracked on them, however, than the panels were gone, vanished, chased away.

Mike rubbed at his eyes, casting a long shadow over the bar before him.

He glanced to his journal, where he'd jotted snippets of his experience over the past few days—no romanticizing, but not much badgering either. Just enough to let ol' Kat know he was still there and that he loved her. Next to the journal was a beer; the beer was empty, and like others before it had been setting there a little too long, was now beginning to mock him. Mike reeled in the urge to swat it off the table, then rose from his chair and got another. It was cold, cool, went down smooth. Absolutely no taste at all. Delicious.

When it was done he tossed it away with the others and stood over the counter, swaying, eyes closed, enjoying what little peace there was to be had in this world. Mike chuckled to himself, opening his eyes and staring down at the only link between him and the reality he'd somehow lost that forgotten night on the road.

Thomas "T.J." Chadwick stared back, his loose-lipped grin frozen in time.

"Keep it up, kid. Stay positive. We'll get out of this yet."

He stumbled to his room, stripped down, tossed his clothes in a corner. The morning would be hard, he knew, but not compared to discovering whatever there was out there concerning that lost night, like some little rock waiting for him to find it and turn it over and see the creepy-crawly truth underneath. Not compared to finding whoever did this to him and bringing them to justice, making them pay. It'd be hard, but he'd be damned if it wouldn't be done, and you could bet your bottom dollar on that. Medical leave his ass.

It was time to get to work.

CHAPTER 11

The burly gentleman with perfectly combed hair shifted in his seat at Canonsburg Hospital. He'd been here over an hour now, and the chair was only getting harder. He checked his watch. For the life of him, he couldn't understand what was taking so long; he'd been in the room himself, had seen the sorry putz laid out there in the bed, unconscious, with all those tubes and the machines beeping and clicking. It was terrible what'd happened—no doubt about that—but, for his two cents, it could've been worse. And besides, was it really that surprising? Lunsmann was a perpetual time bomb, and anytime he hit the juice he went off big time and there was no news in that. Bless his soul, but the man belonged on a booze farm, and if he'd ended up in a hospital instead then that was what Bart Covington called a Good First Step. Still, he couldn't help but feel sorry for the guy...

But then Bart couldn't help but feel sorry for a lot of people right about now.

Hospital waiting rooms are funny things. Part doctor's office, part hotel, they're superficially simple places, and yet Bart had come to know them for what they truly were: private vortexes of the universe where all time stops and one is left to flounder in a limbo of expectant misery and grief. In the days following the last of his father's strokes, he'd spent more than a few hours in one of these curious spaces, had learned well the secret art of power naps and showering from a sink.

He glanced around the room, saw a middle-aged blonde-type flipping through a magazine. Next to her, a man in a Steelers cap sat staring at the ceiling, palms glued to his head as if in mock despair. Two Asian women—one old, one young—were asleep in recliners against the far wall, tips of their feet poking from beneath two blankets. Others came and went, tapping on cell phones or stumbling blindly across the floor and for a second, as if by magic, Bart was taken back ten years in the past. Nothing had changed and he was waiting for word from the doctors, only now he knew the final verdict and this time he promised himself he wouldn't cry.

Then he noticed Kathleen and stood, attempting sympathy as she made her way over through a maze of lamps and plants that would never grow old and die.

"How is he?"

Kathleen's mouth did a little twitch. "Same," she said. They embraced and for a moment she stood back, scrubbing at her eyes.

"The doctor said it's not serious," he said. "Right?"

Kathleen snorted. "Define serious." And then: "No, it's not serious, I'm just…I just feel so bad about everything…"

"Listen, hon, it's not your fault. You can't help it every time Mike decides to go off the deep end. He'll be fine, maybe this is exactly what he needs, you know?"

"I know."

"Then what's the problem?"

"Nothing. I just hate to see anybody like that. So helpless."

"Hey, you're not telling me anything. Why do you think I got out of there?"

Millie had found a comfortable spot on the floor, and was presently ripping a newspaper to little shreds. Bart kept watching, waiting for her to try and slip one of the pieces in her mouth. Either the idea hadn't occurred to her, or she'd been incredibly sneaky about it.

"Has it been bad with her?"

"Not really," he said. "She's been quite the studious worker, our Millie. See that precision? She decided to take something that was white and black and red all over, and just make it all over."

He'd meant it as a joke, but the timing was off. Instead his wife only sniffled once, staring deeper than usual into his calm blue eyes. "Bart," she said, "do you love me?"

"Not at all."

"Bart, I'm *serious*."

"Of course I love you, Kathleen, you're my peaches and cream. Why? Lemme guess, after today you'd like nothing better than to unwind over a nice dinner and a glass of rosé?"

"Well…no," she told him. "I mean, maybe. But that's not why I asked. I asked because it's just that…well, Doug forgot to get a card. You know, for Father's Day."

"Oh?"

"And now he feels terrible, and I was sort of hoping that maybe you wouldn't mind running out and picking one up for him? Please? He's been really quiet today, and I think he blames himself for what happened—"

"Well, he shouldn't and neither should you."

"I know that, Bart, and I've told him so. Still, I think he'd feel better if he had something to leave Mike. Don't you think? I saw an Eckerd's across the street, you could go there. I'm sure they've got something…"

"Doesn't Doug wanna come? Maybe help pick it out?"

Kathleen frowned. "It doesn't much matter to him, just so he has something to leave behind." Then, before he could speak, she flashed her deep brown eyes, a brief reminder of why he'd married her and never looked back. "Would you mind?"

▲ ▲ ▲

There was a moment there—somewhere between "Dad, I don't tell you often enough…" and "When I look back on my life, there's always been that one person who…"—when Bart questioned where he was at that moment, and how he'd gotten there. One of those moments when you realized a hypothetical question was no longer hypothetical. *Say you were the poor dodo who had to select a Father's Day card for the maniac who used to be married to your wife because his own son hadn't bothered to do it and now his tosspot dad had been shot and the boy felt truly horrid—what would you do???*

What an existence he was leading, what a life. Gunman walks in, robs the place blind, aims a hand cannon at Bart Covington's face and yanks the trigger—what a way to go, huh? That's a life worth writing about right there.

He froze, staring down at some whimsical emblem of the perfect father sitting at a perfect table and sipping at his perfect cartoon cup of coffee. He wanted to be angry—anger was easy, to the point—but he wasn't angry. He didn't know what he was.

Starving, for one thing.

It wasn't even that Doug had never given him a Father's Day gift of any kind, not in all the years since he'd married the boy's mother. No, wait, that's not true—there was a tie that one year. Besides that, nothing. But he *didn't care* about that—Bart didn't expect Doug to treat him like a father, not really. So then why did this bug the hell out of him so bad?

For the same reason you can't stand another second in that hospital. Bart, the man broke your nose—three times. You know, you can only garner so much sympathy for a guy like that.

He supposed. But still, that was no way to carry on a life, stuffing that sort of garbage down into his soul. If he wanted to live like that—then why not bring out the gunman now?

He chose a card with a waterfall on the cover, and something inside about how fathers are like river currents or when times get tough you can always count on old dad. He grabbed a fuchsia-colored envelope, decided that was too feminine and went with slate blue instead. He spotted some flowers as he was checking out—a wall of arrangements had been bunched on an endcap—and grabbed those, tossed them on the counter. *Happy Father's Day, Mike.*

▲ ▲ ▲

Later that night, once the dizzying rush of intercourse had faded from his bones and he heard those tiny nasal snores that told him she was asleep, Bart lay in bed thinking about what he'd felt that afternoon. Remembering Mike and the doughy, thrown-away look on his face; staring at him, Bart had imagined the man floating through the blackness of deep space, his body strapped to the hospital bed, one crooked arm held to his heart as the stars went blazing past his headboard.

And despite what he'd told Kathleen earlier, there was a part of Bart—not a small one—that accepted the brunt of the guilt for what had happened.

It was Mike's call, ultimately—he knew that—but he also wasn't so naïve as to believe he'd had no hand in lifting those bottles to Mike's mouth. Sure, Bart knew that.

He found himself thinking of his and Kathleen's relationship, and the small steps that had taken them from what they once were—mere church acquaintances—to now sharing the same bed and a kid in the room down the hall. The months of innocent banter. The playful jabs and her carefully-laid, beating-around-the-bush confessions.

You think it's bad getting him to church, you should try getting him home before midnight.

I'd give anything to actually have dinner with my husband.

Mostly, though, he thought of the kiss.

What was he supposed to have done? The connection was there, they both knew that. But he'd been the one to make the move, because he knew if he didn't then they'd never get the chance again, and would've both walked away unhappy—and if that one little move was all it took then, fine, he would sacrifice a little righteousness to be the one to make it.

Only it had worked, that was the crazy part—*it had actually worked*—and now sometimes he wondered about that little piece of righteousness he'd forfeited all those years before. What kind of person was he anyway? He'd gotten what he wanted: a wife, a family—a damned fine one—even a kid of his own. But what had it cost him? What sort of price had he really paid? And what kind of reception would it get him in the life to come? *Here he is, folks! The one you've all been waiting for! He sold his soul for something but it wasn't rock 'n' roll…that's right—it's Wild Bart Covington! Now grab a pitchfork and dig in…*

Not exactly Bart's idea of eternal rest.

History is written by the winners, isn't that what they say? In Bart's case, he could spin a delicate web and make himself a hero, if not in Doug's eyes (that would never happen) then maybe in Kathleen's, and definitely in Millie's. In his own eyes, however, he would always be closer to how Mike surely must've written him: *a homewrecker.* Nothing new or groundbreaking about that. Sometimes he imagined he'd trade it all to be the good guy again, the responsible businessman with a personality like sewage but integrity like a fifty-story building.

On nights like this—that is, the long ones—Bart liked to play a little game to help himself sleep. He tried keeping his eyes closed and perfectly still, as if he were a kid again and some burglar had wandered into his room and could hear his every breath. If he clenched his eyes too tight, he'd get a headache; not tight enough and the stealthy intruder moved in. Tonight he got the headache. But headaches, he found, would fade; guilt stuck around like a once-fed stray on the porch of his heart. He could pretend it wasn't there, but he'd never feel completely alone again…and never step outside without first taking a good, long look around.

CHAPTER 12

Mike leaned forward, straining to read the streets as he steered the great Buick down Jointner Avenue. He found Easter Street and worked the tires that way, finally pulling to a stop and staring at the address on a faded brick two-story, a well-to-do Georgian-style on a well-to-do street, checking it against the paper held in one hand. Satisfied, he leaned over, removed a bottle from the glove compartment, and took a few hard belts before putting it back.

He cut the ignition.

For a few minutes Mike sat on the street, staring at the Georgian in that curious way he'd learned to look at things, waiting for something, anything to jump out and slap him on the head. Nothing did, and instead he grabbed his cell phone and dialed Kathleen's number, put it to his ear. Listened as the female monotone rattled off her message: *We're sorry, you've dialed a number that has been disconnected or is no longer in service, please hang up and try your call again.* He hung up, dialed another number, listened to the recording. He repeated the process a third time, savoring the slight tingles up his spine, soaking in the words and the even, dronish lilt of the voice on the other end. Somewhere little lightning bolts were firing, brief flares in the impermeable depths of his mind.

He exhaled deeply, closed the phone. By now the whiskey was tapping him on the shoulder, and after tucking a couple sticks of Big Red into his mouth Mike opened the door and climbed out.

Earlier that morning, he'd placed a call to the Craven County Sheriff's Office and requested the name of the detective in charge of the investigation. Frank Holling was no stranger to Mike, the two had known each other a long while and if not close had gotten along well, cooperating on a few cases here and there over the years. Holling might find it interesting to know Mike was tracing his steps, but then Mike doubted he'd make an issue of it. And to be fair, Holling had done more than he'd expected for the case to be only a week fresh, including a twenty-man search through portions of the Creek Bed, a local name for the mass of woods Mike could now see sprouting beyond the Georgian's roof.

He followed the cement path leading to the door, tossing easy glances to the dogwoods and azaleas and listening to the birds do their thing from the trees. His arm was recovering nicely, the blazing pain faded to a throb, though with it lying there like a dead thing in the sling he couldn't help but feel awfully conscious of it as he reached out and rang the bell.

A middle-aged woman in a pea-colored housecoat answered the door. Round-faced with a bush of dyed yellow hair on top, she'd uttered not so much as the first word when Mike sensed the sadness, like a smell it was all over her: the stench of the bereaved. She shuffled forward, heavy-lidded eyes rising slowly to meet Mike's own.

"Yes?"

"Mrs. Chadwick? I was wondering if I might have a few minutes of your time?" He flipped his badge, and for an instant watched the light wash briefly back into the woman's eyes.

"Sure, why not?" she told him, then turned and walked away, leaving the door wide open.

Mike stepped inside, closing the door and following the woman down a main hall into the kitchen. There was some cooked bacon on the stove and some grits in a bowl on the table. She offered him some coffee and he said that would be fine and she poured him a cup.

"Cream or sugar?"

"Please."

As she mixed and stirred, Mike found a trash can and spit out his gum and took a moment to look around the kitchen. An older house, he could tell, but the appliances were fresh and the modifications subtle enough to make one forget the fact. She handed him his coffee and directed him through a threshold to the living room. There was a big TV in the corner and a small child asleep on the couch, a boy with golden blond hair.

Mike introduced himself as Detective Henry Porter of the Glass County Sheriff's Department. He assured her his presence was simply a matter of course, that he'd been contacted by Craven County law enforcement to assist in the investigation. At this juncture, he told her, there was no reason to get overly concerned about what had happened. He rattled off the usual facts about missing persons cases, doing his best to insinuate there was nothing special about his visit. On his way over he'd purchased a new notepad, and following his requisite introduction—no more than a calming mechanism he'd used too many times to remember—he retrieved the pad along with a pen from his shirt pocket. Settling into a chair, it was hard to balance the notepad and manage the pen with one arm, and he was still struggling with the pen cap when the woman said, "Gorry, aren't you busted up. What happened to your arm?"

"Would you believe it if I told you I was rescuing a kitten out of a tree?"

Mrs. Chadwick flashed a smirk, then promptly returned to the humorless droll Mike had become accustomed to in their short time together. He wondered if she'd been like this before, or if her son's disappearance had single-handedly altered her personality.

"No, no," Mike said, "nothing so exciting as that. Kind of embarrassing, but last week I wasn't paying attention and walked out into traffic. I caught myself, but not before this muddy old Ford came along and clipped my arm. It's fine, really, not even broken."

But she wasn't listening. Her eyes were dancing off in the distance, and when Mike looked around the room to get a sense of where she might be, his gaze flashed on a picture of a young T.J. Chadwick, and he sensed that familiar buzz scuttle up his spine.

"This ain't T.J.," she said. "He wouldn't do something like this, I just want you to know that. He knows better."

"What do you mean? Wouldn't do something like what?"

"You know. Runnin' off. Well, that's what everybody's sayin' ain't it?"

Mike laughed. "I'm not sure what anybody's saying, Mrs. Chadwick. I get here, they tell me next to nothing, I'm still trying to sort this whole thing out in my head. In any case, I think it's a little too early to start assuming anything." Mike's eyes slid to the couch, to the quietly sleeping child. "Would you like to move him to another room, or…"

Quick glance, wave of the hand. "He's fine."

Mike nodded. "Well, how about we start with the last time you saw T.J.?"

Assuming a petulant stare apt to turn water to ice, she said, "It was the afternoon of the fourteenth. Saturday. I'd been at work the morning and come home for lunch. Denny and this one here were piddling with their daddy out in the garage. T.J. was still asleep, then came down and we had some burritos before I left. Asked me could he spend the night off with the Rackley's and I told him that was fine. Then I kissed him and walked out the door."

As she talked, Mike sensed these trivial events had reserved an almost sacred place in her heart, the actions both a clue and testament to some greater Happening, some wicked occurrence outside of her control. There was a moment of silence as he scribbled into his pad.

"You mentioned Denny. Who's Denny?"

"Denny's my son. My oldest."

"And where is it you were working that day?"

"I work at the dealership here in town."

"Which one is that?"

"Plymouth-Chrysler-Dodge, off Brinker."

"And your husband?"

"Manager at the new Harris Teeter, over near the high school."

Mike consulted his pad. "According to my notes, T.J. was last seen leaving the house on an old Yamaha four-wheeler. Is that right?"

She nodded. "That's right."

"Who saw this?"

"Denny. He was here when they left."

"They. You mean"—more flipping—"Marius Garber, Blake Rackley, and Craig Rackley?"

"Just the Rackleys. I didn't know about the Garber boy till Sunday night. T.J. knows I don't like him taking up with Marius, so I guess he didn't tell me."

"Why don't you like him taking up with Marius?"

She shrugged. "Just think he's a bad influence, is all."

"He get in a lot of trouble?"

She made a face. "Give him time. And I'll tell you this just like I told the last one, it wouldn't surprise me one bit if this whole business was his fault somehow. I *told* T.J. to stay away from that one." She shook her head, ran a hand through the child's golden hair. "Boys are stubborn inside and out these days."

Mike just nodded and concentrated on a blank space in his pad. "What about your husband?" he asked. "Where was he when they left? Was he here?"

"He was, but he was inside watching TV."

"And this was around…what? Six o'clock?"

She nodded. The tears had started, and she was wiping them away with her sleeve. Then suddenly she excused herself, left the room. Mike stared at the young boy asleep on the couch and took a few sips of his coffee. When Vicky Chadwick returned, her face was a little less red and a little more dry and she seemed to have composed herself. Mike apologized if he'd upset her, but she told him not to worry about it, that it was nothing, she was just an emotional wreck these days. The cup was warm in his hands, and he placed it back on the coaster.

"So let me get this straight," he said. "To your knowledge, T.J. was staying off with"—back to the pad—"Craig and Blake Rackley?"

"As far as we knew, yes. They live just over the river, out in Bayview. The boys do this all the time, they ride their four-wheelers in the woods out there, they get muddy, they go to sleep, get up in the morning and do it all over again."

"And what? They never arrived at the Rackley's?"

She curled her lips. "No, I'd say they didn't. And they never intended to."

Mike frowned. "How's that?"

"Well, because they were pulling a fast one. See, Lena thought Blake and Craig were staying with us. They came here and then the three of them rode off to who the hell knows."

"Along with the Garber kid?"

"According to his mother, yes."

"Ah." Mike nodded. "And then they would come back tomorrow morning and no one would be the wiser. Not the most original play in the book, but it is one of the best."

Mrs. Chadwick was quiet. "I guess so."

They talked awhile longer, until Mike felt he'd plunged the depths of Vicky Chadwick's maternal knowledge. Eventually the child on the couch awoke and his mother sent him to the kitchen to finish his breakfast. Mike finished his coffee and stood, sweeping his eyes once more over the pictures of T.J. and Vicky and the rest of the Chadwick family.

Before he left, Mike turned to her and said, "Mrs. Chadwick, I'm sure you've been thinking about it anyway, so I'm gonna just go ahead and ask. Where do you think your son got off to last Saturday night?"

There was some plug in the woman's body that was knocked loose when Mike asked the question, and she began leaking air. When it was done and she'd lapped enough of it back up again, she said, "I've thought about that and thought about it since this whole thing happened, until I don't even know what to think anymore. But he didn't run away. I'm convinced of that. And wherever he went, Detective Porter, I think he's still there now."

"Oh? And why's that?"

"'Cause if he wasn't, he'd be here."

Mike stared at her, wondering which part felt weirder, being called by someone else's name or the fact that the name was preceded by the word *detective*. Before he could decide, Mike heard footfalls descending the stairs at the end of the hall. He glanced over in time to see an older boy emerge from the stairwell, cheeks and chin touched by hair growth and body widening at the shoulders. He took one look at Mike, another at his mother, then turned and walked out the door.

"Oh, that's Denny," Mrs. Chadwick said. "He's really upset about all this."

Mike watched as the boy skipped down the steps and was gone, then found himself staring through the glass of the storm door and off into the wild, unknowable planet beyond. After a long stretch of silence, he turned back to Mrs. Chadwick.

"I'm sure he is."

Afterwards Mike was hungry and grabbed a hot dog with all the fixings from one of those dusty roadside grills. He got it to go and ate in the parking lot, washing it down with a few light swallows from the bottle in the glove compartment. The chili was cold by the time he finished, but he managed to get it all down without burping up more than air.

He sat for a long time in his car, turning things over and over in his mind and deciding where to go next. It was just past noon and he watched the buzz of traffic on the road, watched the cars pull in and get their fill and pull out. He got out and tossed his trash into a barrel. Back in the car, he shuffled through the Missing Person posters—T.J.'s, one for the Rackley brothers, another for Marius Garber—wondering which of the remaining addresses was closer. A minute later he cranked the engine and followed the nearest line of cars onto the road.

By the time he pulled up outside the Garber house, his stomach had engaged in a little tug-of-war with itself, a dog fight for the ages, so he tried settling things with another drop from the bottle. Then he got out, making his way with icy confidence across the street.

From a distance, the Garber house looked a lot like that of the Georgian he'd visited on Easter Street: relatively well-to-do, birds singing in the trees, flowers in bloom. Adding to this effect was the foreboding presence of the Creek Bed just beyond the backyard. Of course, this particular patch of woods covered better than six square miles; with odds like that, it was no surprise Frank Holling's search had amounted to little more than a litter-fielding operation.

Up close, however, the illusion of similarity began to give way. There was no concrete walk leading up to the porch, for one thing, only those round gravel stepping stones, and the front yard was a little smaller and less manicured than the one he'd seen that morning. The siding could stand a pressure wash, and the roof could've done without the bad weather of the past twenty years. One other difference Mike couldn't help but note was the fact there was no car in the driveway out front. No car, but that didn't stop him from climbing the big wooden porch and giving the door a few hard swings.

At the next house over, there were four or five teenagers playing basketball in the road out front. Their game had stopped, and the oldest of the bunch was looking over at him, the basketball pressed to his shoulder like a black Atlas bearing up the weight of the world. He shouted across the yard, asking if Mike was looking for somebody. Mike told them he was looking for Mr. or Mrs. Garber and the boy walked over.

"What you want with Ms. Garber, man? She ain't home."

"It's about her son. Marius?"

"Shit." He said the word in a way Mike had never heard before, almost like two words. "You straight outta luck, too. Brutha done run off, didn't say nothin', just hauled off and—*chool!* Left." A strange look entered his eyes then, as if some invisible person had whispered a terrible secret into his ear. "You some kinda cop?"

"Something like that. Who are you?"

"Me? Name's Dakeem, I stay up the street."

By now some of the other boys had picked up on the conversation and started over. They were younger, between the ages of maybe twelve and fifteen. One of them asked if Marius was dead, and somebody told him shut up, Wing, you know Marius ain't dead.

Mike turned and asked the older boy about Marius's father.

"Marius ain't got no daddy," one of the others said, a skinny kid with cornrows. "They just stay here all by them self and don't nobody play with Marius 'cept the white kids."

Mike said, "Oh yeah? And why's that?"

"'Cause, man," Dakeem said, "Ms. Garber don't want Marius hanging out with people like us. All these years we lived on this street, how many times you think Marius came over to shoot some hoops? One time, 'bout two years ago." He laughed, shook his head. "We trash, man. Ain't you heard? Ms. Garber wanted her a nice little white boy, so now that's what she got. All the time fishing, shit like that. You ask me, she got just what she deserved."

"What do you mean, got what she deserved?"

He held out his arms. "He ain't here is he?"

"I *like* fishing," said one of the others.

"That's 'cause you white."

"No I ain't!"

They ran with that for a while, and Mike just stood there, wondering what he would ask Ms. Garber if she were home right now. Could she possibly tell him anything he hadn't already heard? Maybe, maybe not. There was nothing about this house that stood out to him, and neither had he felt that instant electric connection with Marius's poster—nor the Rackley's, for that matter—as he had with the Chadwick boy's. Once he found a gap of silence in the teasing, Mike asked Dakeem when he thought Ms. Garber might be home next.

"Shoot, Ms. Garber be home every day," he said. "Then she go to work at the hospital in the evenings."

Mike glanced around. "Well, she's not here now."

The boy lifted his hands. "Hey man, like I said. Ms. Garber don't exactly tell us every time she leave the house, know what I'm sayin'? All I can tell ya is she'll be home later tonight, probably 'bout one o'clock. But I wouldn't be here then if I was you, 'cause trust me Ms. Garber don't like seeing nobody when she get home from work." He laughed again. "Trust me."

Chapter 13

After leaving the Garber's, Mike steered the Buick into an abandoned lot and sat behind the wheel. The liquor had been simmering long enough, and now he wallowed in the upshot of an afternoon of sips and belts, head swimming, stomach full of nails. Slowly, the feeling passed. When it was gone he found himself holding a slip of paper he'd been given earlier that morning, a girl's name and phone number printed precisely along the top.

SHELLY PRATHER/524-9826

The name belonged to a girl T.J. had taken to at some point, though handing him the slip Vicky Chadwick confessed she couldn't be sure just what their relationship was, or if there was much of one at all anymore. T.J., she'd said, kept that secret better than our own government keeps most of theirs.

Acting on a whim, he found a payphone and dialed the number. A perky voice answered, and after a few minutes of moving his mouth and working what little charm he had left—which wasn't much—she'd agreed to meet with him, her only condition that she do it away from home. Her parents, she told him, were pretty nosy. He agreed, and they decided to meet at a small Boston-style deli in the food court at the mall. And though Mama Chadwick may've been kept in the dark, it didn't take Mike long to realize what type of relationship T.J.'d had with the girl. In two words *nothing serious*...but then he wondered at that. Nowadays he didn't know what that meant anymore; gone was the time of you-show-me-yours-I'll-show-you-mine and spin-the-bottle;

in was drugged-out intercourse and mystery make-out sessions in a closet—Seven Minutes in Heaven, they called that one.

Yet from the moment he met her, Mike felt he knew Shelly Prather inside and out. Knew, for instance, that she preferred double dates for dinner and a movie, that her favorite pastime was gabbing on the phone—thing kept going off like a bomb—that she dreamed someday of a white wedding and prepared for it presently by spreading her honey as hard and fast as she possibly could before it came. From where he was sitting, she seemed about as heartbroken over T.J.'s disappearance as she would've a missing cat, and should she discover that cat had been splattered over the pavement down the street, well sure, she'd shed a tear, she'd go through her spacey teenage funk and lament their bitterly cut-short times together, and then she'd move on and remember him one day twenty years from now, a mere figment of her crazy-days past.

"What are the kids saying?" he asked. "What do they think happened?"

"Kids? What kids?"

"Your friends," Mike laughed, perfecting a false grin. "The people who hung around with 'em, what are they saying?"

"Oh. They think they got into a bad drug deal and the drug dealer killed them."

Mike blanched. "*What?*"

"Yeah, that's what Jen and Kenzie think anyway. And Tony."

"What about you?"

She thought. "Mm. Not really. I think they're just off somewhere goofing, y'know? Trying to be *mysterious* or something."

"Does T.J. use drugs, that you know of?"

"T.J.? No. Now Craig, he used to drink cough syrup, and sometimes he'd steal his mom's Percocets. But then his mom thought it was Blake who was taking them and she grounded him, and so Craig stopped."

Mike snickered. "Why didn't Blake just tell her it wasn't him, that it was Craig?"

"I don't know," Shelly said. "Because they're brothers, I guess. But T.J. always works out, so I don't think he does any of that. He works out *a lot*." For the first time, a touch of true sadness moved into her face. After a moment, she said, "I hope he's all right."

Compared to his other conversations that day, this one went well. Nice and light, easy. Still, after a while he couldn't help but feel like a creepy old man, sitting at a tiny table in the food court with a girl young enough to be his daughter and the two of them eating and her too foolish to even know to feel awkward about it. He hurried things along, especially after realizing it was a bust, then thanked her for her time, paid for the meal, and got the hell out of there.

After that Mike called it quits and headed back to Hammond and the prospect of a long hot bath and a half-dozen or so ounces of Jack Daniel's in a glass in his hand. The bath was good and the whiskey better and so he poured himself another, and when it was empty he poured a third and sat at the table to lecture Kat on Henry Porter's unorthodox day on the detection beat.

Finally, he stopped writing and closed the book.

He'd been good with his cigarettes today—still had half a pack—but right now he needed one bad and lit up. He decided on a little fresh air and stepped outside, and when he absently tucked one hand into his pocket and felt the cool skin of the rental car's keys, heard that soft jingle that told him *here we are*—a bolt of electricity went tumbling up his arm. For a long time he ignored it, his mind combing the conversations of earlier that day, calmly sifting the information as a soldier would sift the many parts that make up a gun. Only there was no guarantee these pieces would form anything, and any time he came close to thinking they did his fingers jangled the keys and another cigarette was in order. So he smoked, washing down the stale taste of the cigarettes with more booze, until finally the whiskey softened the cries of the keys and there were no more monsters hiding in the hedges of his mind. He pulled out the keys, gleaming like polished silver in his hand, yellow rental tag still dangling from the chain.

See? Nothing.

Two minutes later he backed out and started down the road, raging at the damned Little Man who had once again risen and taken hold of him in the night. He'd dared to tangle with Captain Jack and now Mike sensed the old man fighting back, a mutiny from within, thrashing around, stomping the gas and turning the wheel and hitting the wipers to wash away the dirt.

When the car stopped, Mike got out and lurked his way over to the building across the street, his legs drawing him like obdurate pistons to the only
window with light burning inside, a smooth golden glow. Standing on tiptoe,
he peered in and saw ten, maybe fifteen people hunched in chairs near the
middle of the room. Scattered over the walls were posters with perfect little
slogans like *One day at a time* and *One drink is too much, a hundred is not enough* and
Man take a drink, then drink take a drink, then drink take the man. Civilized enough
from the outside, only Mike knew what was really going on in there, he knew
because he'd lived it—oh no, not here, but somewhere, and it was all the same
no matter where you went. Bunch of assholes sitting around in a circle-jerk
talking about how they can't quit the juice. Lame. Double lame. Reminded
him too much of real church.

His eyes scanned the room, scanned the losers and their sophomoric *oops-
I-did-it-again* stares. He felt sorry for them, in a way, so wrapped up in their self-
ish melodramatic cycles of suffering. *What gall!* Yeah, he was a boozehound,
what of it? Least he wasn't off somewhere smoking crack, sucking fatties for
cash.

At the front of the room was a banner bearing the words LIFE MAX, and
it was beneath this banner Mike spotted the goon, Goliath the Goon, chatter-
ing away from behind two massive forearms. Mills, his name had been. Once
again he'd attempted to hide his brutish He-Man frame behind loose-fitting
clothes and failed miserably. As he spoke, Mike heard the muffled reverbera-
tions of his voice on the other side of the glass, watched his hands as they described some esoteric situation meant to help these winos get over themselves
and join the human race.

"Gol-ly, getta load of this guy," Mike gushed to himself. "What a super-
prick. What is he, twelve years old? Thirteen? Guy's a comedian."

Mike snickered and licked his lips. He'd left the bottle back at the house,
but if he'd had it now he would've went bottoms up, then maybe knocked on
the glass and asked was anybody thirsty. Boy would they shit! The more he
thought about it the more he realized how much he liked the idea, loved it,
so much that he found himself running the scene in great detail through his
head, an imaginary flask in one hand; he pasted a cruel, blood-shot grin on
his face, feigned a knock, then tipped the flask high for all to see. Only at that

moment the goon's eyes turned, along with several other heads, settling on his silent position outside the glass.

Mike dropped the imaginary flask, dropped his arm, ducked from view. He stuck his back close on the church wall and began inching, comic spy-style, away from the window. Once at a safe distance, he slipped from the building and started across the grass, getting all of ten yards before hearing a sudden voice from behind.

"*Hey! Hey you!*"

He turned in time to see Goliath fuming out the door. There was a terrifying intensity to his walk, and for a split second Mike considered running, fleeing down the street like some kid busted in a game of ding-dong-ditch. Instead he just watched as Mills migrated down the steps and out into the yard, stopping only feet from Mike's slightly heaving frame.

"*Listen, buddy,*" he said, "*if you think this is some kinda…*"

Only he stopped then, his shining green eyes squinting in the darkness. "Wait, I know you…sure, you're that cop that came down about the laptops. Almost didn't recognize you without the uniform…" Mills glanced around, as if expecting a raid of armed policemen from the bushes—something Mike wished he could deliver. "So do you normally creep around knocking on church windows this time of night, or did you just really wanna come in that bad?"

Mike said, "I'm sorry, was just—" He stopped, got a hold of his tongue. "I was just out walking, I saw a light on. I don't know why…I don't know what I was thinking."

"You okay? What happened to your arm?"

Mike shrugged, tried a tentative cornerwise smile. "Banged all to hell, ain't it? Little fender bender's all, you know. It was nothing."

The man made another step. "What was your name again?" Mike told him, and he said, "Mike, are you drunk?"

Mike glanced out over the churchyard; as the green visual fluttered wildly before him, his mind repeated slogans from the posters on the wall. "Maybe," he said. "I don't know anymore—drunk, what does that mean? What does that even mean anymore?"

Another little step, an extended arm. "Hey," the big man said, "why don't you come in, huh? Come on. We can—"

Mike took a step back, swatted the arm from his shoulder. "Forget it, preacher. I've had just about all the help I can stand from your kind. So I'm drunk—you never been *drunk?* Huh? Whattaya—gonna tell me a story now? Teach me about some poor tore up son-of-a-bitch who can't keep his hand out the cookie jar? I don't give a good shit…"

Mike missed a step, stumbled backwards, and as Mills rushed to stabilize him one of Mike's hands flew out, catching him just over the eye. Mills grunted and took a step back, put a finger to his head, looked at it.

"Yeah," he said, "you're drunk, all right."

"Damn straight, sonny. Baptized in beer and whatcha gonna do about it?"

Mills studied him a moment, an unexpected fire buried deep in his eyes; again Mike sensed that strange inner urge to go jogging down the street. Before he'd had time to consider it, Mills took another step back and said, "Door's open anytime you want it, Officer Lunsmann. I don't mean just tonight. I know you think you're not interested, but you should really give it a try. Now as much as I'd like to stay out here and talk…I really would, I'm not kidding when I say that…but I can't. I have a class to finish. I'm guessing you won't be joining us?"

Mike laughed. "Not hardly."

"Are you driving?"

Mike told him not to worry about what he was doing, that maybe he should just get on back inside before all those filthy addicts did something crazy like roll up the rugs and smoke 'em. Huh? How about that?

Another gaze, this one more inscrutable than the last, and Mills turned, walking silently back to the church. Mike watched him go, a mask of victory spread over his face, and then Mills was gone and the mask vanished. He struggled to recall if he'd swung on the guy or if the hit had been unintentional, but the information was lost, irretrievable, and Mike experienced that eerie sensation he had when realizing he'd lost his footing on the night—a floating emotion, laced with dread, cut with fear, drowned in the extinction of hope. *The line has been drawn,* that emotion told him, *from here on all bets are off.* His mind moved back to his little drama at the window, and looking back he couldn't help but wonder had things went further than he remembered. What was it Mills had said, about knocking on church windows? Had his fingers actually *connected* on the glass, had he actually *knocked*...or was that only his mind playing tricks again? What had gotten into him lately? What was he thinking?

Only he wasn't thinking, and he knew it. He stared again to the golden rectangle of the window until finally he could stand it no longer and looked away, his face a splotch of deepest darkness in the night. He ambled back to the Buick and slid behind the wheel. Deep down he was a swell human being, he knew that. He *knew* that. So why didn't he believe it anymore? He knocked the transmission into drive, but for another minute his foot only rested firmly on the brake, eyes locked firmly on the church, mind locked firmly on the image of himself as a younger man with a bright future in this world.

In a moment it all slipped away and the Buick rolled off into the night.

Chapter 14

Doug pumped his Nautica cologne and tugged at his hair with a comb, studying himself with the eye of a trained conservator. Over the last few months he'd perfected a series of choice expressions for the ladies—one for *handsome laughter*, another for *boyish charm*, he had *mysterious sadness* and *passionate contemplative*—and now he performed a stirring medley, checking the angles, the lighting, making sure those annoying folds of skin over his eyes didn't droop down and make him look like a freakin' cartoon. Satisfied, he walked out of the bathroom and down the stairs, where he found Brent Northrup parked next to Bart on the living room couch, the two of them watching TV and snacking on chicken legs.

Brent turned. "'Sup Dougie."

"How long have you been here?"

"Oh, calm down," his mother called from the kitchen. "He's just got inside, we haven't tainted his mind yet."

"Well...ready?" Doug asked.

Brent got up, made his way to the kitchen and tossed the leftover of his meal into the trash. "Thanks for the chicken, Mrs. Covington. It was delicious."

She told him that he was certainly welcome, that he should stay for supper sometime, while Doug did his best to usher Brent out the front door. Before they could make it, however, Doug heard his mom say, "Oh wait! Son, don't you need a little extra money in case you get hungry later on? That bowling alley food must cost a fortune. Here, let me see..."

"Kathleen, he's already had dinner, I'm sure the boy has enough for a snack," Bart offered, the words garbled by the bone of chicken in his mouth.

His eyes remained glued to the television—some courtroom drama with Richard Gere. "You've already given him twenty dollars, dear."

"Here." Kathleen emerged from the kitchen, purse in hand. She revealed a ten dollar bill and pushed it toward her son. "Now you be sure and get something, don't starve yourself. And that goes for you too, Brent—Doug, you share that with him, understand?"

"Yes, ma'am."

"Thanks, Mrs. Covington."

Doug gave his mother a quick hug, then said goodbye and slipped out the door. Sixty seconds later he puffed his menthol to life as Brent backed out and eased down the road. Doug had gotten rather used to this routine over the past few weeks, had gotten used to Brent and the too-much cherry smell of the Pontiac's interior. Had gotten used to the long nights. It was easier now with Gary out of the picture. Not that the two of them never talked—they did—but as it turned out Doug and Gary seemed to have less in common than Doug and Gary's cousin, and as long as his name was thrown around and kept in circulation, Doug's mother didn't seem too concerned about the idea of him and Brent hanging out. Bart...well, Bart hadn't exactly been himself lately. Maybe the guy'd been working too much, he didn't know. Maybe life had finally kicked him in the ass.

Maybe he was depressed.

"Were you having fun in there?" Doug asked. "Thought I told you to keep away from them, did I not? Why didn't you come and get me? Or do you just have a thing for hanging out with my stepdad?"

Brent only laughed. "Hey, he told me to have a seat, I took one. Your mom handed me a chicken leg, I took that, too. Dude, your mom can *cook*—that shit was tasty as hell."

"Oh yeah?"

"Oh yeah. Matter fact, I'm 'bout to go back right now and get some more. Finish that stupid movie with old Bart."

"Well, drop me off before you go. I'm just gonna drain my veins into this ditch."

"Yessuh, will do," Brent said. Then after a moment: "Here, got something for ya."

He tossed a baggie into Doug's lap; Doug picked it up, and inside could see three small pills, two blue and one pink.

"What are they?" he asked.

"Diazepam. You know, muscle relaxers."

Doug sensed a growing tension in his chest, a dark consumption of his innards. He'd never taken drugs—not like this, anyway—and had heard enough stories to make him anxious about taking these. He massaged the bag for a second, making it crinkle and pop.

"What'll they do?"

Brent shrugged. "They'll *relax* you, Doug, whattaya think. Wait till we get to Ray-Ray's to take them though. Don't try and chew 'em up or they'll hit you all at once."

Chew them up? Doug thought. He stared down at the bag, weighing his options on a mental scale he hadn't known existed one year earlier. Only recently that scale had always tipped in his favor, a carousel of dreams, and as far as he was concerned, all signs pointed to fun.

For these, said some movie-guy voice in his head, *are the days of our lives...*

"And Doug, if you tell me you left your weed back at the house again, I swear I'm gonna punch you in the nose."

Doug patted his pocket. "Relax," he said. "Got it right here."

Brent smiled, leaned over and fiddled with some knobs on the radio. "Well, fuck a duck," he said, and then the music was up and the Pontiac was thumping along the road out of Clover.

First stop was Ray-Ray's.

Ray-Ray was a few years older than Brent, and lived in a single-wide trailer off a dirt road in Southbend. Though he'd never met the guy, Doug thought the name was familiar, and no sooner had Brent navigated the muddy road to his house than Doug recalled having been there once before, back in a time when he and Gary had been left to lay farts and play pinochle out in the car. This time he made it through the door, and his first thought upon entering was that someone had left something burning on the stove and it had caught fire, so dense was the swirling, inhuman fog of smoke through the trailer.

They stayed for maybe half an hour—and not a very exciting half hour at that. Five guys sitting around watching UFC, one girl forcing a bottle down a baby's throat. Ray-Ray was a long hair, with a narrow wire of a body spotted with tattoos, lots of skulls, lots of fire. His two friends had joined the club. At one point Ray-Ray motioned to one of them, some guy called Owl, who then reached behind the couch, revealing a strange object which Doug at first thought to be a lamp with no light bulb and no shade. On the TV screen, a massive black man was ring-dancing with an Asian. As if on cue, the girl with the baby moved off down the hall and returned with a Ziploc half-filled with grass; Owl stuffed a portion into a fixture on the funky vase, then placed his mouth over a hole at the top and lifted his lighter. An absurd bubbling noise filled the room as water danced down below, smoke filling its tall glass neck; then Owl inhaled sharply and the smoke was gone and the thing was passed on. A moment later Owl said *ahhhhhh* and the room was again full of smoke and the black man was throwing his fist into the Asian's face.

From the corner of his eye, Doug watched the device being handled by each new set of hands, studying carefully the subtle and seemingly complex motions that made this thing go. *Ah, so smooooth* someone exclaimed, but after Doug had fiddled with it, finally coaxing forth some smoke, he was too exhausted from concentrating on how the damned thing worked to remember if it was smooth or not. At least he hadn't drowned himself...

Then he remembered the pills. And though he wasn't crazy about the idea, he got up and went to the bathroom and used the faucet to swallow them whole. Soon as the small gulp was complete, however, he immediately wished he'd made a different choice, and it was then Doug began to suspect that maybe there was some other force at work in his mind, some Dark Appetite which short-circuited his defenses and sent him stumbling forward through the crazed wilderness of his own desire.

Doug didn't like that feeling, not at all, and for a moment considered jamming a finger down his throat, regurgitating the little devils before they'd had a chance to go down and work their evil magic. Of course he was too high for that, convinced that every sound was a thousand times louder than it actually was, that they'd all hear his ear-splitting gags from the living room and be waiting with their tired laconic quips and sleepy-eyed stares. And what would he say then? Nothing, there was nothing he could say.

So he'd walked out and the room was even thicker than before, saturated with the clingy, grungy stench of pot. The baby was bouncing on her mother's knee and the Asian was standing over the black man and putting his toes into the black man's ribs. Then the match was over, the celebration began, and it was around this time Brent stood and two minutes later they were walking out the door and down the three little steps to the car.

Next they drove over to Eddy G.'s, where there was supposed to be a good-size party that night. The street out front was deserted when they arrived, however, and moments later Eddy G. came hobbling out to their window. He was a big guy with a horizontal gut, long curly hair and a humongous mustache. Though not a particularly old man—early-forties maybe—the rheumy eyes and incessant groans and great dewlaps up his neck told of a rough road ahead. In his usual husky wheeze, he told them sorry, grand bash had been canceled, said Mrs. G. was pissed all to hell and had made everybody leave.

"It's these young girls, y'know? They come over dressed the way they do nowadays, with their shirts too small and their asses hanging out and Diane, y'know, she can't be around all that. She gets all these ideas, crazy things. Last time we had one a these, a couple gals had too much to drink, y'know, got on top a table and danced around a bit, couldn't a been more 'an sixteen. Diane, oh jeez, she about shit a brick when she saw that. What can I say? She's getting old, guess she feels threatened, all that jazz…"

He'd heard most people were heading over to Jackson Lara's house. It was a bit of a drive, however, and by the time they arrived the sky was black, the moon a ghostly half-bulb overhead. Dust-spattered Chevys and Fords sat jammed across the yard, and it took Brent maybe ten minutes to find a place to park. The Lara house was set ridiculously far back from the road, so Brent said he didn't expect having to make a run for it.

"But look," he told Doug after cutting the engine, "why don't you leave your bag in the car, just in case. Just put it under the seat."

"Why?"

Brent peered through the back glass, studying the massive house in the distance.

"Well, if the cops *do* show up and wanna be dicks about it, they'll try and search us. But they won't check the cars."

"Well…are you sure?"

Brent hesitated. "Pretty sure."

Inside the party was raging, a swirling smoke pit of bouncing bodies, bad smells, and the careless laughter of the fallen; loud thumping hip-hop pounded through speakers the size of refrigerators, the subtle underpinnings of chatter working their own clanging melodies through the night. Teenagers roamed, all of them laughing and smoking, some holding beer cans or plastic cups, others slamming shots or drinking straight from the bottle. In one room, a spirited game of beer pong was in progress, with red-eyed spectators cheering on contenders, or else booing their disapproval. Doug recognized one of these from high school—they'd shared two classes the previous semester—and felt a flurry of kinship at her familiar face. There were other familiar faces, he noticed, though most of these were upper classman, and if they noticed Doug Lunsmann at all it was with the sort of irritable passivity he'd grown used to during his freshman year, as if his presence somehow sullied their good time.

To hell with 'em, Doug decided. *Up their ass with a blade of grass.*

He and Brent had gotten separated after arriving, parted by the long arms of too much everything, and at last his good friend emerged. He handed Doug a bottle and then vanished through a mash of bodies, swallowed up once more into the music which seemed to come from everywhere at once. Doug stared at the beer with a dubious expression, wondering what good could possibly come from such a bottle as this.

He popped the top and took a sip. Flinched at the taste, took another.

He stepped out back and stood nipping at his beer, nursing it, making it last. For once, everything in life seemed good. An uncommon peace settled on his shoulders, and for a long time he did not question it. Only after a moment did he notice the constant twitch in his arms, the creeping breed of lethargy washing through his veins, and then remembered the pills and realized they were eating at him, gnawing a numb little hole in his perception. But he didn't mind, he'd felt worse in his life—much worse. Grinning, he swallowed the last of his Busch and then heard the soft squeal of a voice from behind. It took him a moment to realize the squeal was shaped in the form of a name, and that the name was his own.

"Doug Lunsmann? Doug, is that you?"

He turned to see Nicky Collier, the girl he'd spotted playing beer pong minutes earlier. A swift wave of ink black hair fell over her face, swallowing her in a hood of shadow; only as she moved out from the patio into the yard could he make out the dark eyes and smooth particulars of her face. It was a pretty one, he thought, not exceptional, but there had been times when he'd looked at her—with her long bronzed legs, those great golden thighs—and felt that agonized bliss that told him he liked what he saw. Not often, mind, but often enough to make him smile now and walk over, the two of them meeting in a patch of moonlight in the backyard.

"Hey, Nicky."

"*I can't believe you're here!*" she gasped, voice crackling with what he thought rather untoward emotion. She leaned forward and gave him a small hug, their bodies pressed together for an instant, and Doug felt electricity crawl in spirals up his legs. Without realizing it, the beer tumbled from his hands, hitting the grass.

Nicky's expression widened.

"*Oh! Doug, I'm so sorry!*" she cried, and was about to say more when her voice was snapped up in an unruly belch.

He looked down, slower than usual. "No, it's okay," he told her. "It was empty."

"Well, c'mon. I'll take you to get another one…"

And then she had grabbed his arm and pulled him into the house, through the kitchen, into the den. Drums pounded, bass lines danced. She stopped to talk with an older guy Doug recognized from school, a redneck-type who paused long enough to give Doug a once-over and then handed Nicky two Michelob Lights.

"You know that guy?" Doug asked once they'd moved on. His voice sounded far away.

She just laughed. "Uh, *yeah*. That's Jackson. It's his house you dodo head."

He said, "Oh."

They lingered in the kitchen for a while, screaming over the music and pulling at their beers. Nicky explained how she'd come over with her friend Paisley, who come to think of it she hadn't seen in a while, hope she weren't sick, then told him how her parents were going through a divorce. Doug dredged up his own broken-family story, and it had been so long since he'd told it that he actually felt affected. They talked about sophomore year, and teachers they wished were dead. Dabbled in colleges for about two seconds flat. And through it all Doug felt a curious energy moving in the room, pulling at him—pulling at them both, he felt—and recognized it as the loosey-goosey sway of flirtation. No sooner had he paused to register this than she grabbed him by the hand.

"C'mon," she said, pulling him up a flight of stairs and through a closed door on the second floor. He glanced around and saw an empty closet and a bureau backed by dusty mirrors, a stripped bed. Somewhere in the distance the crashing roar of the party continued, but from here it seemed miles away; here it was dark and lonesome, almost quiet.

"Whose room is this?"

Nicky looked around, as if unaware they were even in a room. "Oh, this is Maggie's room. Jackson's sister. She stays in Wilmington now."

Near the window, Doug saw a Queen Anne wingback which seemed so out of place that for some reason it struck him as funny. He made his way over and sat down, lit a cigarette. "So," he said, "sounds like you know this Jackson fella pretty well then."

"Jackson?" She shrugged. "He's my cousin. But he always *says* he's my brother, you know, since I don't have any *real* brothers. Just sisters."

"Ah, the Collier sisters." Doug smirked. "Of course, how could I forget?"

She gave him a look. "What's that supposed to mean?"

"Nothing at all."

"Let me guess—you want me to set you up, right?"

"Set me up? With who?"

"Oh, stop playing, Doug. With Kristen."

"Whoa-ho," Doug said, "I don't want you setting me up with anybody, and I *especially* don't want you setting me up with your sister. Hell no, Nicky— what are you, mental?"

"It's all right," she slurred. "I know Kristen's prettier than me, I don't care. 'Cause she might be pretty but she's dumb as a *stump*."

Doug laughed. "You're crackers, Nicky. Look, your sister's all right, okay? But...I'd rather have Nicky Collier any day of the week. Well, any *night* of the week, ha-ha…"

She was quiet, eyes swirling deep in her head. A subtle grin eased onto her face and she got up, made her way over. She climbed onto Doug's lap, dropping her head onto his chest.

"Doug, Doug, Doug."

For a moment he thought she'd fallen asleep, only then Nicky began shifting on top of him, writhing with a sensuous, almost serpentine grace that told him she was by no means asleep, but rather as if some vital thing were waking up inside.

"You know," he told her, "if Jackson walked in right, he'd probably kick my ass. You know that don't you?"

"No, he wouldn't," she said, speaking with utter assurance. "I wouldn't let him. I would tell him to get out, leave us alone."

He looked at her then, flashing *sexy seductive* and growing a smirk. He snubbed his cigarette into the arm of the chair before lifting his lips to her own, feeling the warm, slimy touch of her tongue dipping in and out of his mouth. They played this game for a while, not knowing exactly what was happening or why, not caring all the same, simply enjoying the slow sensual ride of discovery and exploration, and savoring the ravenous connection forged in the act.

Doug became aware of a silly heat in his body, of a subtle sweat crawling over his skin. Nicky's arms tightened and eventually his kisses moved south, first to her neck, then dropping down to her chest. By this time it was apparent their current position would not do and, as if in mental conspiracy, they rose and stumbled awkwardly across the floor, splashing onto the bed.

He tugged at her blouse, exposing the great lump of her left breast, the dark circle of the areola, a hard little nipple. He put it in his mouth, and a low escalating moan crept from Nicky's throat. He felt her up with his other hand, running it up her shirt and cupping her tit and brushing his thumb gently overtop, not even thinking now but high on wild, blind, screaming-at-the-stars emotion. His mind kept coming back to the idea of her crotch—what it felt like down there, did it smell, was it wet like everybody said—and suddenly he wanted to stick a hand down her beltline more than anything he'd ever wanted in his life. But he didn't. He'd later regret it, but at the time he knew it wasn't right and so didn't do it, just kept working the tit and sucking at her neck and rubbing his pounding erection into her leg, until at last he felt a sharp tingling sensation and his body clenched tight, racked in a sudden, inexplicable spasm of pleasure which seemed to emanate from his groin. He sputtered harshly, clenching at the mattress as the cascading shower of bliss washed over his body. Then, as quickly as it had come, the feeling was gone, trailing softly into the night and leaving his body a limp sardine on top of Nicky's own.

Nicky seemed to have sensed what happened and giggled smugly, and in the minutes that followed things began to wind down: tongues returned to mouths, hands were retracted, clothes fixed and flattened. For a moment they lay there in the silence, until at last Nicky turned to him and said, "Don't know about you, but I could use a cigarette."

Doug agreed he could definitely use a cigarette.

Later that night, as Brent and the other members of the Northrup family lay sleeping in their beds, Doug sat by a window thinking about all that had happened. And what had happened? Nothing he could believe. Nothing that made any sense to him now. He'd had a tit in his mouth—*Nicky Collier's* tit. *What?* But it was true—it really was—and a part of him never wanted to brush his teeth again. Just thinking about it put fire in his bloodstream, and eventually it was too much and so he got up and walked out the door.

Not far behind Brent's house were the bones of a farm long since abandoned, its bins and silos hovering like massive tombstones across the horizon. Doug walked to them now, like a soul awakened from death, stopping at a silo and the bottom of a steel ladder that soared higher and higher into the night, vanishing somewhere between here and the moon. Without quite realizing what he was doing, he placed one hand on a rung overhead…and started climbing.

He did not stop.

He kept his eyes on the next rung up and made one foot follow the next. His hands shook like maracas and his head swelled, higher and higher until finally the temperatures dropped south and at last he turned and looked down, down, down.

"*Oh…*"

Things were small down there, smaller than he'd expected. He hesitated, wanting to turn back and yet also aware of the safety of the small platform only feet away.

He faced the ladder and kept moving.

A moment later he footed the small platform and took a deep breath, turned and looked down. And gazing down at something like that, the houses sprawled like a Monopoly board below, he couldn't help but think what it would be like to throw himself over, to plummet to the ground below, to strike the earth, casting up a thin line of dust like a symbol of the life that had been knocked from his body. Of course he would never do such a thing—he wasn't stupid—but the thought was there, and there was more power in it than he expected. Then he thought about what it would be like to survive such a fall, and in a jagged trajectory his thoughts moved to his father, to his father battered and bruised in that lonesome hospital bed. He'd learned not to feel much for his dad in the past couple years, but seeing him like that Doug couldn't help but feel *something*, though he chose not to delve too much into what that might be. Even now his stomach produced a nervy twitch at the visual and he quickly shoved it away, a forgotten memory in a world of dreams.

Doug stared out over the town below, thinking how small everything looked from this height. Distantly he felt the sticky residue of cum still pasted up his leg, smeared like dried human glue in his boxers. He gazed at the clouds, wondering how such things were formed and why, wondering who he was and knowing that tonight he'd taken some irrevocably profound step toward the person he would one day become…and one step away from the person he'd always been. And nestled between the two there was only tonight—tonight and him standing here high above the earth and with fading clouds in the dark blue sky. He could walk on them, if he wanted. But he wouldn't.

Because here he was free.

And why would he ever leave a thing like that?

Chapter 15

By the time he emerged from the beer cave carrying a six-pack of Coors and two bottles of Mad Dog 20/20, Harvey Slater was already well beyond the legal limit. He knew that. But unlike others too stupidiotic to know better, he didn't advertise. One foot moved perfectly in step with the other, his breaths were neither deep nor shallow, his temper very much in check.

He stood in line, whistling fragments of long-forgotten songs and pulling against an itch at the very center of his back. After a small eternity, the itch abated and the line inched forward and Harvey stepped to the register to check out. A teenager with glasses asked him for his ID.

"Huh?"

"I need to see your ID?"

Harvey glanced back to either side, as if checking for wings. "Me? Are you serious?"

"I have to ask for your ID, sir, I don't—"

"Let me ask you this," Harvey interrupted, calmly. "Just how old do you think I am? How old do I *look* to you?"

The teenager stared back, a vaguely stuporous glint in his eye.

"Well?"

"I really don't know, sir. Maybe if you had your ID…"

With an irritated grunt—but not *too* irritated—Harvey produced a wallet of worn brown leather and flipped it open, flashing an ID. "There," he said. "Happy?"

No reply. The teenager rang him up, accepted the tender and gave him his change.

"Thanks a million," Harvey said. "Now whyn't you get back to mopping up aisle two."

He grabbed the paper bag and walked away, a string of curses filtering the air in his wake. Then he was outside and his feet carried him to his car, a wasted Yugo with too many miles and an ass-end covered in stickers. He slammed the door and fired up the engine, was ready to drive off when a scrappy-looking youngster of about eighteen rushed over, stopping at his window; then a small hush of words, at the end of which the paper bag was lifted (minus the Mad Dog, of course) and passed outside. The boy nodded and then smiled and reached out his hand—but the Yugo was already pulling away, muffler calling out for vengeance as it slid slowly, carefully down the road.

When it was gone the boy opened the bag and looked inside, weighing what he saw against the twenty bucks he'd slipped in Harvey Slater's palm. There was a slow tanking feeling as he peeled back the paper; but it was short-lived, limping away at the sight of the six-pack at the bottom of the bag. He touched them. Cold. Yes, cold was good. With a grin that betrayed his own youthful glee, he closed the bag and then started across the lot.

"Get something good?"

The boy spun at the voice, almost dropping the bag in the process.

"Whoa, whoa. Don't get too excited now, you might break something." With a slightly twisted expression, not really a smirk, Mike shuffled out of the shadows at the side of the building. "So tell me Denny, what's in the bag? Something tells me it's not a pack a gum."

The boy squinted at him. "Hey, I remember you," he said. "You're that guy came asking about T.J., got my mom all worked up again."

"Ah, so you did see me. You were out of there so fast I couldn't tell—didn't even stop and say hello."

Denny seemed to find this amusing. "Say hello? Why *would* I? What do you, work for the cops or something?"

Mike sputtered, a thing that would've been laughter if he wasn't so drunk. "Denny, I *am* the cops."

"Oh yeah? Why ain't you ever dressed up like one then?"

Mike looked down. "You don't call this dressed up?"

"Man, you know what I mean."

"Whattaya think—I'm a *detective*, asshead. That your car?"

Denny glanced to the Mustang, not for long. A couple of different answers floated through his head. It was hard, but he went with the smart one.

"Yeah. So what?"

"Well, would you like to stand out here all night holding that bag of beer, or you wanna go somewhere we can talk?"

Denny stood glaring at the man—a stranger, really—wondering what sort of crazy country paid lunatics like this to walk around with a loaded gun. Serve and Protect, what a joke. After a long moment of silence—a moment taut with the whims and fancies known only to teenagers—he went over and opened the car. They both climbed inside.

No sooner had he cranked the engine than Mike snatched the bag and set it at his feet.

"Hey! What are you—"

"Just drive," Mike told him, voice hard as concrete. "Drive, I said. C'mon, *go go go*."

Mike leaned back and closed his eyes. There was no comfort in the posture, but then comfort meant so little nowadays, comfort was a foreign language. Once again he'd been swept up in the feeling his life was spiraling toward some inexorable point in the future, a point when all things came clicking magically together, making sense once and for all. Sometimes that point seemed more distant than others. And yet, like it or not, it was this dusty road he traveled and so on he rode, confident it was a road that had chosen him and not the other way around.

He'd made more than a few calls in the past week, and made his share of visits, chasing his tail simply for the pleasure of seeing himself run. Nights lying in bed, however, his thoughts turned again and again to young Shelly Prather, and their conversation at the food court. There was nothing obvious about it—no map with meandering dotted lines and a giant red X—though the whole conversation had gotten him thinking in other directions. Thinking about young people and their peculiar loyalties and bonds. Thinking about family. Finally he'd played a hunch, not knowing whether it would pay off but playing it all the same. You lay the cards like so, you flip them over, sometimes you beat the house. Not as often as you'd like, of course, but then that's the game now ain't it?

"All right," Mike said, once they'd found an appropriately spooky leg of country road and stopped the car. "So tell me, Denny, what do you know? What is it you're holding back?"

"I ain't holding nothing back."

With a stoic sort of frustration, Mike reached down with his good hand, snatching a can from the bag in the floorboard. He popped the top and began pouring from the window.

"Hey man! Hey chill out, that stuff cost me twenty bucks!"

"C'mon, you're his brother, you gotta know something. What's the deal Denny, where's he at? He tell you, or did he just leave a note?"

"Please just—stop! I don't know where T.J.'s at, all right?"

He stopped pouring. A trickle of Coors bounced around at the bottom of the can; Mike poured it down his throat, then leaned out and tossed the shell into some weeds outside the car.

Mike said, "Let's try again. What do you know?"

Things went on like this for a while, Denny Chadwick swearing innocence, then just swearing as he watched his booze pissed away outside the window of his own car. It was amazing the sort of power this act had over such an oth-erwise intelligent young man; he might as well have been sending electric cur-rent through the boy's body. After Coors number three, Denny had hit all the superficially private details of T.J.'s life, including his small brush with Shelly Prather (though "brush" was not exactly the euphemism Denny employed). At the appearance of number four from the bag, he was about ready to talk.

"All right, look, there's this one place they might've gone, all right? Marius found it one day, I guess they go there sometimes, go camping. Maybe they went there, I don't know. And even if they did, so what? They're not out there now."

"How would you know if they're out there or not? Have you been there?"

"No, I haven't *been* there. Is your brain busted? It's out in the woods in the middle of nowhere, I'm not going out there."

Mike shook his head. "They've searched the Creek Bed, there's nothing there."

"It's not *in* the Creek Bed. But it doesn't matter, that's what I'm *telling* you, because if that's where they were they would've been back by now. Why would they stay out there?"

"They could be hurt, Dougie. They could be injured, you ever think of that? What if some wild animal happened on them in the middle of the night? A mama bear, or bobcat?"

Denny glared at him. "You wanna stop doing that? My name's Denny."

"Huh?"

"I said my name's *Denny*, all right? You keep calling me Dougie."

"I do?" Mike stopped, staring at his own clenched fists. There were four of them.

"Look," Denny told him, "what T.J. does is his own business. Craig's been talking to some party girl in Boone, I'll bet they all hitched a Greyhound or something. They'll be back."

There was a tiny check in Mike's stomach, something that told him this last statement could not be further from the truth, that indeed, they would never be back, never be found. That they were gone, in some way neither he nor Denny could ever dream to understand. A sheet of dust eddied in that preordained road up ahead, and through it all Mike noticed a glimmering pinpoint of brilliance, drawing him like a drowning man to a raft.

"Take me there," he said. "I want to see it. I want to go there and see it for myself."

"Oh, jeez. I guess you're gonna pour the rest of that out the window if I don't?"

Mike looked at him. "Just start the car, Denny."

Denny groaned. And started the car.

The drive was long. They'd taken a left toward Clarendon when the rains started back, pummeling at the windshield and causing a slow, hypnotic glaze over Mike's face. Frank Holling may've searched a good part of the Creek Bed, but never in a million years would he have wasted his time with wherever it was Denny Chadwick was taking him. As the Mustang rolled deeper into the endless turns and lost stretches of blacktop, Mike realized they were nearing the Craven County line.

Just as he noticed the sign up ahead announcing NOW ENTERING LANCER COUNTY, Denny pulled to a stop at the side of the road. There were deep woods at either side of the car, and through the boy's window Mike saw the tree line pushed back beyond a couple acres of muddy pasture. By now the torrent had slipped off, fading to a gently swirling mist, and in his haze Mike couldn't help but feel trapped in some dewy upholstered bubble.

Denny lifted one hand, pointing through the darkness. "Out there."

"Out there where?"

"Right *there*," Denny told him, his face green in the glare of the dashboard lights.

Mike trained his eyes on the spot, though from his perspective everything looked the same; the entire hedge of forest was silent, muggy, dead. He said, "You bullshittin' me?"

"No, I'm not bullshitting you! Damn, dude, what is your *deal*? Look, this was T.J.'s thing, all right? I've only been out here once—and that was a long friggin' time ago. See those two deadfalls there? No, over there. See? And the one sticking out down there? The clearing is somewhere between them, I can't remember where."

"How far in?"

Denny considered. "Not far enough to be hidden from the road," he said. "I remember 'cause the only time I went back there I took T.J.'s Banshee for a spin through the woods, and I remember seeing the cars on the road out here from one of the paths."

"Banshee? Same four-wheeler he was riding this time?"

Denny nodded. A dull, almost nostalgic sort of gloom fell over his eyes. The past was fine, that look said, he could chat all day and half the night about that; but when it came to the here-and-now and the subject of his missing younger brother, Denny Chadwick clenched up tighter than a clamshell.

"Denny, why haven't you told anyone about this? Why didn't you—"

"Like I said, what T.J. does is his own business." For the first time that night, Denny produced a pack of cigarettes, lit one up and started puffing. "He ain't out there anyway, so what difference does it make?"

In the silence that followed, Mike began to wonder what other information the boy may have neglected to mention—either to his parents or here tonight—and was about to ask when suddenly he felt a steel rod of pain being driven into his head, compliments of Dr. Daniel's. Mike pressed fingertips to the middle of his forehead, as if pulling some psychic tumor from his brain.

Denny's voice, distant: "You all right, mister?"

"Let's go," he said. He sat up, wiping a bit of sleep from his eyes. He unlocked his door. "C'mon, Denny, get out of the car. You know where it is, I want you to show me."

"You crazy? I'm not going out there!"

"Get out of the car, Denny, I'm not messin' around."

Denny shook his head. "Man, what's with you? You got a death wish or something? You don't wanna go out there."

"Sure I do. And you're coming with me."

"Listen, mister—you can't go out there. It's *raining*. It's *dark*. It's *muddy*. Your friggin' *arm* will probably fall off."

Mike reached down, grabbing a Coors. He glared back in what he hoped to be a menacing manner (to him it just felt drunk), but the look fell short and that's when he saw it. Saw that this time it wouldn't work, that the boy would actually let him pour it out, the whole thing, and probably the other two as well. In fact, if Mike's intuition was correct, nothing short of a pointed gun could get Denny into those woods tonight. He was...*scared*.

Mike let out a breath, a long, sweeping breath redolent of whisky and halitosis and little else. The hand moved back to his head, only this time there was more shame than pain in the gesture. What if the world was wrong? he thought. What if you didn't get older and wiser after all, what if you just got older? What if wisdom was perfected in the ignorance of youth? What was that saying—from the mouths of babes? He'd actually been about to drag this poor kid out in the middle of the night, in the middle of a storm, to who the hell knows what in the middle of the woods. Yes, older and wiser seemed a little too old-fashioned for him right now.

"Listen, man, I do have a curfew, you know. I gotta get home..."

For a long time Mike said nothing, watching the mist swirl and dance around them...

CHAPTER 16

B y the time they'd arrived back at the store, it was past midnight and the rains had picked up again. The station was closed and the parking lot empty, Mike's Buick shrouded in windswept darkness at the end of the lot. Denny pulled the Mustang in close and stopped.

"This yours?"

Mike nodded, and had started to open the door when he leaned over, grabbing up the three remaining Coors in the paper bag.

"Yo man! Mind that shit!"

"Sorry, Denny," he said, "but you know I can't let you have this."

No sooner had the words come out than Denny began to fume and curse, a brightly shining ball of teenage fury. Mike calmly slipped his wallet from a pants pocket and fished inside, stuffing a twenty-spot in the cup holder nearest his seat. Though still royally pissed to see his funbag carted off by some bumbling stranger with a gimpy arm, the cash appeared to work its irrefutable magic on the boy's mind, overriding his anger and, for the moment, stilling his rage.

"Why don't you do something constructive with it this time, huh?" Mike asked. "Why don't you go and buy your mother some flowers?"

With some tenderness out of place with the ferocity of seconds earlier, Denny lifted the bill from the holder, stretching it solemnly between his two hands. For a moment Mike only watched, drinking up that crazed passion—for what, he didn't know—buried somewhere deep in the boy's eyes. "Life is full of mystery," he told him. "At your age, that sort of mystery comes easy. It *flows*. Cherish that. 'Cause someday you'll be old and life will be every bit as mysterious as it is for you right now…only you will have forgotten that, somehow, and life will have gotten old right along with you. Old and boring." He reached over, placing a firm hand on Denny's shoulder. *"Cherish it, son."*

Denny was quiet. "You're flippin' nuts, you know that?"

Mike grinned, a grossly inebriated and yet genuinely peaceful grin. He opened the door.

"Thanks for the time, Denny."

He'd stepped into the rain and was about to shut the door when he heard Denny call out, "Hey! What's your name anyway?"

Mike thought about that.

"Mike," he told him. "My name's Mike."

Afterwards he sat behind the wheel, staring ahead to nowhere at all and the solid rhythm of his heartbeat *thump-thump-thumping* in his head. A quarter-full bottle of Jack Daniel's rested next to him in the passenger seat, along with his recent addition of Coors beers.

Don't even think about it.

Look away.

It's only there if you want it to be there.

Only there was no looking away—the Little Man made sure of that—and when at last Captain Jack completed his hollow transformation, Mike dropped the bottle to the floor and felt the rain come washing gently inside the car, flooding his mind. He plunged the key into the ignition, gave it a little turn; the motor roared to life. Snapped on the headlights…and froze.

Mike gazed ahead through the storm, small fingers climbing up the ladder of his spine at the rumble of rain battering away from above. Responding to some silent yet instinctual command, he reached out his hand and twisted a knob, the wipers springing to life outside. Whiskey flooded his perception, fierce as ever, and without warning he reached over, popping the glove compartment and running one hand inside, searching for something that wasn't there.

He turned, striking the automatic lock on the doors. There was some memory struggling to resurface in his mind, and for the first time Mike wondered was it a memory he really wanted to retain? Or were some rocks better left unturned after all?

Sweat beaded down his face, touching like ice on his neck.

Mike closed his eyes, waiting for whatever death this was to come and take him away, and when he opened them again he was leaned over in the seat, listening to a sound his barely-conscious mind could not quite place. He sat up, at a loss as to whose car this was and how had he gotten here and why on earth was everything so damned *bright?* Then another question, one which trumped all others: what oh what had he done the night before?

Then it came, piece by excruciating piece, as he gazed at the wipers and listened to the endless screech of their arms scrubbing at the glass: *whhcckk! whhcckk! whhcckk!*

He turned a knob, and the wipers stopped. Outside his car the rain was no more, the sun brimming on the horizon and people waking to another day of business as usual. With a touch of nostalgia, Mike wondered what that was like. Staring through the glass, he sensed a familiar burning sensation near the middle of his chest; he recognized it as the total rape and pillage of what little self-respect he had left.

He turned back the key, shutting down the engine and then wiping his eyes. Just for kicks, he wondered how long he'd been out. Four hours? Five? Long enough for the gas needle to have dipped down to E, and the wipers to have etched precise and permanent arcs into the glass. Mike turned and saw the harsh fluorescents of the gas station spilling through the windows, the solid hulk of a tanker coughing its deep, unholy idle into the morning.

He got out and made his way inside, heading straight for the shitter. It was locked, and back at the counter a gawky-looking teenager handed him a paddle with the word GENTS written in black magic marker down one side, a ridiculously small key dangling at the bottom.

"It's locked," the kid told him.

Mike thanked him for the heads-up, then returned past racks of junk food and overpriced light bulbs to the restroom. In the mirror, he observed a haggard creature with foreign eyes: a man who'd once been sole survivor of a nuclear blast, only to wake one morning and find the world had rebuilt itself overnight. He did his best to freshen up, washing his face and flattening his hair. The head beneath felt brutalized, however, and there was little he could do about that, though something told him a couple Excedrin and a piss-hot Coors might point him in the right direction. He leaned over the toilet and threw up, then sat down and let the other end have it. Twice the little prick out front came knocking on the door; Mike assured him everything was under control, then asked him in the most condescending tone possible to please, please leave him the hell alone. Soon the smell was too much and Mike gathered the plank and walked out.

He paid in advance and pumped a couple gallons into the Buick, then walked to the payphone at the side of the building, checked his messages. There was one from Norma Rackley, mother of the famous Vanishing Rackley Brothers. She'd found some recent pictures of the boys, she said, and some of the Kawasaki four-wheeler as well—did he think they could possibly help with the investigation? It was still early, but he took a chance and called her back, said he would be by later that morning to pick them up. Not because he felt the pictures would help with the case, of course, but because after all the time he'd spent talking with torn-apart mothers—women who'd come to know and nurture these children a whole nine months before the rest of the world had so much as set eyes on them—he'd learned that to humor them was not the same as spitting in their face. Hope, he'd realized, was pretty much all these people had left, and if he could dole out even a little of that spirit at the risk of being cutesy or indulgent, then so be it.

He thanked her and said goodbye, and had no sooner hung up the phone than he heard a gravelly voice from behind.

"Mike? That you, old buddy?"

He turned to see the towering figure of Frank Holling, a gentle smile tacked on his face. The features were sharper than Mike remembered, thinner somehow, giving the local detective's head an angled, almost dangerous appearance.

Mike returned the smile, hesitantly, and Frank walked over and knocked him on the shoulder, asked how the hell he'd been. Mike yanked a couple answers out of his ear about that, told a story about his busted arm, then conjured some half-assed reason he was in town at such a butt-early time on a Tuesday morning, looking like Hammond PD's answer to *Bad Lieutenant*.

"This was a '73 Corvette," Mike told him. "*Near-mint* the ad said, leather seats, the whole bit. But I'd say the only thing near-mint about it was the rear-view mirror. Frank, the guy should be arrested, really, it was that bad. *Total crackpot*."

"Listen, you had breakfast?" Frank asked, the word alone bringing up the gorge in Mike's throat. He told him he had, and Frank said, "Well, how about a cup of coffee then? C'mon, I know a good place…"

Minutes later he was back in the Buick, choking down a Winston as he followed Holling's company cruiser across town. Billy's Ham n' Eggs was a homey, exceptionally cold breakfast joint in the Glenburnie area, and no sooner had they settled in a booth overlooking the morning traffic than Mike's gorge sunk and his appetite came roaring up in place.

"Best eggs I've ever had *in my life*, Mike, no kidding. Get a side of bacon, some grits—" Frank kissed the air with the sort of excitement Mike could no longer understand, not stemming from food anyway.

"How's the ham?"

Frank shrugged. "Ham's okay. But the eggs, Mike, I'm telling you they're out of this *world*…"

Mike went with the pancakes, and by the time the food arrived they'd settled into the usual conversations about work. He assumed Frank had heard he was no longer detective, though Frank never brought it up if he had and Mike didn't bother offering the information. Instead they talked about crime and violence, and mutual acquaintances who'd had heart attacks or been gunned down or retired. Soon they'd started shop-talk on old cases, remember this, remember that, and before long Mike steered the conversation to the missing teens, then sat back and listened to what Holling had to say.

"Initially I assumed it was just another case of four kids skipping town, you know, same as always. Now, Mike…I'm not so sure."

"Gut feeling?"

"I guess you could call it that, yeah. But, in the same breath, most mornings I wake up and keep hoping I'm wrong and they'll turn up like nothing's happened. I want to believe that, you know, because it makes things easier all around."

"The stubborn optimist, huh?"

Frank smiled, sipped his coffee. "The stubborn optimist," he said, signaling for a refill. "I'll have to remember that. Sounds like something my wife would say." A waitress with bright curly hair walked over, showing some teeth and filling his cup. When she was gone, he looked at Mike and said, "Makes me nervous, though. How long they've been gone. It's been—what? Fifteen days now? Sixteen? Kids go on crazy jaunts all the time, but they don't stay there, not usually."

"C'mon, Frank," Mike said. "Really, though, what more can you do?"

He'd thought about it, and after much consideration had decided on keeping his conversation with Denny Chadwick to himself. For starters, there was simply no plausible way for it ever to have taken place, not without spilling a whole can of beans all over Frank Holling's shoes. Which really wasn't worth the trouble it was printed on, considering the entire lead could prove a dead-end. And besides, even if there *was* something waiting for him out there in those woods, some prescient part of himself demanded Mike go alone. A smoky question mark as to why that was existed at the back of his mind, but he did not press for an answer. "I mean, you've asked the questions, you've followed up. You searched the Creek Bed. What else is there?"

Holling offered a quizzical stare. "How did you know about that?"

"About what?"

"The Creek Bed?"

Mike looked him over and said, "Twenty-man search tends to get attention, *inside* and *outside* the force. There was a story about it on the local news, am I right? Channel twelve, channel five, something like that?"

Holling nodded pathetically. "There was, but I couldn't watch it. It always makes me feel dirty, watching myself on TV. Sheryl thinks I'm neurotic. But the way I look at it, other than those few times I'm on because something good has happened—"

"Like the time you found that kid stuck in the tunnel."

"—right, something like that, no problem. But when I'm on because somebody had their lungs ripped out and we don't know who did it, or some sicko burned down a house with the kids inside, I mean…call me crazy, I can't really get into that."

After a couple more cups of coffee, Mike started feeling jittery and thought he might throw up. He excused himself and then hovered over the toilet in the restroom, a picture of Holling's talking head floating back and forth in his brain. *Maybe Frank was right*, he thought, *maybe I should've went with the eggs*. By the time he got back, Frank was standing at the register near the door. Mike tossed a couple dollars tip on the table before joining him.

"No, no," Frank said, when Mike opened his wallet. "My turf, my treat."

If there was one thing he'd learned as a police officer it was how to take a hand when the world offered one, and Mike took this one without a fight. Once outside, he thanked Frank again for the meal, exchanged a couple rough slaps on the shoulder and then walked back to his car, doing his absolute best to hold down the vomit at the back of his throat.

CHAPTER 17

S eeing Holling had been good for him.

Just being around the man had cleared Mike's head, made him start to think more like a cop. He hadn't realized the meeting had this effect until back in the Buick and speeding down the road, but once discovered Mike at last felt the torpor of the morning slip from his bones, the hangover falling like a shadow from under his feet. Postponing his stop to the Rackley's, he instead followed the curving route he'd traveled with Denny Chadwick the night before, and not long after found himself trekking the muddy slop of pasture which gave on the woods.

He spotted the first deadfall, its jumble of ivory logs and rotted-through trunks glowing like bones against the deep green of the forest. Mike had started in that direction when he glanced down, noticing a pair of synchronized tracks etched across the earth. After seeing the first, others leapt out at him from below—three pairs in all, each zigging and zagging through the others and forming a giant latticework of the field. Rather than washing away the tracks as he would've thought, the rain had instead pooled inside the ruts, as if fossilizing them, and after a careful study of the prints Mike decided these were exactly what they appeared to be: the fading remnants of four-wheelers.

Three four-wheelers, to be exact.

Slowly Mike picked his way forward, following the tracks in a meandering route up the pasture and into the trees, finally vanishing among the endless blankets of pine straw farther in. Only by then it didn't matter, the stark blue bubble of a tent appearing up ahead—then another, this one in red. Other items came into view as he approached: the charred leftovers of a fire, a jug of gasoline, the sodden remains of sleeping bags.

Mike stopped.

His mind flashed on Denny Chadwick, on that subtle, creeping fear he'd sensed in the boy the night before, and suddenly Mike got it, suddenly he understood. He understood why a person like Denny would wish to avoid this place. And though he'd come this far, now Mike had to stop and ask himself this same question all over: did he *really* want to know?

It didn't matter what he wanted. He was a cop, and this was what he was built for, this right here, right now. Without thinking he walked over, unzipping the first of the tents—the blue bubble—with one quick motion, knocking back the flap. Inside he saw a dark camouflage comforter spread across the floor, damp with the smell of mildew rising off. He fished around and came up with a couple bags of potato chips and a pack of licorice, that was it. The second tent was bigger and had more snacks, as well as a close-to-empty two-liter of Sprite. No bodies, however, no blood, no guts. He stood in the clearing with his one hand held over his eyes.

They'd been here, no doubt about that.

So where'd they go?

Mike began an orderly probe of the clearing, starting at the fire pit and working his way in concentric circles to the rim. When he'd finished, he started again. On the third trip, the circles grew to include the first few yards outside the clearing, and it was here Mike again noticed the meandering trails of four-wheeler tracks. He followed them once more, tracing their madcap journey through the trees and realizing deep down he knew *exactly* what had happened to the boys—that soon he'd find their four-wheelers plowed into a pine or else flipped to the side, their smelly cadavers crumpled like rag dolls.

Only that never happened.

Instead he followed the tracks up a small hill, and just over this embankment the forest opened on a fresh series of poplar trees stretching proudly to the sky. Only when he looked, the tracks never quite made it to those trees; they spun up the embankment, ripping over the earth and rain pooling in the ridges, creating a perfect print…and then…

And then vanished.

Mike stopped, staring down at this apparent discrepancy in reality.

He assumed the boys may've jumped the rise and landed farther on— only that wasn't the tale his eyes told. What he saw instead were three pairs of tracks—each distinct from the next, all mushily intact—vanished into thin air, just as the riders themselves seemed to have vanished into thin air. What he saw was six lines here and—two inches over—six lines gone, as if they'd never been at all. As if the four-wheelers had never reached that other side of the trees.

Six lines, untouched, here and then gone.

...but how could that be?

He strolled among the poplars, searching for tracks and finding only a wilderness dappled with sunlight and limbs bobbing softly in the gentle hands of the wind. His stomach rumbled, bowels dangerously close to rebellion as he wiped his eyes, confused and angered and ashamed at the sudden appearance of tears. As if some psychic picking up visages of an extinguished life, he reached out with one hand, propping himself on the sturdy reality of a nearby tree.

Finally the feeling passed and he turned, blinded suddenly by the sun glinting off something in the brush below. He walked over, plucking the item from the earth and turning it in his hands. Had the bottle been full, Mike's trek in these woods may've taken a sudden ghastly turn, but as it were the bottle was empty and the cap was gone and without being told he knew what had happened to what was once inside. His mind flashed on the near-empty two-liter back at camp.

Back at camp...

Camping...

And just what might a word like that mean to a group of teenagers on a Saturday night?

With furtive eyes, Mike traced a line from the bottle to the vanishing tracks in the soil, to the faded pink ribbon he saw tied to the poplar he'd leaned on not two minutes before. Then back to the bottle, where one sprawling word jumped out at him from the label: SMIRNOFF.

He stopped at the old Exxon on his way back into town, using the same payphone he'd used to call Norma Rackley earlier that morning. This time he dialed the Chadwick house, and no sooner had Vicky's voice touched the line than Mike groaned and hung up the phone. He stepped inside and saw a young lady with heavy eyeliner behind the register, fetching cigarettes and handing out change. He grabbed a deuce from the beer cave in back, stood in line and then paid and walked out.

By the time he arrived at the Rackley house, the deuce was empty and his arm was on fire. He munched a couple painkillers, then rumbled out and climbed the steps to the door. Only after knocking did he glance down and notice his shoes covered helplessly in mud; he slapped them twice on the brick steps, turning in time to see the door swing open and Mrs. Rackley emerge with a drifting, joyless grin. She welcomed him inside.

"I'm, uh, sort of in a hurry here," he told her. "If you have the pictures…"

"Oh, of course," she said, and disappeared into the house.

Of all the mothers he'd talked to, Mike believed this was the only one who still held some dim hope for her sons' return. Not that the others had told him as much, of course, but after twenty years in the business of reading people, he didn't have to be told. The eyes, they say, are the doors of the soul, and if that were true then one would think these mothers were born in a spiritual barn: *whatever ye seek, fair traveler, look no further than this grief-blistered face…*

Moments later Norma Rackley returned to the door, manila envelope in hand.

"Here you are, Detective Porter. These are the most recent of the boys I could find." She turned a wistful gaze to the front lawn, as if some sultry-eyed specter had appeared there out of thin air. "They're out there right now, Detective. Helpless. Afraid. Maybe starving…I do wish they'd come home." Then, with a subtle turn, she shifted her gaze to Mike; he'd have felt no less uncomfortable had someone driven a lit cigar into his cheek. "We *should* have kept a better watch on them," she implored, "we *should* have been more strict about that damn-forsaken four-wheeler instead of letting them coast all over creation. Who knows where they went? *Who?*"

Mike turned, glancing across the yard. Nope, no specters here.

"We should have been better parents, Detective. Simple as that. You don't think anything like this can happen, not to you, not in such a small town. But it can, it *does*, and I just…I hope we have their forgiveness for letting it happen to them."

Mike looked at her. "What'd you say?"

"I'm sorry. I'm talking to myself again, aren't I?"

"No, but what'd you say just now? Something about forgiveness?"

"I just hope we have their forgiveness…"

Mike mumbled something to himself. Forgiveness. Something about forgiveness. Forgiveness isn't something, isn't what? Then it hit him, a subtle sledgehammer to the heart. "Forgiveness isn't enough," he said.

"Excuse me?"

Mike turned, looking at her. "Huh? Oh, nothing, nothing." He mumbled something more to himself, then thanked Mrs. Rackley for her time and hurried away, mumbles turning to gibberish as he rushed to the Buick and hopped inside.

Forgiveness is not enough.

He sat there a moment, silent, struggling against something and not knowing what it was. At last something clicked in his mind. That click was a long time coming, and when it hit home he knew it to be true and awesome and right. He cranked the car and sped off, unaware of the sweaty-shaky grip of his hands over the wheel.

Mike stared ahead, his thoughts on a wild rodeo of the soul. At the center of this cyclone were four words, four simple words—*forgiveness is not enough*—only they may as well have been open sesame. Another of those tumblers had been knocked loose and now Mike was downloading, soaking in their vague shapes and intimations. Then a faint buzzing sound—a distant plane, he assumed, or a lowrider perhaps with one of those annoying scooter-pooter mufflers. Only it wasn't either of those things and as he kept down the street the noises grew thick and guttural, swelling to one excruciating din in his ears.

Mike floundered in his seat, at last managing to steer the car to a stop at the nearest curb. He loosed his seatbelt, swept up suddenly in the incessant growl of faraway motors; not just one but three of them now, three separate strands of noise. He closed his eyes, and when he saw the reel of images flickering there in the darkness—so *living*, so *real*—one hand clapped to his face. Gradually the images sharpened, focused, and with grim conviction Mike realized these were no fantasies, were not dream visions or images conjured by a bottle, and he knew this because—

Because he'd been there.

Because it had happened to him and now, finally, it was all coming back.

Sudden knowledge blossomed in his head, some cruel red flower spreading its petals to the darkest corners of his soul—and then it happened, that lost door of memory flinging open and spilling his eyes with a splendorous staccato-blur of sights and sounds. Then a quick buzzing roar, and Mike turned but a little too late and the four-wheeler caught him in the gut, tipped him and kept going. He stood, making his slow way to the familiar form of the Banshee. Felt the silent weight of T.J. Chadwick in his arms, saw the boy's blood-spattered chest; then the sharp bite in his arm and T.J. was collapsed to the dirt, and with unbelieving eyes Mike watched himself crawl, cloaking himself among the endless dark of the night. Then a figure emerging, a flashing glint of steel. Mike watched in horror as the knife entered T.J.'s tender throat, the resulting spurt of blood so awful and muddy in the glare of the full moon overhead.

"*No-oooo,*" he moaned, throat shuddering as the reel trembled once and then snapped to a total-black end. "*Dead,*" he sputtered, "*they're all dead, the sonofabitch killed them…*"

Mike dropped his head in what appeared to be a gesture of penance, and for a long time there it remained, tears streaming down his face. *A twenty-two,* he thought, the bastard had actually shot them with a *twenty-two,* like lousy rats eating at the garbage.

He opened his eyes, surprised to find himself safely back in the Buick. Everything—the dull crimson of the sun, the wind through the trees, the trees' secret whisper to themselves—all of it seemed too perfect to him now, too lovely in light of the terror he'd been through and survived and not helped others to do the same. Looking down, his left arm seemed somehow different, no longer a mystery but a casualty of some visceral warfare of the night.

Dead, the word kept repeating itself again and again, echoing down these newly inherited halls, weeks of searching wrapped up in that one decisive word. It was soon followed by four more: *Forgiveness is not enough.*

The tombstone, he thought. Mike closed his eyes, remembering the letters carved with endless care into the rock. He remembered the house, measuring his renewed memories of that night against his memory of weeks earlier, and the miserable old man with creaky lungs stuffing Pabst beers into his fridge. His memory shifted, and there he saw the embroidered message hung over the man's gleaming bald head: FORGIVENESS IS NOT ENOUGH.

The pieces fell into place with a little snap, leaving only small holes here and there, holes bearing questions such as how four-wheelers could suddenly sprout wings and vanish into thin air; of how two houses could be separate and distinct, yet one and the same; and most important, just who else the old geezer had staying with him in that house. Mike wanted a name, but settled for a face: some crew-cut asshole who hadn't thought twice about sticking a knife through a young man's neck, about slaughtering teens or tossing a bullet into Mike's arm.

Too much, he thought.

Too much…

And it was. It was all too much and now he felt nauseous and as if to prove the fact he opened his door and puked into the street. He wiped his mouth, and performed an encore. At last, when it was over, Mike cranked the Buick and started down the road.

After two weeks, he finally knew where he was going.

PART THREE

CHAPTER 18

Mike shifted uneasily in the blazing heat of the Buick, sweat glistening like small diamonds down his skin. A pair of binoculars were pressed to his face, and through them he peered past acres of swaying green earth to the house he'd entered only weeks before. There was nothing spectacular about the house—nothing overt, anyway—and so it was no surprise that a murderer had existed there for so long without being discovered. Especially, Mike thought, when his crimes were committed in a world halfway removed from our own...

He glanced at his watch. Quarter of two. Time to move.

He cranked the car, reversed and started back along the old logging road that had brought him here. He stopped at the pavement of the Slocum Road and turned left, away from the Jessup house, and then took his time driving the five or six miles to the local Stop & Go, a homegrown station surrounded by deserts of faded dirt.

Mike parked out of sight and lit a Winston. He was still smoking it minutes later when an extended-cab Chevy with a flatbed trailer attached came roaring into the lot, grinding to a stop at one of four pumps arranged out front. Three young men in ripped denim and t-shirts piled out of the truck; the oldest, a competent-looking man with a curly drip of facial hair, grabbed a nozzle and started pumping as the others headed inside. Mike got out and made his way over.

"You Jim?"

The man cocked an eyebrow, spat a ball of something into the dirt. "Porter?"

Mike nodded, glancing casually to the store. "How was the drive?"

"Long," Jim said. "You don't mind me asking, why the hell'd you pull us out here in the middle of nowheres for anyhow? Don't get me wrong, mister, we're glad to do it, especially we get to keep the haul like you said…that *is* what you said?"

"That's right."

"All the same, there's plenty a scrappers right here in Lancer. Why call us?"

"What can I say," Mike told him, "you've got a stellar reputation."

Jim grinned, his big brown beard reaching from his jaw in a perfect spike. "Fair enough, fair enough. You a cop?"

"Not at the time. Check back a little later though."

Big Jim jammed the nozzle back into the pump. "Be a buck-fifty, up front. Would be less, you understand, but"—he gestured to the pump—"what and all with the drive…"

Mike told him it wasn't a problem, then counted out the paper and handed it over. By now the others had emerged from the store, cold sodas in hand, and as Jim headed inside to pay Mike introduced himself. They were twins, they told him, though for the life of him Mike couldn't see the resemblance, and started to think that maybe they were putting him on; he didn't care if they were. They'd started a little wrestling match when Jim reappeared from the store, cursing the heat and lifting his shirt to reveal a sweat-shined bay window. Minutes later all four piled into the truck and were moving down the road.

They were approaching the turn-off to the Jessup house when Mike leaned forward and said, "This may sound a little strange, fellas, but once we get to where we're going you gentleman may notice a…slight change in my character. At some point I'll probably get in your way, and possibly make a mess of things, including myself." Mike reached down and revealed a portrait of Ulysses S. Grant, handed one to each of the men. He asked, "Is this going to be a problem?"

The men looked down at the bills, made them disappear into their pockets.

"No."

"Hell no."

"Not at all."

Mike nodded, but he didn't smile. "Good. I didn't think it would."

"This guy some type a criminal?" one of the twins asked, keyed-up at the thought.

Mike stared out the window, watching as the house loomed closer and closer through dancing green fields. "Not him," he answered. And then thought: *Just the one he lives with...*

Minutes later they parked and, gesturing to the old Farmall row-crop still collapsed against a shed, Mike climbed the front stairs and gave a few hard knocks at the door. From his early morning reconnaissance, he knew Jessup was inside—had been all day, minus one trip to the pickup—and so there was little surprise when the door squeaked open and there the old prune stood. Even after seventy-two hours of observation, however, Mike still found himself unduly perturbed in the man's presence: the wrinkles were more wrinkly, the clothes more threadbare, the eyes more dead.

"*Howdy-howdy!*" Mike boomed, attempting that same country-wise accent he'd affected at their first encounter. "Took me longer than I 'spected, but here I am! So tell it to me straight, mister—is she still up for grabs?"

For one endless moment Jessup gazed back dumbly, his rheumy eyes creeping past Mike to the faded Chevy with its long black tail and its three young men cutting across the yard. He stepped onto the porch, brushing past Mike and over to the steps and his empty stare cruising a reckless tour of the unknown land beyond.

"Damned tractor ain't worth a hoot," he breathed, the words slurred and scattering oddly like dry leaves against the wind. "You don't believe it, sonny, then...by all means have at it. She's only gettin' older as it is. Just like me..."

Mike laughed pleasantly and slapped at his knee, gushing on about some poor uncle down in Jaw-juh who didn't exist and the measure of sheer joy the shitty row-crop would soon bring to his life. They strolled to the barn, where the good ole boys from Carolina Movers had now backed the trailer and were going about the business of readying the old wreck to be winched.

Then it was done and they went at it with gusto, huffing and puffing as the burning sweat rolled down. It was slow work, the tires dry-rotted and seeming to lumber rather than roll, and soon Mike was in on the act, doing whatever one arm and one wide mouth would allow. Jessup, meanwhile, had fetched a cool sixer of Pabst and taken a seat on a dilapidated kitchen chair, a chair that under normal circumstances had no business in a withered front yard but which fit in nicely here.

Mike watched him from the corner of his eye, confident that time was simply moving too fast and would soon be gone as he waited for just the right moment to make his move. Then he saw his chance and took it, managing a great glob of grease into one eye; he cursed loudly and spun, tumbling to the ground.

"You okay, Henry?" asked one of the twins, running over. "Get ya in the eye?"

Mike scrubbed at his face, feeling more and more like some bad actor in a slapstick.

"Better wash it out," the twin said gravely. "Shit'll screw with your vision, you let it set long enough…"

Mike struggled to his feet, stumbling blindly across the yard. He turned to Jessup—still milking a Pabst from his wooden chair—and made a perfectly nuanced gesture toward the house. The old man waved him inside, and it was all Mike had not to break character and bolt for the door; instead he took it slow and easy, inching up the porch and walking inside.

Standing in the front hall, he was struck once more by the cold depression of what he saw, which was less a house than a ruin: a demolition-ready edifice that appeared just as used up as its current owner. More than this, however, was the eternally gray feeling which seemed to rest over the innards of the house, a bleakness that defied logic, and wading through it Mike felt inches smaller than he actually was, and shrinking with every step.

"Hello? Anybody here?"

Only the droning whir of an air conditioner.

As if to satisfy any remaining doubt to his sanity, he moved silently to the kitchen and found the embroidered fabric still dangled from the fridge: *Forgiveness Is Not Enough.* Mike held out a finger to the phrase, cocked his thumb and fired: "*Pow.*"

After dousing his face in the kitchen sink, he found a stairwell and rushed the steps. Picked his way down a darkened hall and found the room he wanted. Inside he saw a bed dropped like a sleeping dog against one wall, a light bulb dangling impotently overhead. Sunlight spilled from two windows facing the sun, one of these partially blocked by an object which cast an oblong shadow over the bed. At the sight of it Mike grinned, pulling a sheet of paper from his pocket and staring at something printed near the top. He compared what he saw on the page with what was in the window, grunted once, and tucked away the paper.

Moving closer, he peered down and saw the young men on the ground below, still working the old row-crop inch by grueling inch onto the trailer, while yards away sat poor Saul Jessup, a near-corpse baking in the sun. What Mike didn't see was the twisted oak where two cadavers turned in a non-existent breeze—only a stump. What he didn't see was a tombstone carved with some cryptic sign-off—only a bare mound of grass. No lost handgun gleaming in the weeds. No chickens, no bones. Instead of being discouraged, however, these things and more only served to tell him he was heading in the right direction after all...

Another step and now he could make out the peculiar symbols, like hi-eroglyphics, carved into the strange gilt-bronze of the object in the window. *Candelabrum* was the official name, he thought, though Mike judged the term far too innocent for the piece he saw before him now, too simple...too safe. There were three spreading branches—*left-right-middle*—all falling to a sturdy molten base formed into the shape of some fantastical beast which reminded Mike of a dragon, save for the flat face and three coiled horns. The metal-work was filled out by a cast of coiling gothic creatures, most of these equally ambiguous as members of the animal kingdom—gorgons and griffins and chimeras—all of them melded into one writhing mass and mouths hung wide in the throes of some inexplicable anguish.

Mike shut his eyes, and in the faraway reaches of memory saw an explo-sion of bright blue light; without thinking he reached out, fingers extended. Another small step and now he sensed the object's shrewdly welcoming warmth, had come within inches of contact when a sudden rumble opened his eyes, snapping him back to reality.

He stared down, and far below saw the twins securing the old Farmall to the trailer, saw Big Jim behind the wheel and Jessup walking his slow, dejected walk toward the house. Mike faltered, the sweat crawling like a warm blanket down his face as he came to himself and then slowly turned away, hurrying from the room and down the endless stairs beyond…

▲ ▲ ▲

Later that evening, long after the boys from Carolina Movers had taken their loot and vanished to the horizon, Mike entered the library where he'd spent most every night since that single phrase—FORGIVENESS IS NOT ENOUGH—had taken his life and turned it inside out. He moved efficiently through the bubble of silence, pausing momentarily in the stacks and pulling a spine and reading the jacket. He'd never been much of a reader, and stomaching such copy helped him understand why. Maybe it was the smug pretentiousness of the author photo on the back flap (*I am to be taken seriously*, that photo said, *I am an amazingly intelligent human who is utterly worthy of your time*), or the dumb little come-hither plot summary. But really it was the Advance Praise that did him in, because no matter how hard he tried Mike just didn't understand how a novel could be brave, much less generous. These were not terms he used to describe a book—taking a bullet was *brave*, leaving a good tip was *generous*. Those things up there were just words on a page. Besides, in his opinion the only good stories were the bloody ones— the shorter the better. He occasionally bought a bloody book off the spinner rack at drugstores.

He shook his head and continued along his usual path to the Kellenberger Room, an annexed research area specializing in local history and genealogy.

"Evening, Mike," Mrs. Darby called, and he waved and took his usual seat near the window, within spitting distance of the microfiche reader. On the outside, he was engaging in the same sort of information hide-and-go-seek he'd perfected in his years as a detective. On the inside, however, Mike knew some vital switch had occurred; that he was no longer working after the usual fashion but instead relying on some pseudo-spiritualesque new instinct, inching forward like a thief in a darkened room. The old order (that is, the one he'd lived in all his life and stepped out of that evening on Mrs. Rackley's stoop) had quickly faded, and now Mike Lunsmann found himself in a new world where the impossible was not only possible, but likely.

As if to remind himself of this, Mike pulled the folded paper from his pocket and stared at it once more, eyes marching up the blown-up image in the middle of the page. Poring over it the way he'd pored over his own surreptitious journals, tracing this uncanny saga back to where it truly began—to his late-night stroll in the Harlow Boonies.

But if that was where the story started, then Mike had come to believe it ended there as well, only not in the Boonies themselves—but in all of Lancer County. It was the boys' campsite that turned him onto it, that and the four-wheelers with their peculiar vanishing act in the woods. Only it wasn't so peculiar when considering what he'd experienced after leaving The 19th Hole, and less peculiar still after taking a good look at a map of the county itself. Mike did so, and discovered the eastern Lancer/Craven border—the line along which T.J. Chadwick and his friends were camping—had once been formed by a southward-running stream through what was formally known as the Black Hill Woods. That stream had dried up in the Twenties, perishing as the nation squirmed under the shaky thumb of Prohibition, and along its banks were planted a meandering line of poplars. Sometime over the next forty years—the consensus was '67, though some experts pegged the date at '62—these same trees had assumed the accepted borders. Mike's mind tinkered with that for a while, images of the pink ribbon still dancing in his head.

He began looking into the history of missing persons in Lancer and the surrounding areas. What he found was a disturbing mash-up of people who had, in one fashion or another, been eradicated from the earth. Over the past decade alone, there'd been no less than *fifty-six* unsolved missing persons cases in Lancer County—an exorbitant number, Mike thought, when considering that forty percent of the county consisted of sweeping farmland.

It would've helped had there been something connecting the cases, an M.O., only the disappearances seemed to cross all sorts of boundaries: the old, the young, women and men and everyone in-between. There was no *consistency*, which is what every good detective would be searching for: *a pattern*. On the surface, there wasn't one.

But maybe, Mike thought, maybe there was some connection no one had made. A connection they *couldn't* make. A devil in the details…

And Mike had seen the devil. He had a crew cut and carried a rifle and lived in a sandbox the color of fire, a mysterious plane that existed somewhere between this world and the business end of the next. And the threshold between the two, just maybe, was in an upstairs room of a house in Lancer County.

Which led him to Edward DeFelice.

Following the Depression, Eddie DeFelice had grown his Lancer County farm from a dinky five-field operation into a respectable business producing the usual southern staples—cotton, corn, soy beans. In the late Forties he'd dabbled in potatoes, finally branching out into tobacco; within three years he would become among the three largest producers of tobacco in the state. By the time of the Army-McCarthy hearings, DeFelice Farms was a business set to rival any corporate enterprise, covering several hundred acres and with fingertips in four counties.

In another world this is where the story ended, and DeFelice and his wife and two young sons enjoyed privileged lives which he'd wrested honestly from the earth. In this present world, however, Eddie had come home one night high on Dutch courage and put a Luger in his shaky hand. He'd woken his family sometime after two a.m., led them downstairs to the den, ordered them on their knees, and did it execution-style to the back of the head. *Bam, bam, bam.* When it was over, he turned the gun on himself. Astonishingly, DeFelice's youngest son—only twelve at the time—survived the encounter; woken by the shots, a neighbor by the name of Loomis had entered to find the boy stumbling down corridors and bumping into walls, babbling like a fool as the tears ran down mixing with the blood. Joshua DeFelice never returned to the house, and ten years later would sell both it and the land at an embarrassingly cut-rate price. The fields went to various local farmers, the house itself to a young man named Saul Jessup.

Here the paper trail thinned, though from his research Mike gathered Saul had been married at the time, with an infant son. The Jessups were poor, and apparently the big house and big yard did little to improve their situation; what acreage was included with the lot Jessup rented-out piecemeal, and eventually sold. Then in August of '79, Chase Jessup went suddenly missing and—despite a thorough county-wide search—was never heard from again. No traces, no leads, only an eventual presumption of death notice in the local paper.

Ten years later, Mariah Jessup would take her own life.

But none of this is what Mike found most interesting. Most interesting of all was the object he'd seen earlier that afternoon, with its curving stalks and frozen-jawed grotesqueries. Thinking of it now, his fingers gripped the paper in one hand, eyes drawn to the image of a grinning Edward DeFelice riding a fresh wave of agricultural success. His gaze narrowed on something in the picture, past DeFelice's head and into the small square of an upstairs window. What he saw there—grainy, insubstantial, more or less a blob of black-and-white—was enough to make him grit his mental teeth: three small lines, half-obscured by sunlight.

The candelabrum.

The same lampstand Henry Porter had seen and so tentatively reached out for in what was now the Jessup house. Still there, after all these years…

He folded the paper and put it away, then opened the book in front of him: *Lancer County Heritage 1950-1975*. He read a few articles and scribbled into his pad, took a few well-timed sips from the flask in his pocket, chewed some gum.

When he noticed Mrs. Darby shutting down for the night, Mike stood and gathered his things. A thick old woman with glasses like windshields, Mrs. Darby had become an unlikely accomplice in the past week, helping him to gather whatever obscure information he required. For the same reason he'd hired Big Jim and the Twins from out of town, Mike had been hesitant about mentioning the Jessup name, never knowing what sort of his-momma-my-aunt connections folks might have with one another. Mrs. Darby had only measured the name with a vague recognition, however, recalling the missing child before moving on. Now he turned to her and said, "Mrs. Darby? You said you remember the DeFelice murders?"

"Oh, certainly. Doesn't get much nastier than that. My grandparents lived in Lancer at the time, and as I recall the whole town was shook up. Poor boys, they were *so* young…"

"Whatever happened to Joshua DeFelice?"

"Moved away, last I heard." She shuffled down a line of computers, snapping off the glowing lights of the monitors. "But then, that was years and years ago, honey. He still has family here—not much, a few cousins, I believe. I'm sure they would know."

"Do you remember their names?"

She thought about that. "One of them became principal of a middle school down in Pamlico, I believe. Blackerby, his name was. And who was that other girl? Had a flower business went sour, oh what was her name?" She frowned, shook her head. "It's gone. Pretty girl, though. Blackerby, *that* one I know of. But I'm afraid that's the best I can do."

After getting home, he took a shower and drank a tall glass of whisky. When the glass was through, he moved to the bed and lay wondering what sort of wild, wonderful, terrible things existed in this world which we knew nothing of...and, just maybe, didn't want to know. Again and again his thoughts turned to the newsprint image of Edward DeFelice, chest puffed, arms crossed as if in defiance of all the world as he stood before his then-elegant home on the Slocum Road. What had made a shrewd, successful, and apparently happy man such as this go suddenly feral and murder his own family? What sort of thing could do that to a man? As his breathing slowed and he drifted softly into sleep, Mike imagined asking these questions to someone who might just have an answer. A better solution, as it were. He thought of young Joshua DeFelice and the bullet he'd survived, and where his older self could be found...

Chapter 19

Shane Blackerby was a rotund man with hairy forearms and a shirt that expressed open hostility toward its wearer. There was a port-wine stain roughly the size of a walnut on the left side of his face, and the unmistakable glint in his eye of a man who did not ask for but commanded authority. Mike found him listed in the Stonewall area of Pamlico County, and paid him a surprise visit the following afternoon.

"Who are you?" Blackerby demanded. "Are you a cop, or just some reporter trying to rummage up the past and sell some papers?"

Mike went with the first one, then produced a badge and a story about how he thought Blackerby's cousin may be able to provide assistance in a police matter which it would be untoward of him to discuss. Blackerby's tune changed a little at the sight of the badge, but not much. He still refused to give an address for Joshua DeFelice, offering only a telephone number. Mike could take it up from there with Joshua himself, Blackerby said, and if his cousin decided to meet with him, then fine, and if not then that was his prerogative. Mike said all righty, then thanked him for his time and strolled away.

He recognized the area code as somewhere in Virginia—Richmond digits, if he remembered correctly. As soon as he got home he dialed the number, listened to an electronic message, hung up. After a few minutes he picked up the phone and dialed another number, and this time a male voice said, "Hello?"

"Denny?"

"Yeah? Who's this?"

"This is Mike Lunsmann. You took me for a spin the other night, remember?"

Mike heard muted swearing across the line. "Dude, what are you doing calling here? Please, my mom's had all she can—"

"I didn't call for your mom, Denny. I called to talk to you."

"Well…what the heck *for?*"

"Shh. One quick question, I'll let you go. Got to thinking about the way we met the other night and, I don't know, something occurred to me. Maybe it's nothing, but…being T.J.'s older brother and all, did you by chance happen to…obtain for him the same sort of beverage you had the other night? Maybe something stronger?"

A moment of silence, stretching into eternity.

"Denny? You there?"

"Look, I…what T.J. does is—"

"Is his business. Yeah, I know. Listen, I'm just asking, it's nothing serious."

"Did you go there? In the woods, I mean? Did you go where I told you?"

"Yeah, I went. But there was nothing there to see—sure you didn't get mixed up, show me the wrong spot? I mean, maybe I missed something, maybe I wasn't looking in the right—"

"They wanted some liquor," Denny said, his voice a whisper. "I said no, but then T.J. got all nuts like he always does, and anyway I got him something, I don't even remember what it was. Some of that flavored shit, I don't know. I didn't think that…I didn't think…"

For a moment Mike considered that the boy was close to tears—if not already there. Before he could find out, Mike heard himself say, "Hey, don't worry about it. Like you said, they're probably out goofing somewhere, just being kids. They'll get home. Appreciate the honesty, Denny. Take care of yourself."

He hung up, and for a long time sat nursing a beer, trying to convince himself he'd performed some merciful—nay, even noble—act in sparing Denny the hard news of his brother's death. But really, what choice did he have? What was he supposed to do? *Hi, Frank Holling? Mike Lunsmann. Remember that pack of missing teens you're looking for? Well, I think I found them. That's right, a half-realm, Frank, one with invisible borders. Nope, no sasquatch, but there was this strange cat with a twenty-two and one hell of a nightlight.*

Sure, he could see that. That'd go over *real* nice.

Besides, he knew how these things worked. Eventually somebody would stumble over that mess out in the Black Hill Woods, and they'd put two and two together themselves—if not the whole picture then at least enough to know the score.

He munched another painkiller, grinding it to a bitter powder between his teeth and then washing it down. Another hour and he'd forgotten all about Denny and slaughtered teens and most everybody else in the world, his thoughts settling on two people and two people alone. One had tossed a bullet into Mike's left arm, and the other was busy hiding from his own demons somewhere far, far away from here. Mike tried DeFelice's number again, got the message, hung up. He spent the rest of the night spinning his wheels for Kat, writing long, too-elaborate theories about whatever the hell was happening in his life. Soon the words jumbled together on the page, and after another quick beer down the gullet he called it a night and closed his eyes.

He talked to DeFelice the following afternoon.

He wasn't sure what he expected—some paranoid shut-in, perhaps, not delusional but moving right along in that direction—but the voice on the other end seemed less a shut-in than a man endued with sharp wits plus little stock in the human race. He'd already talked to Shane, he told Mike, and didn't see any possible way he could possibly help anybody do anything. Mike told him he understood that, and though he was a cop this was actually more of a personal request and had nothing to do with his job.

"A personal request? Then what's the holdup? Spit it out, cowboy."

"Actually, I'd...I'd rather speak to you in person about this."

"Is that right?"

"That's right."

"And why is that?"

Because I want to read you, he wanted to say. *Because I want to know if you're lying, and if you are then about what and why. Because you're my only source to whatever the truth might be and I want to tap your brain until I'm positive there's nothing left.* Only he didn't say any of that, he said, "Because I want you to look me in the eye and know that I'm serious, and that you can trust me. Something tells me you've learned to let go of trust over the years—only because you had to, of course, and I don't blame you for that; I would have too. But in a situation like this trust is important, and I want you to feel comfortable giving it to me."

Mike could hear the man breathing on the other end, a narrow whistle, in and out, in and out. "Well," he said, "I guess that's all up to you, Officer Lungsman. You wanna come, then come on. My door's open."

After jotting an address and a few directions into his pad, Mike returned the receiver to its cradle and stood to his feet. Defying the slight tremble in his arms, he took a deep breath and blew out the smell of his early morning beer, and then set about the business of packing for the journey ahead.

Chapter 20

Kathleen whirled about her kitchen with a gracefulness bordering on the obscene, displaying the casual but intimate familiarity of surroundings known only to short-order cooks and stay-at-home moms. Every so often she caught a glimpse of herself in some passing reflection, and didn't know whether to laugh or cry at the face she saw staring back. Yesterday she had been a youthful, vibrant, flowering eighteen-year-old with life full-speed ahead and damn the leftovers. Twenty years and two surnames later she was an old hen with two kids by two different fathers and a body she'd promised herself would never be hers. And yet, fate of all fates, it was; she owned it, and no matter how much she struggled the bloated mess just wouldn't budge. And what could she do about it? Nothing at all.

Once she'd finished scraping away at the microwave and dutifully polishing the stove, Kathleen grabbed the last of the dishes from the dishwasher and put them with the others. If nothing else had improved in the last twenty years, at least they had. Look at this china, she told herself. Does china like this lie? No, ma'am.

She entered the living room and found Millie sprawled awkwardly across the sofa, her breathing soft and even as she slept. Running her fingers through the child's silky-soft hair, Kathleen felt that uncommon love rise up and take hold, a love so strong it was somehow dangerous. She kissed the top of Millie's head and then switched off the television, thrusting the house into a rare silence, at first peaceful, then oppressive. Soon she found herself at the window and staring through the blinds, staring in that way she hadn't stared since she was twenty-one and a newlywed, a stare replete with half-formed dreams and a bubbly giddiness over what lay ahead. There was none of that now, of course…so why the stare? Forty was still a good year-and-change away, so why the stare? But the issue was a moot one and she knew it, because whether she liked it or not Kathleen had reached one of those peculiar pit-stops in life, one of those cometh the creeping darkness periods when self-reflection was inevitable and, more often than not, quite sordid. She'd become familiar with them since her blissful towheaded time as a teen, and with middle-age storming the beaches and razing the strongholds of her life like the ruthless mob she'd always known it was, the creeping darkness had never cometh so often.

Stuck in aphelion again, she thought.

Only this was different, somehow, and by the time she knew why Kathleen had already scrapped together an impromptu new direction for her day. Doug had stayed off the night, and Bart was away at the Willard County courthouse, where he would remain for most of the afternoon. After eating an early lunch, smacking away as she nursed her own erratic fears, she picked up the phone and dialed, both hands unreasonably slick with sweat. She hung up without speaking, dialed again, and this time was met by an electronic message; she waited for the beep, then spoke a quick message of her own into the receiver. When it was done she hung up and dialed yet a third number, though by now her hands were dry, the gentle voice greeting her on the other end a familiar one she'd heard all her life.

"Hey, Mom?" she said. "What are you doing right now?"

▲ ▲ ▲

An hour later Kathleen steered out onto the highway, wondering was she actually as stone-cold batty as she felt. Why now? Why, after all this time, did she suddenly feel the need to check up on Michael Lunsmann? Was it guilt? Is that what this was all about? Possibly, maybe. If not for the sins of the past—they'd been down that road and back again—then maybe just the long silences of the present.

Things had gotten a whole lot worse before they'd gotten better between Mike and the Covington clan, but now their relationship—including the one between Doug and his father—had entered a curious state of limbo. It was a Cold War of sorts, and that on both sides—but now, if not ever again, Kathleen felt the sudden urge to reach out to her former husband, to reach out in a way she hadn't since the separation had first moved out of thought and into action and gained its irreparable momentum.

Was it wrong, what she'd done? Certainly. She knew that. Surely Mike hadn't deserved what happened, she'd faced that demon a hundredfold. But then it didn't matter, because she would never care for Mike that way again, it just wasn't in her to do so. It's not that she didn't love him, because she did; they'd had a child together, after all, and once that sort of bond has been made—a bond which has nothing to do with physical intimacy—there's really no going back. She would always cherish the good years they'd had, and there were lots of them, but good as those early days were, she would not canonize the bad times: the lonely evenings at home, the long nights not knowing if her husband was alive or dead or somewhere in-between. Those memories were not worthy of her time, not anymore, and in the end the love she felt then had now become a thing she despised, and would gratefully escape if only given the chance.

So why the sudden road trip? Why the need to do it alone, without her daughter in tow but instead left back in Gatlin with her mother and a shabbily-built, easily-toppled pack of lies?

Was it love?

Guilt?

Fear?

All of the above?

Or was it only to stare once more into the empty cave from which this silence had been radiating for so long? Whatever it was, the feeling was not a good one, oddly coiling, and when at last she'd reached his house the sight of a Buick in the driveway out front gave Kathleen a slight chill along the nape of her neck.

She parked on the street, stopping a moment to brush at her hair before climbing out and starting for the door. Without consciously doing so, she uttered a silent prayer, hoping beyond hope not to be met there by the cloying stench of decay, not to find her ex-husband stashed away somewhere inside, his body snowball white, flanked by bottles, splashed in vomit, one more throwaway in a room already brimming with trash.

She mounted the steps and knocked on the door. When no one answered, she knocked again and then stood waiting under a too-hot sun slipping down a perfect blue sky, assured of the worst, until finally the door swung open and Mike stepped out and said, "Kathleen."

His appearance was escorted by the thick, indefinable smell he'd picked up since living on his own—not quite decay, but it wasn't roses either—and for once the odor was a comfort rather than merely a stench. His left arm lay cradled in a sling, a stage prop of the body, and when her eyes moved from it to his face, she noticed the deep blush of burst capillaries around his nose, the blue-black bags beneath his eyes. For a moment she stared, saying nothing, not sure she *could* speak had she wanted to.

"I called," she blurted. "I left a message, but I guess…I guess you didn't get it?"

A quick glance into the house. "Well, yeah, you know…I've been sort of caught up around here…" Mike laughed. "What are you doing here, Kathleen?"

And for some reason just then she felt like crying, as if all the doors in all the world had been curtly slammed in her face. She turned away, not knowing how to answer, and for a few uncanny seconds couldn't believe where she was, couldn't understand how she'd gotten here. But this sun, she had to get out of this *sun.*

"Mike…can I come in?"

He stood aside, waving his hand in a welcome gesture. She hadn't gone far before being struck by the choking stench of cigarettes—that and another, more familiar smell it occurred to her only men living on their own can acquire; it was the smell of dirty carpet and filthier dishes and tighty-whities with skid marks rotting away in a corner. It had been a long time since she'd been over and for a second she wondered if the place had always seemed so darned *empty,* barely a skeleton of everything a house should be. She counted a total of three (3) framed pictures—one she recognized as the family portrait from the year before they separated—and there were ragged holes in the kitchen linoleum, and cobwebs festooned along the ceiling. There were notebooks and newspapers, and a map, and a single suitcase standing upright near the TV.

"Sorry about the place," he said. "It's a mess, I know."

"It's all right, Mike. But you should really try and clean every couple of months or so."

"I'll have to remember that. You said you called?"

She nodded. "Even tried your cell a couple times, but the line was busy."

"Yeah, it's broke. How's the fam?"

"They're fine. Millie's with my mother, Bart's at work."

"And Dougie?"

"Fine, I guess," she told him. "Don't see too much of him nowadays, it being summertime and all. He's usually off somewhere…"

Mike grunted softly.

When he did that, Kathleen's skin seemed to pull a little tighter against her bones. *Great*, she thought, *here we go again*, and then gritted her teeth, waiting for the deluge…only it never came. She asked, "Whose car?"

"Huh?"

"In the driveway. That yours?"

"For the moment, anyway. Just a rental till I get something else."

She was about to ask the fate of his Oldsmobile when Mike pushed a button on the answering machine and her message played back. It was awkward, hearing herself on tape; it seemed to be a different woman who had spoken those words, and a million years in the past.

"Sounds pretty serious," he said, after deleting the message. "What's the matter, you and Bart need a spot of cash till the first of the month? If so, I could—"

"Mike, please."

"What? There's no need to be ashamed if—"

"Could you just sit down a minute? Could we just talk?"

Mike stared back, his face a stone wall of blistering non-emotion. She wondered what was going through his mind at that moment, and decided she probably didn't want to know. Finally the stare loosened and he walked to the couch, shuffled some boxes and had a seat.

"Sure," he said. "Let's talk."

Kathleen turned to stare out the window, and in doing so caught her first whiff of alcohol, the ghost of it tracing gently up her nose and throwing shivers down her soul.

"How's your arm?"

He shrugged. "Doing. Better than the last time you saw me, that's for sure. At least, I assume you were there—I got the card, and the flowers…"

Kathleen nodded. "We were there. You looked bad, Mike."

"Well, thank you, the flowers worked wonders. What did Dougie have to say?"

"Not much. But he hasn't been himself ever since. Nobody has, really."

"I think I know what you mean."

"What about work?"

"A good ass-paddling from Palmer, that's about it. On medical leave till the doc says I'm all healed up."

Kathleen stared at him. "What were you thinking, Mike—haven't you learned your lesson? What *happened* to you that night?"

He gave her some story about getting lost in a bar, about pig-haters and evil eyes and of being whacked hard on the back of the head. The tale made her sick to her stomach, a squalid affair worthy of derelicts and university kids but not a grown man. When it was over, she asked, "So how long have you been off the wagon again, Mike? How long since you've had your last drink? Today? Have you drank today?"

Mike laughed. "Naw, Ma. Ain't been drinkin'."

"Mike, I'm serious."

"I know you are, and that's what I can't understand, Kathleen. Why should you care? That's not really something you have to worry about anymore."

"Then what about Doug? Doesn't he deserve a father who isn't always hiding in some bottle somewhere? Somebody he doesn't have to worry about showing up dead in some newspaper one morning?"

"Yeah, sure, he deserves that. He deserves all that. In fact, he deserves so much that one father just doesn't cut it, so you know what? He gets two."

She let out a breath. "You haven't changed a bit, you know that? Still the same old bullheaded Mike. It's good to know that some things—"

"Aw, cut the shit, Kathleen. Why'd you drive all the way the hell out here for anyway? You know I've been drinking, I know it, so what. You never seemed to mind before."

"Believe it or not I still care about you, Mike, and I don't want to see—"

"*Care* about me—you don't *care* about *me*. You're set, you've got it all. I'm like a dirty rag, baby, you used me up and threw me away."

"I did not."

"Look, just tell me what this is really about so we can both—"

"*I don't know!*" she screamed, feeling the warm rush of blood up her face. "I don't know what this is about, Mike, I wish I did. I just felt like I should come, so I came. I *lied* to Millie and I *lied* to my mother and I'll probably lie to Bart if it comes to that, so don't you *dare* make me sit here and lie to you. So how about this, how about you tell me, Mike—why *am* I here? What's going on with you?"

For a long time he was quiet, his eyes as hollow and sober as she'd seen them in years. Somewhere deep in those eyes she caught glimpses of the fun, attractive man she'd married twenty years before. The face had changed since then—as most things had over the past so many years—but the truth remained lost somewhere inside…and if she stared too long, Kathleen wondered if she might forget all about her current life, and discover a world where she and Mike were still together and laughing and maybe doing better than either of them were doing now. Only then the lights changed, and instead she was living with Bart Covington on a renegade ranch in Clover, with a stolen son and the daughter she'd always wanted.

Mike spoke, interrupting her convoluted train of thought.

"I don't know what you're talking about, Kathleen." He leaned back on the couch, rummaging a pack of cigarettes from his pocket. "Work is hell, but that's to be expected. A new car would be nice. Otherwise I'm fine, really, just had a bad run of things. Life goes on."

Kathleen smiled wryly. "Bullshit."

Mike sighed, held out a hand. A small cloud of smoke hovered in the air over his head.

"Plan on going somewhere?" She pointed to the suitcase.

"Eh, been thinking about it. Just get away, you know?"

"Any place in particular, or…?"

"Not really. Anyplace but here, more like it. Figured I already have the medical leave, might as well take a vacation."

"Sounds nice."

He looked at her in a funny way. "All right, you asked me, now it's my turn. What's going on?"

"I told you, Mike—"

"Apart from all that, apart from me. Where is Kathleen at?"

She sat looking at her hands. For the first time in over six years, she found herself yearning for a cigarette. "I don't know. Usually I'm fine. No, usually I'm too busy to feel much of anything at all, if we're being honest. Then sometimes something happens and, I don't know, I get…stuck in aphelion."

"Come again?"

She waved a hand. "Oh, I just mean that—"

"I know what you mean. But what's…whatever-it-is you said?"

"Well, you know—*aphelion*. Like astronomy. It's the part of something's orbit when it's farthest from the sun. It's cold out there, and dark. And there's no sound in space, so that means no singing. Life just…seems to stop. So, whenever I feel this way, I say I'm stuck in aphelion."

Mike just looked at her. "Good gravy, lady. That's morbid."

Kathleen looked away, hiding a small smile behind her hand. "Give me a break, Mike."

"Who's joking? That's the saddest thing I think I've heard this year. Sounds like you're in serious need of a vacation yourself."

"Ha. Tell me about it. No, actually it's not that bad. I'm just…I don't know what's the matter with me. Mind if I get one of those?"

Mike tossed her his pack of cigarettes, said have at it.

They talked awhile longer, Mike puffing cigarettes on the couch, her in the kitchen, the sun sinking low in the sky outside. All told, it was probably the best hour of conversation they'd had in years—including during the last of their marriage. He was lying to her about some things—the story of his arm, for instance, and probably the luggage as well—but something told her he'd weighed his options about those things and made a calculated decision to fib, and that he was well aware of the fact that she knew it. She could press him, but if there was one thing she'd learned in their time together, it was that Mike didn't take well to pressure.

At last she looked at her watch and stood. "I need to go," she announced.

"No need to hurry off, white rabbit. Stay, relax. Bart can do take-out just like the rest of us every once in a while."

She made a face. "Here," she said, and walked over, handing him a small slip of paper from her pocket.

"What's this?"

"It's Doug's cell number. Why not do both of you a favor and call sometime?"

Mike stood, jamming his cigarette into a nearby tray. "When'd this happen? I thought it would take an act of Congress to—"

"It was Bart's idea, believe it or not."

"Oh…but I thought he's the one who said Dougie was too young to have a cell phone in the first place?"

"He was. Now he's been practically badgering me about adding him onto the plan, so today I finally did. I have the phone out in the car, I'll give it to him as soon as I get home. Or later tonight, if he's not there."

They looked at each other a moment, a silent exchange, and when he moved in to give her a hug she allowed him that, just as she'd allowed another man to move in on their marriage and give her a kiss one late night at a church four years before. The hug was clumsy and awkward, a confirmation of the gulf that had formed between them, and when it was over she pulled away, staring him in the eyes.

"Please take care of yourself, Mike," she said. He told her he would do just that, and after a lingering moment the stare was broken. A moment after that she offered a final goodbye and was walking out the door.

▲ ▲ ▲

By the time she arrived back in Clover, the sun was straight ahead on the horizon. She'd swung by Smithfield's on the way home, picked up some barbecue and coleslaw, and though she'd feared the worst, Kathleen found the house just as empty as she'd left it. When Bart pulled into the driveway fifteen minutes later, the table was set, Millie had taken her place in front the TV, and Kathleen felt run-over exhausted from her long hours on the road. What had happened to her today? she wondered as she leaned in and kissed her husband, a man she loved and cherished and adored. What sort of thing was this she had done? And why did she feel so dirty inside?

As they settled down to eat, her mind flashed once more on Mike with his alcohol-ravaged face and that preternaturally tired look in his eyes, the image of him sharpening in her mind. Among all others, it was this image of Michael Lunsmann she would remember most in the coming years, no matter how often she attempted to replace it with those of other, happier times. What, she asked herself, had he been thinking in this dusky photograph of the mind? And why was he so opposed to sharing it with her? There was no fitting answer to such questions, however, and in the end she would look back on this day—ever foggy as the years grew on and her hair went slowly to gray—with an ever-growing sense of wonder, aware only of the fact that it had been the last time she'd ever set eyes on her former husband.

PART FOUR

CHAPTER 21

Once he was bored of lying in the grass and staring up at the sun, the child with bushy brown hair and a splash of freckles over his perfectly round face stood and yawned. He picked his way lackadaisically across the yard, twirling once, twice, falling. He giggled. Silly. He was busy counting clouds when he heard the sharp slap of the screen door and turned, watching as his father moved past large Doric columns and down the front porch steps.

"Hey Pa!" he called, lifting his hand.

But Pa kept moving, forehead glistening like ice in the hot summer sun. The boy watched him go, heard the squawky clucks of the chickens as they scrambled in the dooryard next to the house. Then he was gone, back into the old barn where he was supposed to be busy, busy, busy working on Things. But he knew what his Pa really did in there. He knew because one night he'd peeked through the hole in the boards, the hole nobody knew about, and had seen him doing it.

Pa was Drinking.

But Mama didn't like it when Pa Drank, and he guessed that was why Pa went in the old barn to do it. When he came out he was always DRUNK AS A SKUNK and sometimes Mama got punished because she told him so. Sometimes Mama got hurt. And one time Pa had gotten really Drunk and called him a Peckerhead and then slapped him in the face. That night he'd told Pa that he hated his stinky old guts, and Pa had started crying. When Pa acted like that, the boy wished he could take his Mama and they could both run away and never be found ever, ever again.

Suddenly the boy didn't feel so well. He felt sick. Maybe it was the sun, maybe he'd stayed out too long. He started toward the house, was still climbing the front steps when he couldn't help it anymore and turned, staring at the old barn. The door had been closed, and through it he heard Pa hammering away, then stopping, then starting again, and the boy felt a slimy feeling in his throat that he didn't like. He went inside and, moving past his mother, she patted him on the head and sang, *"Somebody's got a birthday coming up, I won't say whooo-oo…"*

He giggled and ran past her up the stairs. He wasn't *really* giggling though, just pretending because he didn't want Mama to know he was sad. He topped the stairs, and upon entering his parents' room opened a pair of louvered closet doors. He stepped inside and shut the doors, making positive the slats were closed, and then pushed his way through the darkness: past hanging bundles of clothes and shoes scattered over the floor, until finally reaching his collection of baseball cards and cowboy action figures in back. His hand found the small flashlight he kept there and clicked the button, bathing the closet in pale blue light. He always came here when Pa Drank and when he was lonesome or sad, and stayed real quiet just like Mama told him, in case Pa got *bullydrent*. That's the word Mama used when Pa got mad and started hitting the walls.

He hoped Pa wouldn't get *bullydrent*, not today, please not today.

But he would stay here just in case.

CHAPTER 22

H e should've been on the road by now.

For a long time Mike remained still, staring at the floor and thinking what strange curveballs life sometimes tossed at you. Thinking he'd never seen Kathleen as beautiful as she'd been today, thinking he should've been on the road by now. He'd woken with the intention of leaving before noon and reaching Virginia by five. He'd get a hotel for the night, meet with Joshua DeFelice sometime early the next morning, hopefully be done in time to make a straight shot of it back home.

By the time she'd left, however, Mike instead found himself emotionally affected by the encounter, as if suddenly the past four years were nothing but a dream and he'd somehow achieved a SECOND CHANCE—only for that door to be slammed once more, reality hitting like a cold slap to the face. He spent the next thirty minutes in a funk, thinking of all that had been said and all that hadn't. Thinking of aphelion.

Thinking of his son.

Not long into Kathleen's visit, Mike had already decided on postponing his trip, at least until the following morning. Suddenly he was having second thoughts. Truth be told, talking to his ex had opened some of those vintage doors of the soul, doors which he'd trained himself to avoid when traversing those inner halls, and now he reasoned that maybe he would leave after all. There was a place on the way to Kelky he'd like to see and it would be easy enough to stop there for the night, then pick up where he left off the next morning.

He checked his watch, waiting for some internal buzzer to sound off and turn him on his heels. That buzzer never came, however, and five minutes later Mike gathered his things, locked the door, and stepped off the porch.

Two hours later he passed a discreet green sign welcoming him to Reelsboro County. He followed the road at a slower pace than usual, parting his window and breathing in the rural Carolina wilderness much as would a criminal recently released from prison. These surroundings had changed a bit since he'd last seen them—some for the better, others not so much—but not even Mike could shrug off the feeling that in some peculiar way he was coming home.

This was where Mike had gotten his start in law enforcement, working as deputy for the local sheriff's department. The move from Jacksonville to quaint, shit-kicking Reelsboro had been easy enough, if not much fun at first. For eight long years—right up until the year after Dougie was born—he'd worked these streets, and loved it. Looking back, Mike realized with remorse they'd been some of the best times of his life.

Mike smiled a grin that was too big for his face and quietly drove on, for the next forty-five minutes hitting all the famous still-frames of his past: he cruised the crumbling masses of Arapahoe and Grayson Fields, the fish's-ass stench of Fairfield Harbor; he visited rich Grantham and Riverside. Last of all he steered down the familiar lanes of Trent Woods, where he parked the Buick at a curb and sat staring, mesmerized, at a faded two-story across the street.

Well, I'll be damned...

Still there. After all these years the house was still there and actually not looking so bad for its age—and it was no toddler when he and Kathleen first rented it back in the summer of '85. The trim had changed colors, from slate blue to white, though the house itself appeared as stunningly green as ever, and staring at it—some missing piece of his soul that he could never reach out and snap into place—Mike felt suddenly overcome with grief. The water-works were coming, but before they could arrive he reached over and dragged the old bottle of Jack from under the seat. Knocked down a swallow, blew out and took another. He lit a cigarette and sat smoking until at last he felt the eyes upon him, he couldn't tell from where; it could've been this house or the next one over or any of the fresh duplexes across the street. Finally he took a last gulping glance of his former home before cranking the motor and driving off.

He found the boulevard and parked in the lot of what had formally been known as Ernul's Oyster Bar, only now Ernul's had been nixed and the place was just called BUSTER'S. A queer feeling of camaraderie washed over Mike as he clambered out of the car and in through the screeching front door, a sense that in this place—if nowhere else on earth—names and paint colors may change, but the essence of a thing remains forever. He grabbed a seat at the bar, slapped the counter and said, "What's a man gotta do around here to get a drink?"

The old bartender looked up. For a moment his eyes remained frozen, an expressionless stare drawn tightly down the drooping folds of his face. "Mike, is that you?" He started over, lips curving in a tentative smile. "Sure is, ain't it? Mike, Mike, welcome back old pal, how ya been?"

Mike told him he'd been fine, just fine, and when Buster pointed to his arm, Mike rattled off some story about getting gnawed at by a Rottweiler. Though never exactly call-me-at-eight buddies, he and Buster went back a long time. It was odd seeing him again, but good, and Mike wondered if his own face had aged with the same reckless abandon that shown on Buster's. He ordered a Coors, and Buster filled a glass and handed it over.

"So what the hell brings you this way?"

Mike told him he was just passing through. "Headed up Virginia-ways on a case," he said, "someplace called Kelky."

"Sure, I know Kelky. Nice little town."

"So I've heard."

"Nice little drive, too. Hope you're not trying to go all night?"

"No, Buster, this is it for me, at least for tonight." Mike yawned and lit a cigarette. "Figured I'd…drop in on things, see what's changed."

"Not much, huh?"

"The name on the sign out front."

Buster laughed. "And that's about it, too."

"Congratulations."

Buster waved his hand. "Finally managed to buy myself out from under Smithey Junior. The Twit, we used to call him, remember that? Turns out the bastard ain't a total prick after all. Who knew?"

They shared a laugh about that and afterwards talked of business and politics (four legs good, two legs bad, they both agreed); they celebrated memories and lamented the curse of time; they spoke of old friends and new directions. After his third beer, Mike's tongue was loosened about his own problems, about perpetual suffering and his own strained relations with his son.

"Yeah, I'd heard you and Kathleen were on the break," Buster told him, an apologetic curve turning his voice to something low and soft. "A thing like that does hell on the kid, you know? Wasn't your fault, don't get me wrong—it was *her* fault. I've at least heard as much, correct me if I'm wrong. But the kids gets it no matter what, get what I'm saying?"

Mike told him he got it, and moments later when Buster offered one on the house, he took it. "Buster, what the hell happened? Can I ask you that? I mean, I thought being a father was hardest when they were little, you know, just babies. Now he's grown up and I *really* don't know what I'm doing."

"Hey, none of us do. You think our parents had any idea what they were doing when we were growing up? Hell, they were kids themselves, most of 'em. They didn't know. Didn't have a clue. But we *believed* they knew, we *trusted*, because we were the kids and they were the grown-ups and grown-ups know best. Daddy was fifty feet tall. Momma could tackle the world and still have time for supper—real mac n' cheese and dessert."

"I know, but still…this might sound crazy, Buster, but sometimes I think I'd give just about anything to live the past five years over again. Do it different this time. I wish I would've been a better father, instead of being so…"

"Mike, Mike, you gotta wake up. Who doesn't wish that? Listen, you think Mister Rogers ain't sitting somewhere right now, wishing he'd spent more time with his kids instead of being all day in a stuffy studio singing a bunch of slaphappy songs? You think Timothy McVeigh's pops don't wish maybe he'd said I love you a little more often? It's a tale as old as time, Mike. Remember that story Hemingway wrote? Old man puts out an ad in the city paper: 'Son, all is forgiven! I love you! Meet me at noon tomorrow at the hotel such-and-such!' Didn't sign it, no name, nothing. Next day there's *eight hundred men* waiting there at that hotel to meet their daddies. That's a great story, but it's only great because it's true."

"Yeah, I guess you're right."

"Sure I'm right. Now excuse me while I go tell these bozos to quiet down."

Mike watched as the old man shuffled around the battle-scarred bar, then vanished from the corner of his eye. Faintly he heard the sounds of Buster scolding someone, then someone else talking back, but he wasn't listening to that. Mike tilted his glass of beer, peering down inside as if maybe there'd be a message written for him somewhere at the bottom of the mug.

He pulled out the slip of paper with Dougie's number on it.

He stared, face scrunched, finally turning to the payphone at the back of the bar. He made his way over and dialed the number.

It rang four times, and was connected to a voice mailbox.

He hung up the phone and stared out over the bar. For one lingering moment Mike felt like he was dreaming; then the moment passed and he was back on his stool, his mind spooling to nothingness and trying to forget about the persistent problem of himself. Soon the bar would be closed and he would have to find another sinkhole for his misery. Probably a hotel room. Not an expensive one.

Then he thought of something, and out of curiosity decided to act on it.

He dropped some money on the counter and walked over to where Buster was fiddling with the TV set. They traded goodbyes, shaking hands and staring each other in the eye as only two people who have been harshly briefed on their own mortality are able to do. Moments later he carried that look out to his car, cranked the motor and started down the road.

Minutes later he stopped, climbing out and for a long time staring past the long silence of the trees. Crickets chirps, a chorus of too-high voices jangling against the moon. Snatching the last of his whisky from the Buick, Mike started forward until at last the looming shadow of the mountain appeared against the stars, rising sharply across the night and seeming to brood like a ghost over Reelsboro County.

By the time he reached the top he was twenty minutes older and his body was greased with sweat. Staring ahead, Mike could make out the yawning shadow of the barn in the distance, its form stranded wraith-like among the prison-bar stalks of the trees; if he'd been surprised by the sight of his own house in Trent Woods, the existence of this one was a borderline miracle.

Believe it or not, fifteen years ago and in a different world this old shack had been something of a hot-spot, drawing hipsters like gypsy caravans from places far and wide. There was a band, loud and reckless, its name forgotten with the years, and as the live music roared and pulsed from a makeshift stage together they'd dance and get drunk and screw and who knows what else they did up here. Not him; he was a cop, after all, and in those days cops were not exactly welcome at these heights. In the field below was a different story—most weekends he'd stop there and share a cold one with the rest of the laymen: hillbillies and degenerates and all other grovelers of the crumb. But here? At the throne of worship? No way, not happening.

He made his way over, pushing through the sudden heavy fog that had settled over the barn and stumbling through the door. His foot touched on something on the floor and he bent forward, picking up a large candle still in its stand. He lit the candle and placed it on a shelf, glancing over the ruins before him. There wasn't much left of the place—a few couches, a couple straight-back chairs, a collapsed table in the corner. An empty stage sulked across the room, and set off to one side he noticed the rusted heaps of two generators which had once powered the night, coughing up the desolate crunch of electric guitars and drum palpitations and howling vocals over the crowd and down the mountain and out into the streets.

He lit a cigarette and grabbed a seat on one of the couches near the stage, then uncapped his bottle and swallowed some of what was inside. A couple minutes passed, and he took out the slip of paper with Dougie's number on it. He stared at it, studying the cutesy-curly hand Kathleen had written it in. How many times had he read her words and thought nothing of it? These seemed eerily alive, however, as if somehow each letter had been infused with her essence and now only waited there, magically encapsulating her until someone brought her out again. Was it possible? With enough money and a little time, could he make it happen? He tugged a final drag from his cigarette, savoring the stale taste of smoke and his own delusions, then without thinking dropped the butt down into his bottle: *hsssss*.

He glanced and in the soft glow of candlelight saw the butt swimming along in the last of his Jack, a dark slug in a silent black ocean. Mike damned it all to hell, tucking away the number and then grabbing his bottle and tossing it across the room, listening with some sick pleasure as it crashed and knocked and tumbled to the floor. He slipped from his jacket and laid it at his head, stretched out on the couch. After ten minutes his darkness was complete and the barn was filled with the music of Mike's guttural snores, beating its own sporadic rhythm into the night…

CHAPTER 23

Hours later Mike parked a few spaces down from Noel's, a low-key diner just off Kelky's main street. He'd spoken to Joshua DeFelice two hours earlier from a payphone in Chesterton; they'd planned a one o'clock lunch, and checking his watch Mike saw it was quarter past noon.

Instead of waiting inside he wandered the streets, exploring the delicate downtown paradise he'd observed through the Buick's scarred windshield. He strolled up Broad Street, smiling at locals and peering in shop windows and wondering who the hell had money for this crap anymore. One store, Maury's Place, housed a collection of the most horrid homemade dolls he'd ever seen, in addition to a bizarre display of garden shears and other assorted pruning tools. Another specialized in cotton candy, and Mike bought a stick of the stuff and went to gobbling. He passed two stories worth of steak joint, and when a college-age boy brushed past him out the door a waft of booze filled his nostrils and Mike kept on gobbling.

By the time he'd arrived back at the diner, DeFelice was waiting for him in a booth near the door. A waitress pointed him out and Mike tentatively made his way over. Joshua DeFelice was a towering figure, with thin little arms and legs buried beneath two denim blankets and attached to his waist by a thin line of leather. A ball cap boasting the emblem of a bucketmouth bass sat atop his head, dusty black hair running in a pony-tail out the back. Then the brim shifted and what Mike saw beneath produced a jolt as true as any electric current, swirling back and forth in his chest. Struggling to keep his voice even, he said, "Mr. DeFelice?"

"Call me Joshua," the man said, "and I guess you'd be Mike?" The two shook hands, and DeFelice gestured to the seat opposite his own. "Go on and rest your heels."

He slid into the booth, and from here the sunlight from outside danced over DeFelice's face in just such a way that Mike almost lost his gorge all over the table. Many times his mind had played the scenario of Edward DeFelice carrying out his gruesome acts in the middle of the night, but never in his wildest dreams had he imagined the results being so grotesque as the face which existed before him now. Best Mike could tell, the bullet had come out somewhere between DeFelice's nose and his upper lip. The teeth were falsies for sure, and were about the best things the man had going from the neck up; his expression retained a perpetual sort of pinched grimace, as if gravity had started a small rebellion near the center of his face. DeFelice had been twelve at the time of the massacre; he was now close to sixty and over the years the scars seemed to have dried into drawn-out runnels over his deeply tanned skin, forming a haywire mash-up of wrinkly, dimpled mutilation.

Mike said, "Look, I really appreciate you meeting me like this—" and was promptly cut off by DeFelice's upraised hand.

"Sure thing, don't mention it. Now why ain't you look at the menu here and choose a number? So hungry I could eat the hind legs off a hobby horse, so try and make it snappy, huh?"

Mike went with the burger and fries and a Diet Coke. DeFelice ordered a fried chicken meal with string beans and cheesy mashed taters, and no sooner had the old waitress scuttled away than he said, "All right then, let's have it. What's been tickling your brain so damned bad you had to drive up here and tell me all about it?"

Before leaving the day before, Mike had printed off a clean copy of the newsprint photo he'd been carrying for almost a week. He removed it now and slid it across the table, wondering if maybe the image alone would be enough to make Joshua DeFelice stand and leave the room. Instead he only stared at the paper with a curious sort of detachment, as if the person smiling back jovially were some stranger instead of his own father, a man who had murdered his mother and his only brother and who had done his very best to end him as well.

"What's this?"

"That's your old house," Mike told him, pointing. "And that's your father."

DeFelice looked up, a peculiar sort of glaze forming over his eyes. "No kiddin'. You drive all the way up here to show me this? Wasted your time if you did."

"Not quite," Mike told him, and leaned forward, rotating the picture. His fingers shifted to the bright sun-cast lines in the background window. "I want to know about this. What is it, how it got there. Why it was left behind."

DeFelice stared down at the copy. After a while, his nose began a low whistling sound that seemed to swirl up toward the ceiling. His fingers tapped a fast rhythm on the table.

"*Aw, hell…*"

"What's the matter?"

"Nothing," he said, shaking his head. He dragged a bony hand down his face. "I just…call me crazy, but somehow I *knew* that's what this was all about, *knew* that's why you came."

"I don't understand. What would make you think that?"

"Nothing much. Except t'other night I had a dream about the damned thing, first time in years. I was looking for something in my cellar, you know, in the dream, but couldn't remember what it was I was looking for. Then something knocked at my door and when I opened it there was this *thing*"—he flipped the photo with his hand—"just sitting there on my doorstep. And I just knew…it was like a warning."

"Come again?"

"Ya know, a warning not to talk to you."

"A warning? From *who?*"

DeFelice only stared. "How should I know—the Jolly Green Giant. I don't know who." Another whistling breath and now Mike could make out the red irritation that had shifted over DeFelice's features, his eyes like two gray pearls peering out from within. He glanced back to the picture, his gaze lingering for the slightest of moments on his father.

Time ticked away.

This was it, Mike thought. This was where the rubber met the road. Either DeFelice would shake him off and move on with his life, or there would be more than just a good tip on the table when they left. There would be blood, the kind that came out thick, and just maybe a small sliver of Joshua DeFelice's soul.

As he thought it over, DeFelice rapped his knuckles on the table. Almost as an afterthought, he asked, "What happened to your arm?"

"I was shot."

DeFelice seemed to smile, only his face never changed. "Stings, dudn't it?"

"Only I don't know by who. That makes a difference, you know. Eats at you. See, I keep telling myself I'm gonna figure out somehow who did it, then I'm gonna find them and I'm gonna kill them. Kind of demented, huh?"

But he might as well have been speaking to the dead.

All of a sudden DeFelice arched up in the booth, leaned forward and said, "What do you know about this thing anyway? You're here, you're asking about it, so what do you know?"

"Not much," Mike told him. "Nothing at all, if you wanna get right down to it. But I've got some bad vibes, real bad ones, and something tells me they were coming from this." He tapped the picture. "Sounds crazy as hell, I know, but it's the truth."

"You said it's still there?"

Mike nodded. "Sure is, still bolted right into the sill. Remember the family who bought the house? The Jessups?"

"Vaguely."

"Vaguely like how?"

He shrugged. "Nice enough family in need of a cheap place to stay. That was most of forty years ago though, and I haven't seen or heard from them since."

"Well, they've hit on some hard times, and I'm just curious whether or not this had anything to do with it."

A funny look on DeFelice's face. "Kind of hard times?"

"A son that went missing and never returned. A wife that somewhere along the way decided she'd rather be dead than alive, and acted on it. A poor old man with a whole lot of house and nobody to share it with."

Joshua DeFelice's eyes fell to the table. He adjusted the hat on his head, but the action seemed to have been performed underwater. Before he could say anything, the waitress arrived with their food, juggling the plates onto the table.

"Watch your tongues," she told them. "Food's pipin' hot."

When she was gone, DeFelice looked at him and said, "All right, listen. You wanna know about this thing, let me put it to you simple as I know how. You ever hear that expression about how many angels can dance on the head of a pin? Well, there's something dancing inside a that thing—but it ain't no angels, I'll tell ya that."

"What is it?"

"What is anything?" He shrugged. "It is what it is, I don't know what it is. Something we won't ever understand, my guess. Something that don't want us to understand it."

The way he talked about it—as if it were alive, as if it had any say in what anyone knew or would come to know about it—didn't settle well with Mike. That wasn't the way he worked. But then why had he been thinking in similar notions about the object himself?

Mike asked, "Where'd it come from?"

"That's the key question, now ain't it? If we knew that, I guess we'd both sleep better at night."

"So you're saying it was always there?"

He shook his head. "That's not what I meant. My daddy, see he was a collector. Rare items, artifacts. I think it started during the war, you know, him collecting all sorts a stuff from over in the Pacific, from Europe. Coins, Kraut helmets, that sort of thing. It was just a hobby at first—we didn't have the money for it to be anything else. After a while, though, he got pretty fanatical about it. In the end, he would've bought Hitler's left nut if he coulda found it."

"I wasn't aware that he served."

"He didn't. Gimp leg, you know. But he knew a buncha guys in the service who had contacts and anyway that was how this guy showed up. All we knew, he was just another trader sent by one of my father's friends. Looking back, I know he wasn't, but at the time I was just a kid, what did I know?"

"Who was it?"

He shook his head, eyes spiraling out through the glass and down the street. "I'll never forget the day he came," he said. "I was out making mud pies when this long sleek car, black as pitch, drives into the yard, and out steps this tall monster of a man with long dark hair." He gestured with a thumb to his own back. "Hangin' loose too, not even ponied. Common thing, nowadays, but back then I'd say it turned more 'an a few heads. But he came up with his long black hair and his big black car and he looks at me and he says, 'Joshua, is your father home?' Which near about turned my gut, him using my name and all, seeing as I'd never set eyes on this fella in my life—and neither had Daddy, I'm sure of it."

"So what'd you do?"

"What do you think? I ran inside before I watered my pajamas and got my daddy. Then I went straight upstairs and never saw the man again. Hope I never do. See, evil brings a cloud with it, Mike, and that man...that man had it all over. Eyes as cold as steel, eyes that could look right through you and then back out the way they came. But he had that...*thing*, that damned *relic* with him when he drove in, and when he left it stayed behind. Daddy had it installed in the upstairs window."

"Your father never said where it came from? Never mentioned—"

"If he did, he didn't say it to me—or Davey, for that matter. Davey was my brother. You know, it's funny. My father had all sorts of artifacts, from all over the world, but he was always most protective about that one, it's like he didn't even want us around it. Maybe because it gave us all the creeps and he knew it. When the booze finally snagged him good, he'd give us a whoopin' just for being in the same room with the thing. It's not that he was a crazy man, don't think that. In some ways he could even be considered brilliant, a genius when it came to business. Industry was his expertise. You know he bought almost seventy percent of all the land he ever owned during the Depression? Weren't exactly pennies on the acre, but damn near."

"Which is about what you sold it for, right?"

DeFelice smiled. "You know, even if you hadn't told me I coulda made you for a cop from a mile away, plainclothes and all."

"What makes you say that?"

"'Cause you talk like one. Think like one. I can see all the little wheels spinning in your head. But yeah, you're right. I sold the land cheap, just like it was bought."

"Why?"

DeFelice seemed to pull away from the conversation then. He watched a middle-aged couple walk by holding hands, a Mexican girl with a bag of books. Returning to the table, he measured Mike with a gaze as obscurely penetrating as any he'd ever received. "The only reason I sold in the first place was because I got sick and tired of being hassled by every farmer with a padded wallet and more greed than nature ought to allow. That's all. What I got from the sale I took and made a few people happy with it, but personally I didn't see a red cent. And I did it that way 'cause I wanted no part in the land. Not in the house, the fields, nothing."

"Why wouldn't you?"

DeFelice laughed. "Short answer? Because the land is cursed. Always has been."

The words hung in the air between them, dangling there like formless shadows on a pale gray wall. Mike asked, "You really believe that or—"

"I really honestly truly do. I don't expect *you* to believe that. But let me ask you this—did you know Lancer County was where the Tuscaroras lost their last battle before being run off to New York? That was back in the 1700s. Once me and my buddy, we even found a couple arrowheads in the woods out back of the house. And maybe it's just me, but I've always wondered if maybe those redskins didn't leave more than just arrowheads, if maybe they didn't leave a nice whammy on the whole lot before finally being pushed into the sunset—a parting gift for whitey. Maybe that's what brought that damn man with his totems to our house in the first place. Or maybe the land was never cursed till that thing came along. Who knows?"

"Weren't they supposed to be the peaceful ones?"

"Who's that? The Tuscaroras?"

"Or Native Americans in general?"

"Well, how would you like it if somebody came into your neighborhood, caused all sorts a hell in your backyard, then broke into your house and told your family to move it along? Don't know about you, but for me that's not exactly conducive to feelings of rainbows and butterflies."

"I see your point."

He nodded, forked some mashed potatoes into his mouth. "Then again, I've thought about it a long time and you know, look at it like this. Every force needs something to power it. Tires just don't roll down the highway, they need an engine. Engines need fuel. Maybe that thing in the window, whatever it is and whatever it can do, maybe it's like a dead battery—useless until it has something to feed off of, something to *charge it*. And maybe this one feeds off a land cursed by bloodshed—or vice versa. Either way, as I sit here it's damnable. Forsaken. I'd always thought it, even as a child, but I don't think I ever really believed it until I got nice and old. Age won't let you get away with a lot, and silly real-world delusions are usually one of the first things to go."

And then Mike asked the one thing he'd promised himself he could never ask, the question his own mind had been surreptitiously scouting for the past couple of days: "Could it bring a person back to life?"

Joshua DeFelice's eyes widened. "Beg pardon?"

"Could it bring somebody back to life?" Mike asked, doing his very best to hold DeFelice's gaze. "Could it do something like that, you think? Or is its power limited merely to driving otherwise healthy people over the edge, making them insane?"

DeFelice laughed, glancing out the window. "Life and death, what's the difference? I wouldn't be surprised if the thing made pancakes. How should I know what it can do? It can kill a person, I believe that, but bring 'em back to life?" He shrugged and passed a fork through the food on his plate, moving it back and forth. "Why not bring 'em back?"

▲ ▲ ▲

They talked awhile longer, forming tall theories about things they'd each experienced but neither truly understood. Both seemed rather comfortable discussing such things, knowing perhaps on some deeper level it was probably the only time in their lives they would ever have such a discussion. Coffee came and went. When DeFelice excused himself for the second time after cleaning his plate, Mike took his cue and paid the check and tossed a couple five-spots on the table. He stood waiting for DeFelice to emerge from the restroom, and when he did they shook hands and Mike thanked him again for the conversation.

"Talking's never been a problem," DeFelice told him, "it's finding the right people to do it with I can't seem to figure out. Hope you got your money's worth."

Mike told him he thought he had, and gazing back into the greying folds and impossible flaps of the man's dried-out face, he sensed an odd wave of relief—however fleeting—wash over them. Walking out the door moments later, Mike had the peculiar sensation of emerging from an endless slumber and into a world so much bigger than he'd imagined. He stopped at a stationary store not far from Noel's and bought a notebook, and for a long time sat in the Buick, filling its pages with whatever strange notions came into his head. When it was over, one arm felt just as deplorable as the other and the notebook seemed a little less trivial and his mind not so full. Moments later the Little Man appeared from the shadows, whispering some unintelligible thing out into the void. The urge to drink hit him like a cannonball to the chest.

He pushed it away and started the car.

It was a couple hours before midnight when he arrived back in Hammond. He undressed and then looked on the shelf and found a fine old bottle with a good ten or so ounces of brandy left inside, brought it to the table. He reached to unscrew the cap…and then stopped, his hand shaking restlessly over the bottle. *Please*, he begged, *please please not tonight…*

He stared at his reflection in the kitchen window, a stranger with too-dark eyes and a life he could not comprehend. Only then that reflection changed, replaced by the image of another man, someone he knew. It was Saul Jessup. The likeness was marred, however, not Jessup's own, and after a moment Mike realized it wasn't Saul Jessup he was seeing at all—but rather some manufactured notion of Saul Jessup's son, his face bearing the scars that had settled like physical thunder over Joshua DeFelice's wasted visage.

Slowly that face morphed into the one he'd witnessed on the balcony almost a month before, eyes sinking inward, jowls thickening, hair peeling back to a nicely-trimmed crew cut.

Mike shook himself, pulling out of the trance, and looking down noticed his hand still tremoring softly over the bottle.

He grabbed the brandy and put it back on the shelf.

Chapter 24

He was woken by sunlight.

He rolled out of bed and went first thing and ate two of his painkillers, crunching them to a fine powder between his teeth before swallowing a glass of SunnyD. He waited patiently for their little kick in the ass, and when it came Mike gathered his things and drove over to Ogburn's Funeral Home in Lancer County. He did not call ahead.

Entering the parlor, Mike found himself in a large high-ceilinged room which somehow seemed more tailored for cocktail parties than funerary arrangements; along with the usual Queen Annes, several plush couches lay scattered across the carpet, each flanked by mahogany end tables with useless lamps plopped on top. If dust ever gathered here, someone had made a point to conceal the fact. Across the room he noticed a pale-eyed blonde seated behind a desk just massive enough to make her seem childish; she sat twirling her long Alice-in-Wonderland curls.

"Yes? May I help you?"

He walked over and asked to speak with Ross Ogburn.

"Of course," the girl told him, moving from behind the desk. "Feel free to have a seat if you'd like, I'll be right back…"

Mike didn't have a seat. He walked around and stared at the pictures on the wall, bucolic scenes which had existed in some artist's head and which they'd toiled to show the rest of the world. Lots of sunsets, lots of autumn trees touched but never ravaged by an unseen wind. There was a coffee set-up on a table near the door, with a stack of Styrofoam cups beside the pot. Mike grabbed up a cup and poured himself some coffee, and when he'd finished a bald man with a weathered face and two floppy ears came walking toward him from across the room. Two melancholy eyes stared back from his face, and Mike had a feeling the eyes were melancholy not because the man himself was sad, but because melancholy eyes were an assumed thing in a business like his, and after a while he'd simply forgotten how to turn them off.

"Ross Ogburn, nice to meet you," the man said. He was moving in for the shake when he noticed Mike's cup of coffee in one hand and the light blue sling which told him the other was OUT OF ORDER, and silently slipped his hand back from where it came. "What is it I can help you with today, sir?"

Mike said, "Nice place you have here. Building's a little old, but I'd have never known it stepping through the door. How long you been in business?"

Ross Ogburn smiled, but it was an uncomfortable one. "My father started his business in the long-ago year of 1974. The Grant Ogburn Mortuary," he said with a flourish. "I changed the name once I took over for him, of course. I never did like that word, mortuary. Sounds horrid, if you ask me." He tried another smile. Nope, still not right. "Of course, we've only been in this present building since 1994. It is spectacular, isn't it, mister...?"

Mike introduced himself, setting down his coffee long enough to reach out and swap palms. There was little magic in this contemporary ritual of hand-wagging, Mike knew, but much to be said for man's common neurosis that such societal trappings—however absurd—be followed to a T. Extend an arm, grip and pump. Show some teeth.

"I was wondering if you could give me information about someone you laid to rest."

"Yes?"

"This must've been, sheesh, what is it now? Twenty-five years ago? His name was Chase Jessup. A local kid, grew up over in—"

"Oh, I remember him quite well. Of course. Except you couldn't properly say we laid him to rest, now could you? There was a coffin, but unfortunately it was empty as a poor man's stomach."

"You remember what happened then?"

"To the boy, you mean? A little of it, yes. My own father had a passing acquaintance with the boy's. Oh, what was his name? John or Paul or something Biblical like that."

"Saul."

"Excuse me?"

"Saul Jessup."

"Oh, yes. Saul, that's right. Like I said, my father knew a little of him, not much. I was barely more than a teenager at the time, but by then I'd been assisting in the business for years. By eleven, I'd seen more dead bodies than most people see their whole lives. Only the Jessup boy, that was the first time I remember there being no body to lay in the coffin, and I thought that was just the strangest thing. It was also one of the first times I'd seen a child's coffin up close—*ugh!*—I've hated them ever since. What did you say the boy's name was again?"

"Chase."

"Chase Jessup." He seemed to muse on that a moment, as if summoning some cherished childhood memory. "Yes, he was lost, if I recall correctly. He wandered off and I believe the whole town was searching for him at one point, but he was never found. Some say he was kidnapped. Or that he must've fallen in one of the streams in the woods out back their house, that he drowned and his body was washed away."

"Is that what you think?"

"Me? Oh goodness, I really wouldn't know what became of the poor boy. Whatever happened, it tore their family apart. The father scuttled off to some bottle or other and the mother…now let me see, what was her name? Mariah. Yes, that's it. Well, she committed suicide some time ago, and I *do* remember that because we handled the arrangements."

"You remember how she did it?"

"Carved a couple lines in her wrist, if memory serves. Shaving accident, must've been."

"Do you have the exact dates for all of this?"

Ogburn led Mike away from the desk and down a darkened hall with even darker rooms spiraling left and right. After rummaging around a bit, he retrieved a large album-sized ledger from one of the rooms and flipped through its pages until finding the respective dates.

As Mike scribbled them into his pad, Ogburn asked, "Did you know Chase Jessup?"

"No."

"A friend of the family?"

"Not exactly."

"Well then…?" A peculiar expression appeared suddenly on the bald man's face; his mouth snapped shut. "Oh, I do feel dumb. You're a police officer, aren't you?" he asked, voice betraying his own excitement. "A detective, am I right? Of course you are. Who else should come in asking all these questions?"

Mike flipped away his notepad, lifting his coffee cup from where he'd set it on a shelf. He finished what was inside and then tossed it in a small receptacle near the door. He asked if there was anything else Ogburn could tell him about Chase Jessup.

"About the boy? No, I'm afraid not. But if you'll wait just a second, perhaps I can find you someone who can." He flipped through more folders, turning pages, muttering to himself as he went along. After some searching, he said, "Ah yes! Here it is. Natalie Hollister."

Natalie Hollister, he explained, was the woman who had taken care of Mariah Jessup's funeral arrangements. Daddy Jessup had devoured too many skinfuls by then to be of much use, and Hollister had been Mariah's closest friend during most of her time in Lancer County. "If you'd really like to know more about Chase Jessup, she'd be a fine place to start. Of course, you could always talk to the father, though I doubt he would be much help. Assuming he's still alive, that is. But then you're a detective so I suppose you've thought of that already…"

Mike wrote down Natalie Hollister's information, but he wasn't expecting much. The records were almost fifteen years old, after all; for all he knew, Hollister was as thoroughly deceased as Saul Jesup's better half. He chatted with Ross Ogburn awhile longer—about police procedure, mostly, with a couple short anecdotes thrown in—before finally turning and following the darkened hall to its genesis, where the pretty blond was engaged in a riveting phone call at the front desk. She told him to have a nice afternoon and Mike lifted a hand in return, stepping outside into the blistering heat of a sunny mid-July.

He drove in silence, placing little pieces like so in his head, forming pictures that three months earlier he would've deemed the work of a mental patient on a bad day in hell. Now those pictures made sense, and he didn't know how to feel about that. Worried? Scared? Like maybe the Little Man had performed his greatest feat of all, infiltrating not only his emotions but now his intellect as well? Whatever it was, he knew he couldn't stop—not now—because, horrible as they seemed, those pictures in his head were reality. His other life—the one with a stable existence of house and job, with holidays and buffet restaurants and classics on the tube—had faded; at best, he was left ducking from one alcohol-inspired mania to the next, devoid of even the simple pleasures of insight and the ability to act on one's will. His wife was another man's lover. His son had let him go in favor of another applicant. He'd once owned a dog, but it ran away. He'd burned all his grass and it never grew back. He was driving a car that wasn't his own. Soon his life would be over, and suddenly that didn't seem so bad. There was much to be done before that time, but none of it seemed very important. Except this. This he would finish.

It was all he had left.

CHAPTER 25

Parents really are *the craziest people on earth.*

This was Doug Lunsmann's poignant if biased insight as he powered off his cell phone and plugged it to the charger near his bed. It was only three months ago he'd finally grown tired of begging and pleading for one of these magical cellular machines and now suddenly, out of the clear blue sky, he was given one without so much as asking. *Crazy people*, he thought, *ruled not by logic but by their own belly of power, their appetite for domination.* His mother had told him it was Bart's idea, but Doug wasn't so sure he believed that. How could he? The Christmas Spirit was still five months away, after all, and Bart himself as wigged-out as ever; why would he do such a thing? And wouldn't he ask for something in return?

"C'mon, Doug. I'm tired, let's go to *sleep…*"

Doug glanced over and saw Gary curled into his blankets on the floor, hands splayed over his eyes to block out the light.

"All right, all right," he said. "Shut your trap, I'll be ready in a second."

"That's what you said thirty *minutes* ago…"

"I said quiet, you dunce." Then in his best crazed robot voice: "You will sleep when I tell you to sleep. Understood?"

Gary groaned and rolled onto his stomach.

"Right, go ahead, roll over. That's your answer to everything, ain't it?" Doug smiled, pleased with the measure of his own wit. The feeling didn't last, however, and a moment later his face was as slack as it had been all day.

He lit some incense and placed it in a holder, smoke dancing in a wispy gray ribbon toward the ceiling. Then came the smell, rich and dark, and when it settled Doug moved to the window and stared outside, eyes creeping past the muted greens of the yard and out across the street and finally up to a star-littered sky.

Only he wasn't thinking about the yard or the dumb neighbors across the street or even about the Big Questions. He was thinking about tomorrow, and what sort of untold journeys lay awaiting him beyond sunset. It was a Saturday, and Brent would swing by sometime after two to pick them up. Doug wasn't exactly sure how he felt about that. Not because of Brent—of course not, Brent was a good person, thoroughly cool, if a little unfinished. It was just that, well…he was getting a little *tired* of all those late nights. They were fun, of course they were fun, no getting around that…but they were also exhausting. Not just physically, but on some deeper level Doug had never known existed until now.

Consider tomorrow, for example. He knew what they'd do—it was no mystery, they'd done it often enough. A stop at Ray-Ray's for a quick toke or couple bong rips. Maybe drive around listening to Brent's bass rattle the trunk and not talking for an hour. Then it's off to some greaser joint to order scraps off the dollar menu. Hell, he'd probably gained ten pounds in the last two weeks.

He tried not to think about it.

But then maybe tomorrow would be different; maybe Gary tagging along would change things. He considered perhaps this was the whole reason he'd invited Gary over in the first place. Well, that and to brag about his wild night with Nicky Collier. Gary had taken the news well enough, not so much jealous as filled with wonder at what kuh-razy things life sometimes crapped into your lap. Naturally he'd started a blurred recitation of his round with Shirley Temple a few weeks back, until Doug chimed in with a few more choice adjectives of the shape and texture of Nicky's nipple. *Hard. Swollen. Slightly ovoid.*

That had shut him up.

There were worse things than these orbiting the dark space of Doug Lunsmann's universe, however. He knew they were there, though it was easier to pretend they weren't; these were not, after all, exactly the types of things you looked in the face. Yet he'd had glimpses of their ragged forms, and something in the reflections cast off their eyes—reflections of *him*—told

Doug he'd been at the table too long, yes sir, that he was in too deep and there was no pulling out now. That maybe he wasn't just getting tired of this rollercoaster life he was on, but that maybe he'd been tired of it a long time before now. It was that Dark Appetite again, and maybe he felt scared at the prospect that he owned it and it owned him and that this was a cruel and ferocious relationship, some twisted liaison only someone in his skin could ever understand.

The sudden rumble of Gary's snores rose from the floor. Doug let out a breath and fished his cigarettes from under the mattress. He cracked the window and for a long time sat smoking at the ledge, staring across the desert of his own withered soul and wondering what had happened to the world that once existed there. The moon shone down brightly, casting its light over the small town below and forming it all into some glorious miracle gone wrong. What had happened to him? he wondered. *How had things gotten so fucked up?*

▲ ▲ ▲

He talked to Nicky the following afternoon.

Nicky Collier, he'd found, was a lot different than the person he'd always imagined back in school. For starters, she was smart. Not smart enough to keep her mother from finding her bag of grass, as it turns out, but still pretty darn smart. Because of the baggie incident, however, she'd been on lockdown for the past week, and tonight didn't look much better.

"Well, see if you can get out anyway. I wanna see you."

"I'll try, Doug," she told him. "No promises though, my mom's been a real robo-bitch lately. How about you just come sneak in my window, we can make our own fun."

Doug laughed. "Hey, that could work too…"

No sooner had he hung up than Doug had all but dismissed his feelings of the night before. He'd been in a bad spot, that's all, and he'd let it get to him. For his part, Gary had spent most of the morning subtly campaigning against going out with Brent at all, doing his best to convince Doug that what would really be boss would be a few funny movies—*American Pie? Freddy Got Fingered?*—and some nachos and cheese and maybe some bottle rockets for later. Wouldn't that be fun?

Finally Brent arrived, not a minute too soon, and after dropping Gary off at his house for a quick shower and change of clothes, he and Brent cruised around and blared some bass and burned down a doob. Afterwards they went to Taco Bell and ate in the parking lot, the stench of pot still lingering like a ghost. Doug was working through his second burrito when Brent rummaged around, revealing a paper from his pocket and tossing it across the seat.

"What's that?"

"Read it."

Doug lifted the paper, turning it in his hand. At first glance it appeared to be some sort of flyer, one of those standard gutter-stoppers he'd sometimes see taped along drink machines or on storefronts. Only it wasn't that—it was an invitation, Brent's name hand-written along the top of the page. It read:

WANT SOME SUMMER EXCITEMENT? CAN I GET A HELL YEAH!
YOU ARE CORDIALLY INVITED TO OUR SWEATY SUMMER SHINDIG,
FEATURING LIVE MUSIC BY HOTT LOCAL
BANDS, A BEST OF THE BUSTIES WET T-SHIRT CONTEST,
A POTATO-GUN SALUTE, AND DID WE MENTION ALL THE BOOZE
MONEY CAN BUY?

WHERE: ABILENE PLANTATION (*see directions below*)

WHEN: SATURDAY, JULY 12th

MUSIC STARTS AT 6:00 PM! DON'T MISS THE HOTTEST
PARTY OF THE SUMMER!

Beneath this was a list of local bands scheduled to perform, as well as a few choice directions surrounded by clip art of brown beer bottles. And written at the bottom of the page: ADMISSION $10!

"This is tonight."

"I know. Flyer came with the mail just this afternoon. What do you think?"

Doug swallowed down the last of his burrito. "You know these people?"

"Yeah, sure. You know that boy Roddy? Stops by sometimes over at Ray-Rays? Got those dumb-looking plugs in his ears? Anyway, it's his parents. They usually throw one every summer, only last year something happened—some bullshit with the scheduling—and anyway they never did it. But I went to the one before that."

"Was it cool?"

"Aw—you crazy? It was *awesome*. What they do, they rent this kick-ass house out in the boonies, and they have all this music and wild shit going on all night. Horny chicks *everywhere*."

Doug hesitated. "What about Gary?"

"What about him?"

"I mean—"

"We'll tell him about it, if he wants to come, who cares? So what, we'll let him. And if he doesn't, then forget him."

Doug thought about it. His mouth felt like sandpaper, and after a few gulps from his watered-down soda he asked, "You think Nicky could come?"

"Yeah, she could come. I mean, I don't see why not."

Doug nodded, staring at the paper.

"All right," he said. He balled up the last of his trash, stuffed it in the bag. "Let's do it."

Gary was on the porch eating a sausage dog when they pulled up back at his house. "Where've you guys been?" he called. "Gosh, I've been waiting out here *forever*."

Brent leaned out the window and said, "Shut up and get in the car!"

Gary smiled and got in. Due to some tectonic shift in the boys' dynamic, however, his residence was now the backseat—maybe because Doug was already up front, or maybe because Gary was just the type of person who belonged in the backseat.

Brent steered the Pontiac out of the driveway and away from the house. He'd driven little more than a mile when his eyes darted to the rearview mirror, and after lighting a cigarette he tossed the invitation over his shoulder. Gary snapped it up and started reading.

"*Heeyyyyy*, cool," he said, his voice slightly higher than usual. "Wet t-shirt contest! Are we going?"

"*We're* going," Brent said. "I'm dropping you off at the bowling alley, bitch."

"What?" Gary groaned. "Aw, c'mon Brent!"

"Are you kidding? You know what Aunt Karen would do to me if she knew I took you to something like that? She'd have my frickin' balls in a sling and don't even act like she wouldn't."

"C'mon, Brent, she ain't gonna find out nothing—"

"Bullshit."

"She won't! Brent, I swear she won't!"

He glanced in the rearview. "You have ten dollars?"

"I've got twenty!"

Brent was silent, letting the moment play itself out. Doug lit a cigarette and stared out the window. No hurry, ladies and gentleman, no hurry at all…

"*Please…?*"

Brent let out a breath. "All right, Gary. But I'm serious, if you open your fat mouth—"

"I won't, I won't, I promise."

"All right, fine. Then I guess we're going."

"*All riiiight,*" Gary sang, his eyes set a little wider than they were made. "Thanks, Brent, this is gonna be great. Doug, ain't this gonna be great?" After a moment, his face clouded over and he sat forward in the seat. "Hey Brent?" he asked. "What's a busty?"

Chapter 26

"**Excuse me? May** I help you?"

Mike stared across the bright linoleum of the Clearview Rest Home, observing a cold place that seemed a little less cold as his eyes caught on the doe-eyed brunette. Her hair was pulled back in a bun, and in it he spied out the first withered strands of gray, as if the building itself were draining that last bit of youth from her bones.

"I'm looking for someone I've been told is staying here," he told her. "Name of Natalie Hollister?"

A gentle grin flashed on the woman's face. "You mean Nattie. Sure, Nattie's been a fixture here for some time. She's quite a lady."

"So I've heard."

"Oh, you've never met?"

Mike shook his head. "We haven't. But I talked with her daughter, Amy, she said it would be all right if I came on down and asked a few questions. Is it all right if I see her?"

The woman had been standing near a linens cart loaded down like a camel; now she pushed it aside and walked over. "Sure," she said. "Not that it's any of my business, but mind if I ask what for? We try to run a smooth enough ship, keep everybody happy. I suppose if Amy told you it was okay…"

"Oh, nothing so serious as that, I'm afraid. Mostly I'm just curious—I've been doing a spot of research on some local history and I'd like to pick her brain is all, about some things that happened a long time ago." Mike smiled his most subtle of smiles, easy on the teeth. He'd considered flashing his shield, but saw that wasn't necessary; shields carried a weight of respect, sure thing, but they also made people tense up, made them suspicious, defensive—all things he wanted to avoid.

"Well, when you're done with Nattie, how about start on the others?"

"Come again?"

"I'm just saying, these folks in here, they have nothing but time. Everything to say and nobody to say it to. They've heard all their own stories about a hundred times by now, some days I think they'd rather somebody just up and die so they'll have something new to chat about." A touch of pink rose in the lady's cheeks. "That sounds horrible doesn't it?"

"Not at all."

"Sure it does. I'm sorry, it's just that…well, it gets to you sometimes, working in here. Anyway, it's really sweet of you to come visit Nattie, whatever the reason."

Mike shrugged. "My pleasure."

"Well, c'mon then," she said, smiling. "Nattie's right this way…"

She led Mike down a series of twisting corridors, each more disturbingly clinical than the last. The smell wasn't septic, not exactly, but some fresh air wouldn't hurt. Finally they came to an empty room and the brunette welcomed Mike to have a seat, then spun and left the room.

She returned minutes later, her tiny charge clutching a walker as she followed close behind, laughing along to some unheard joke before stopping to stare at him with two dusky gray eyes. Mike introduced himself and held out a hand, and Nattie Hollister smiled and shook it and moved past him, taking it nice and easy into a chair near the room's only window. The brunette gave Mike a nod and left the room.

He said, "Mrs. Hollister, I hope I'm not disturbing you…"

"Not disturbing," she said. "Not at all. They make us watch those same old terrible movies every year, I was glad to get out. Every now and then they'll show us something worth seeing but most of it's pure-t trash, from beginning to end."

"Well," Mike asked, feeling his tongue loosen just a snatch, "what kinds of movies do you like? *Casablanca? Streetcar Named Desire? Singin' in the Rain?*"

"Heavens no! That's the sort of garbage they have on in there. Always with the Fred Astaire and the John Wayne and Marilyn Mon-roe. Who do they think we are—dinosaurs? I don't want *John Wayne*, I want *Clint Eastwood*. And forget Marilyn, give me *Julia Roberts* or *Meg Ryan* or somebody—enough of that skirt-tippin' floozy. Haven't we had enough after fifty years?"

"You like Clint Eastwood?"

Her face softened to a smile. "*Love* Clint Eastwood. This day I would marry that man and have all of his babies, as many as he wants. My husband, rest his soul, but he would understand."

"Situation like that, I guess he'd have to wouldn't he?"

"Oh, he would, he would."

Mike gave a little laugh. "You know, your daughter warned me about you, but I'm starting to think she didn't do a very good job of it."

"You know Amy?"

"No, but I spoke with her on the phone yesterday evening. She told me you'd be open to talking to me. She also seemed to indicate that you were 'the most kick-ass mom' I'd ever meet."

Another smile, small but powerful. There was enough joy in the expression that, at first glance, one might miss the tiny glints of sadness he detected lurking just beneath. Strangely, the sadness seemed somehow outside of herself, and immediately Mike took her for a woman who, though very much at peace with her own life, was at the same time acutely aware of the wealth of suffering around her. "Amy's a sweet girl," she said. "And a good mother, too. Four kids in as many years is hard on anybody, but she's handled it. And better than most people—why, I had my hands full with just the two."

"Two? I wasn't aware—"

"My first daughter died when she was seventeen. Drowned."

"I didn't know that. I'm sorry."

"No reason to be sorry, dear. We're all headed in the same direction, just some of us get there a little sooner than others."

Mike looked down at his hands. "Listen, Mrs. Hollister, I drove over from Glass County today. I was hoping you might be able to help me with something."

"I hope I can help you too, sonny. You're the first young man's come to visit me in…well, in quite some time. I went to figuring you must be desperate for something. What is it?"

"I was hoping you could tell me about Mariah DeFelice."

The elderly woman held his gaze, and already Mike could sense in her eyes those tiny circles of darkness bubbling ever so slowly to the top, as if some deeply buried artifact had been joggled loose and was quietly creaking in the depths. Her face clouded, and when she spoke next her voice had lost some subtle vigor that had been present before. "What did you say your name was, dear?"

He told her.

"Never heard it before. Are you kin of Mariah's?"

"No, ma'am, I'm not. But I've recently spent a large portion of my time tracing the history of Lancer County, and particularly the house where Mrs. DeFelice lived. Over on Slocum Road? I was hoping you might be able to tell me about the things I wouldn't read in any newspaper."

"I suppose you mean...the bad times?"

He cleared his throat. "Yes, ma'am," he said. "I do."

She gazed at him, her dusky eyes searching for something Mike wasn't so sure he wanted her to find. Her head tilted imperceptibly to the left, and with a curious gleam the old woman said, "You've felt it, haven't you?"

Mike shifted in his seat. "Ma'am?"

"Once you've felt it, you get a certain look about you. And I'd say you've got that look all over, Mr. Lunsmann."

"Felt what?"

A long breath oozed from her body as she turned, staring out the window. She peered out there, a pretty green lawn, pretty blue sky, birds on the wire, all things working together to make this place feel a little bit less like a cage: a fine place to spend one's final hours before THE END. She said, "Mariah was a troubled person. She started out that way back when we first met, and only got worse as time went on and everything came falling down around her. She didn't deserve the things that life gave her. But it happened and she saw it happening and decided she couldn't look the other way. No matter how hard she tried, she couldn't get out from under." The old woman shifted, pouring herself into Mike's eyes. "I've spent so much of my life trying to forget those things, and I here I am about to drag them right back out again..."

"Mrs. Hollister, if you don't feel—"

"Hush, hush. If I didn't feel like it then I'd be back in the day room snoozing. And if I didn't like you, I'd tell you to leave. Now I see you brought a pad of paper there—are you gonna whip that sucker out, or just sit there staring at the walls?"

Like an obedient child, Mike revealed his small notebook, uncapped his pen.

"Where do we start?"

They started with her.

Born in the hopeless grip of the Dirty Thirties, Nattie Hollister had spent her early years fast-acquainted with the plight of the poor. She'd been only eight when those friendly Japanese pilots dropped their surprise on Pearl Harbor, and recalled being terrified at the certainty that her own town—a desperate place with the unlikely name of Stahl, Kansas—would be next. Her father had entered the war along with the rest of the nation, and by the time our own amiable pilots had conjured hell in Hiroshima and Nagasaki, the Hollister family had crawled from the pit of degradation and found a better world waiting at the top. Soon she'd found a husband of her own, and after sputtering here and there across the South they'd eventually settled in tiny Lancer County, North Carolina. They'd been here all of six months when Edward DeFelice made his gruesome attempt to erase his lineage from the face of the earth.

"That one got national coverage," she told him. "Well, for about two seconds anyway. I can still remember the feeling in town after that. It's like the whole place changed. We all tried to come together because…well, because I suppose you have to after something like that. But the grief was so thick, it was suffocating; the innocence was lost. Tragedy had touched us, and we felt violated by it. Those murders, they left something on that town. I don't believe I ever truly believed that until I got out, and I've never spoken the words until now. But they're true, those words, and if they're not I still believe them. You know what I'm talking about, or you wouldn't be here right now asking me these questions."

Without realizing it, Mike had begun to nod. He knew the feeling, of course—one of despair, and hopelessness, some bleak emotion that filled you up and threatened to break you in half. Only to him the emotion was not a vague free-floating one, but rather one with a definite source, a source covered in some ancient version of tic-tac-toe and all of nature's hobgoblins of the past. That part he decided to keep to himself.

"Whatever it is," Nattie continued, "those killings brought it on, and I guess it's been there ever since. And the genesis of it all was that house. The son—the one that survived—he'd been taken in by some aunt or another, and because of some inheritance loophole there couldn't anything be done with the property till he came of age. A lot of people wouldn't even look at the place when they passed it on the road. Then it got worked out so the Jessup clan bought it—at a good price, after the bloodbath—and I suppose we all tried to move on and forget the whole thing. Sort of like spitting in the wind, but we tried."

"Did the Jessups know about the murders when they moved in?"

"They were told. Even after a decade in the bush the house was still worth more than they paid—a lot more—so yes, they knew. But Chase had just been born and they needed a bigger place, someplace to start fresh. They didn't like it that something so gruesome had happened there, I know it made Mariah sick to her stomach. But she did just like the rest of us and tried not to worry much about it."

"Would you say they were a happy family?"

"Happy?" A knowing smile creased the old woman's face. "For a long time I guess they were happy, if you could call it that. They settled in and set themselves to build a life together—and for a while there were doing a pretty nice job of it. I met Mariah the week they moved in and we talked at least three, four times a week till the day she died. Yes, I believe she was genuinely happy in those early years, only then...all that changed. Happened so fast you would've thought somebody waved a magic wand. Saul took to drinking, something he'd never done much of before. Started losing his temper. That, I think, was the beginning. Before long he was drunk most of the day, and from what I gather not too pleasant a person to be around after sunset. He resurrected what little bit of property came with the house, only to sell it off acre by acre. Got a straight job, lost it. Got another one, then lost that. Mariah'd received a small inheritance when her father died, and for a while they used that to make ends meet."

"You said Saul had a temper. Did he beat her?"

"Oh, of course," Nattie said. "Mariah never told me so outright, but then I could see the bruises, so why would she? Besides the bruises, I could see it in her eyes. Eventually I could hear it in her voice. But anytime I tried bringing it up she just got quiet and said it wasn't so bad as it seemed. One time she got defensive and said something snippy, and that was the last I ever said about it. I wish now I could take that back. It's like she was fading a little at a time, and I let her do it on account of some dumb old hissy fit. It got so I was too damned proud to speak up."

Mike hesitated. "Mrs. Hollister, do you know why Mariah killed herself?"

"There's no reason for no one to kill themselves. People just get mixed up sometimes and they think that would be the better way, so they go on and do it. Like I told you, Mariah saw the walls, in her mind she thought they were too high, so she opted out. No one thing pushed her to that—just a lot of little things, with some big ones along the way that we can stand back and point to and say, 'That was it.' But we won't ever know everything that went into her death."

"Can you tell me about some of the ones you do know of?"

"After Chase went missing," she said, "that was the biggest. Mariah wasn't herself after that. It was like watching somebody *slowly…shut…down.*"

"What else?"

"Second to that? Saul himself, no question. She used to love him, I'm sure of that…but eventually she started to hate him, I think, to truly *hate* the man. After Chase was gone his drinking only got worse, and I picture her whole life becoming like a mental house with no Out door. Then one day I guess she just snapped and made one herself."

"Tell me about Chase."

"What do you want to know?"

Everything, he wanted to say, *whatever memories your precious mind can dredge up so I can take them and study them and glean their secret meanings.* Only that was ridiculous and he knew it, and so he settled for something a little less ambitious:

"Tell me about August 8, 1979. About the night he disappeared. Do you have any idea what happened to him?"

"We will never know what happened to that boy, Mr. Lunsmann. Nobody disappears into thin air, but Chase Jessup comes about as close as I've ever seen."

"The papers I've read, they seemed to indicate that at the time of the disappearance both parents thought Chase was still in the house. Is that what you remember?"

She had to think about that one. "Yes...yes, I suppose they *had* assumed he was still inside. Of course, it was past nightfall before anyone ever noticed him missing in the first place. Mariah called me when she'd figured it out and I rushed right over, hadn't got three steps in the door when I realized Saul had been boozing. Oh, he'd tried to cover it up, of course, but there was no covering up that sort of pollution. I remember thinking to myself, how hard has he been pounding on her tonight? And what about Chase? Had he tried the old belt out on him too, is that what had made the boy so scarce? There's no telling how long we searched those woods for him that night—hours and hours. It was a Wednesday night and there was a full moon in the sky—I remember that part clear as a bell, since on account of it we were able to search straight into morning. But we never found a trace; he'd vanished."

"And you don't have any doubts about his death?"

"None."

"Sure about that?"

She laughed, amused. "Well, I was at the funeral, wouldn't a-been there otherwise. I'm not sure what else you want me to say."

He was about to dig into that when the image of something else stuck in his mind. He asked, "You say there was a full moon?"

"As big as I've ever seen. But it was no use anyway—Chase was gone."

Mike paused, gathering his thoughts. He considered he had a pretty good idea of where the boy might be, but then that wasn't possible was it? An image of the sunken face Mike had witnessed in the window a few nights back flashed through his mind, leering madly against the moon; then the image faded, but not soon enough, and before it was gone Mike heard himself saying, "The picture they had in the papers, was that the last known photo of the boy? It's the only one I've ever seen of him, I was wondering if you happened to have any?"

She told him she was sure she did. "Photographs," she said, "are one of the few things I do have left. No one else seems to want them, and when I keel over I'm sure most of them will go down with me. Worse things have happened, I suppose."

She guided him to the bottom drawer of a bureau along the far wall. Inside he found three albums of varying size, along with a shopping bag of empty frames and an assortment of old-fashioned ceramic ducks. She wasn't sure which album might hold what he was looking for, she told him, and so he passed her the smallest of the three, taking the next for himself. He'd gotten halfway through when she made a small sound.

"Here," she said. "This picture was taken only a few weeks before he went missing."

Mike gazed down at the small five-by-seven, its age screaming out from the page. He found himself staring into the eyes of a young boy with bushy brown hair; the smile was strong, the eyes simple and pure, and for a moment Mike studied them with an intensity bordering on mania. Nattie flipped the page and there was another photo, this one of the boy standing next to a rail-thin woman it took Mike all of two seconds to realize was the same as the old lady sitting before him now, pointing her finger and describing the scenes he saw as if each had been firmly fixed in her mind, bound there by the fact of the photograph.

The next picture showed Chase peering from a second floor balcony, arms flung high in faux-victory over his head. Mike remained silent, a small chill creeping down his spine as he recognized the towering portico, the thick Doric columns and three windows burning bright at the young boy's back. He pointed to the picture.

"What's this? This whole thing, the balcony—it's not there anymore."

Nattie nodded. "Yes, Saul eventually had it torn down. Mariah loved that balcony, used to sit on it every morning…but after Chase, she never used it. He did build a new porch later on, nowhere near as nice as this one."

"And without the balcony."

"That's right."

Mike thought about that.

Another flip of the page, only this time when his eyes met the photo they were drawn not to the small boy in ragtag jeans but instead to the gentleman propped carelessly at his side, his dark eyes and tall lantern jaw and the perfect edge of a crew cut. Mike's breath caught in his throat, producing a raspy bug-on-windshield noise that seemed louder to him than it actually was. From far away, Nattie Hollister rattled on about something he could no longer bring himself to hear, and when at last he spoke the words came out rushed and garbled, another language.

"Who is that?"

"Oh, well that's Chase, honey."

"Not the boy, *him*. This one right here, who is *that?*"

For a moment Mrs. Hollister stared, a queer expression drawn down her face.

"Don't you know, dear? That's his father. That's Saul."

He took the album in his hand, pulling it close, standing for the first time face-to-face with the stranger who had implanted a bullet in his arm. Only if what Nattie had said was true that wasn't entirely accurate, was it? No, no, he'd met the bastard before...

"When was this picture taken?"

Nattie faltered. "Oh, late seventies would be my guess. Why?"

Breathe, he told himself, *take it slow*, he said, *play it nice and easy and cool.*

He tugged down a swallow and opened his mouth, pulled in air.

The album began to shake in his hand.

"Mr. Lunsmann? Are you all right?"

He wasn't all right. He was nowhere near it, peace and all that jazz seemed a thousand miles away. He struggled to answer, couldn't make it happen. The album tumbled from his hand, splashing awkwardly to the floor, and Nattie gasped.

"Dear, are you okay?"

"Never better," he muttered. "Listen, Mrs. Hollister, I've just remembered something. Something important I have to do today. Would it be all right if I came back another time?"

She told him of course, dear, it would be fine, but was he quite sure he was *all right?*

Just fine, and before she could say anything more Mike swiped the album from the floor, placed it on the bureau and snatched the photo from the sleeve. He sputtered his apologies, pausing long enough to plant a quick smooch on Nattie Hollister's cheek before turning and taking off down the hall, the old photograph still gripped in one hand...

Chapter 27

Pieces floating in darkness, drifting in his head.

Pieces bigger than they used to be, and not as many. The edges fixed in his mind.

Following his exit from Clearview, Mike spent the better part of ten minutes sitting quietly in the Buick's front seat, staring at a stained photo from another time and struggling to comprehend whatever it was he'd walked into that first night in the Harlow Boonies.

Now, fifteen minutes later and on his way home, he still hadn't pulled it off.

Mike fished a handkerchief from his pocket, ran it across his forehead. Traffic whirred by in watercolor outside his window, only he couldn't be bothered with that. A dented Cavalier appeared in his rearview, moved to pass, and was blocked by an oncoming pick-up; Mike watched it all with a dreamy sort of detachment. Calloused, unflinching. Worse than the traffic was the sudden ferocity of his own thoughts, figments and snatches of the past three months rolling back in a dark tide of something like madness.

He thought of the day he'd first laid eyes on Saul Jessup, of the old man's surly strut to the house and those twin cases of Pabst. The way he'd solemnly—nay, *reverentially*—stacked the beers into the fridge. Fast-forward six or seven or eight hours and Mike had witnessed the Saul of twenty years earlier pumping bullets into four teenagers, people who had breached some unseen boundary between this world and the next, and who paid the price.

His mind flashed on the others he'd seen that night, their flayed corpses strung from an oak and gleaming brightly against the moon, and Mike thought of all those unknown drivers and passengers who had made this same trip over the past ten or fifteen or who knows how many years.

He thought about Joshua DeFelice with his deep tan and butchered face, and of what he'd said about batteries. About preternatural forces and what sorts of things they might feed on.

He thought about a relic with a dubious past and some sinister power over the hearts of man. He thought about family, and what made a life truly significant.

He thought about FORGIVENESS IS NOT ENOUGH.

And as he sat thinking something began to bother Michael Lunsmann. Something the Hollister lady had said, buried way down now, kicking around back there in some peripheral part of his mind. What was it? He thought long and hard about what it might be, and soon his brain throbbed sickly and he could feel his heartbeat in his eyes. Then it came, and this time when his foot went down hard on the pedal he didn't restrain it but tightened his grip on the wheel and squinted into the early afternoon sun.

Twelve minutes later Mike climbed his front porch and walked through the door. He went to a cabinet and ripped back the door, watching as a deluge of zebra-colored notebooks washed over the floor. *So this*, he thought, *is what three years of therapeutic journaling looks like.* He sank to his knees, rifling through pages until finding the entries he was looking for, checking the dates.

The date of his midnight stroll in the Harlow Boonies—May 16th.

The night of his blackout and T.J. Chadwick's fateful ride into eternity—June 14th.

He moved to the kitchen, checking the calendar against his own foregone conclusions, and was not surprised to find accompanying each of these dates that small white circle indicating a full moon. He gathered his own memories of those nights, remembering the pale glow of moonlight shining bright from above—just as it had the night Jessup's son passed his own mysterious point of no return. Finally Mike flipped to July's calendar, trailed a finger to the next white circle and—

And his heart sank and went black in his chest.

July twelfth.

The date was today.

Chapter 28

A small crowd had gathered in the yard, whooping and cheering as the prestigious potato gun salute officially got under way. For several minutes Doug watched in amazement as the men fired away, each holding in their hands some form of elongated contraption formed of PVC pipes and adolescent glee. There were seven this year, no two alike, one of the machines an over-the-shoulder deal coated in camouflage, another small enough to be held in one hand. The barrels were pointed toward a wooded area across the yard, a distance of about fifty yards, and when the potatoes came blasting out, heralded by spurts of blue fire, they made the distance with ease.

Doug hooted and raised his cup in solidarity, not entirely sure he understood the purpose of such potato-flinging machines, but drunkenly determined that someday he would make one of his own. Gary stood next to him, eyes glazed as he observed the spectacle with an unmistakable expression of disgust.

"What…is wrong with the world?" he asked. "This is so lame, Doug. I'm serious, I can actually *feel* myself getting dumber just watching this."

"I think it's wonderful," Doug told him.

"Yeah, well, *you've* been drinking too much. What is that now, your fourth cup? Fifth? Why don't you lay off it, huh? And stand up straight, you look like my dead uncle."

Across the yard, Doug noticed Brent lounging on the steps of a massive back porch. He was surrounded by a group of young girls—pretty ones—and staring at them now Doug sensed a familiar surge of frustration. Of course Brent didn't mind if Gary tagged along, of course he didn't care if Gary spent the whole night buzzing around like some blood-hungry mosquito, because at least it wouldn't be in his ear. See, he didn't have to baby-sit—that was Doug's job.

Still, the party had been good so far, if not quite the bacchanal the flyer seemed to indicate (though the wet t-shirt contest had proved wildly stimulating). He'd started drinking soon after they arrived—besides the kegs, there were several barrels of homemade PJ set up around the grounds—and by the time the busty beauty with the winning assets had taken her bow, Doug was buzzing hard and ready for takeoff.

Finally the last of the potatoes fell splattering through the pines, and minutes later a new band mounted the stage across the yard and started pounding away. They were a nü-metal band, though not a very talented one, and were joined onstage by a couple of lady dancers with what appeared to be mullets and who reminded Doug a lot of some bad guys you'd be roughing up in a Double Dragon video game.

He'd stopped for a refill at another barrel of P.J. when his phone rang and Doug snapped it up, said hello, and no sooner had the word left his mouth than his eyes were open and his back was straight and the world came sharply into focus. The conversation continued for maybe two minutes, Doug pacing back and forth with one finger plugged to his ear, until finally he grinned for no reason at all, said love you, goodnight, and hung up.

Gary asked, "Who was that?"

Doug closed the phone and slipped it into his pocket. "My mom."

"Again? What is that, like the fourth time she's called?"

Doug nodded, but it was against his will. "Third. I don't know, they're acting weird again. Did I sound drunk?"

"Wasted. You sounded *wasted*, Doug."

"Be for real."

"I *am* being for real!"

Doug let him have it in the arm, had started in on his back when the phone buzzed again and he whipped it out, pausing long enough to check the display this time. An evil smirk crept over his face.

"Hello?"

"Doug, what are you doing?"

"Oh, hi Nicky," he beamed. "Not doing too much here, you know, just necking with some girls at this party. Too bad you couldn't make it. Gary says they're sluts but I keep trying to tell him that's not true, that—"

"Doug, I'm seriously about to hang up on you right now. You better be joking."

"Joking? Do you really think I'd joke about—"

"Because if that's the way it is, I can go party with someone else tonight."

"Wait—what're you talkin' about? I thought your mom wouldn't let you out."

She made a noise. "I talked her into it. But since it looks like you have other plans—"

"Whoa, *whoa*. Nicky, I take it back."

"Oh yeah?"

"Yeah. Gary was right—they're *total* sluts."

Once he finally got Nicky back on the line—and after affirming his thorough disgust of all other girls—Doug could sense some wild electricity working over his body, hot and tingling. It was getting late, after all, and there was just enough booze in his system to make him believe anything was not only possible, but damn well likely.

"Where are you?" he asked.

"I'm at Sissy's."

"Sissy? Who's Sissy?"

"Sissy Parker. You know Sissy. She moved away last year, remember? To Lancer? Anyway, she lives just down the road from…what's it called again? Abilena Plantation? Abilene? I can never remember."

"Yeah, Abilene."

"Well, whatever it's called, Sissy lives like four miles down the road."

Doug smiled. "So we can come scoop you up?"

A funny noise then, sort of like a grunt. "Well…not exactly," she told him, and Doug let out a breath he hadn't realized he'd been holding.

"What do you mean?"

"Doug, calm down. It's just that—well, I figured Brent could come pick us up and we could hang out awhile there at the party, but Sissy's parents…" Her voice grew low, almost a whisper. "Doug, her parents are really *old*. I mean, they're like *sixty*. Sissy said they won't let us leave with anybody unless they meet them first."

Doug glanced over and found Brent still telling stories on the porch, his audience swept away by his numb little smile and demonically bloodshot eyes. His arm was now slipped snugly around the hip of one of the girls.

Doug said, "I don't think that's happening, Nicky."

"Yeah, no shit. You could've come by yourself but you've been drinking, you dumbass."

"Who says I've been drinking?"

"Doug, please. I can smell it over the phone."

Doug shook his head, staring out over the too-green grass of the back-yard, at the mullet dancers still grooving on the stage. His gaze flipped to Gary, who was now busy chatting with two forty-plus women at the side of the house, bellies bubbling from beneath their skimpy black halters. "Nicky, I want to see you," he told her.

"I want to see you, too."

"Then what's the problem?"

Then a clutter on the other end. "Hold on," Nicky said. He heard muffled talking, and a moment later she came back on. "Hey, lemme call you back."

As he waited, Doug found another barrel and filled his cup. Gary waved him over and Doug ignored him, wandering instead to a small garden featuring ripe tomatoes and cucumbers. He picked one of the tomatoes, was about to take a bite but at the last second tried hurling it against a tree instead. He missed. Minutes later the phone rang and he said, "Hello?"

"Hey, it's me. Sissy says her parents should be in bed by ten o'clock."

"And?"

"*And* so then you can come over, duh."

"How?"

"Just get Brent to drop you off or something—and bring Gary. We'll meet you in the backyard, Sissy says we can sneak you inside."

He asked where Sissy lived, and after a few muffled words a new voice came on the line—thinner than Nicky's, more nasal.

"Doug? This is Sissy. Okay, here's what you wanna do…"

When it was over, Doug sat sipping his cup and configuring the route more clearly in his head. He checked the time. Eight o'clock. He glanced again at Brent, started in that direction…then changed his mind and made his way over to Gary instead. Doug could already sense a few obstacles forming in the back of his mind; even these, however, were insignificant in light of what was happening on the other side of his brain: images and reels of a booze-induced romp in some stranger's house, of a sight and smell and taste of things he'd thought much about—too much, actually—and which now seemed torturously within grasp.

By the time he reached Gary, his latest cup was empty and deep in his mind Doug had become convinced of one thing: tonight would be a night to remember.

He would make sure of it.

Chapter 29

It was just after eight p.m. when Mike saw the old pickup stir to life, trailing a line of dun-colored dust through the fields. He watched as the truck veered left onto Slocum Road, rolling soundlessly out of sight. Finally he slipped the binoculars from his face and rolled up the windows, and after a moment's hesitation decided on leaving the keys where they were in the ignition. Waiting patiently in the seat next to his own was a small brown paper bag, folded over at the top; he snatched it now and stepped out of the car.

He started forward, thighs burning like fire as he pushed across the fields. Were his assumptions correct, Jessup had embarked on no more than a summary trip to the Stop & Go for a quick stockpile of Pabst and—if Mike were lucky—a spot of gas and a couple jerky sticks beyond that. Having all the social graces of a baboon, Jessup was unlikely to be held up by anything less than a flat tire, and Mike calculated he had anywhere from seven to ten minutes, fifteen on the outside, before the old man returned.

He'd made it halfway to the house when those first searing claws dug into his shoulders and scuttled up his back; other times it was his legs who betrayed him, turned to rubber beneath the scorching summer heat. Just his nerves, Mike knew, always getting the better of him, always fooling around. Back in his street beat days he'd dealt with such hysteria by forming a small mental compartment, fashioned only of the sturdiest mental material. An image of it fixed in his mind, he would pour into it all such nervousness, all the debilitating fears of death, and paranoia, and every other anxiety which would cripple any normal human being. He found that box now, dusted it clean and crammed away.

Three minutes later he was climbing the front porch steps. His arm ached from the weight of the bag in one hand, and approaching the door he juggled it awkwardly and tried the knob.

Locked.

He fished a credit card from his wallet, dragged it along the space between the door and the jamb—and then froze, petrified by the blaring alarm he heard from inside. Only the alarm wasn't real and he knew it—just his nerves again, hamming it up with another sleight-of-mind display. He turned the knob and with a lingering creak the door slid open, and he realized the real trick was in not tearing the damn thing off the hinges when he walked inside.

He closed the door behind him, locked it.

The house swept over him in waves, turning his mind to misfortune and his heart to all the terrible things of the past few years; an image of Kathleen floated up through the darkness, and he deftly swatted it away. Then came Dougie, and that image was a bit more agile, more resilient, resisting him with raised voice until finally being mashed into Mike's Little Box.

He checked his watch. Eight minutes down.

He shifted the bag and rushed the stairs, taking them two at a time. Made a right down the hall and stopped, his eyes drawn once more to the shining candelabrum with its taunting cuneiform script, the anguished beasts and drooling molds of wax. He took a step, two, three steps forward, one arm reaching out blindly before at last his eyes snapped away...

Focus.

He went to the window, staring out across the dusty yard below; where once had stood an oak and a small copse of woods, now offered only the remains of a single crumbling stump. Panning the twilight sky, he could already make out the looming disk of the moon, burgeoning cold and full overhead. Mike tossed the bag onto the bed, opened it and took out what was inside. There were two bottles—one glass, one plastic. He cracked the seal on the first and took down a gulp, then reached inside his jacket for the forty-five he'd brought along for the occasion. He checked the sights, the ammo, tucked the pistol back into the holster on his shoulder.

He swept the items back into the bag and then turned, moving to the closet he'd noticed his last time here. Opening the old-fashioned louvered doors, he found the closet offered even more space than he'd hoped. No sooner had a thin smile touched his face, however, than a sudden reflection of light crossed the ceiling—here and then gone—and he heard the quick rumble of an engine shutting off, followed by the hard slam of a door.

Mike pushed his way inside, carefully closing the louvered doors and then maneuvering past forgotten clothes on his way toward the back. He'd almost made it when he stumbled over something on the floor, picked it up and saw a small classic-era Matchbox car. There were other things here as well—a flashlight, a couple action figures, a smattering of Topps cards—and brushing them aside Mike settled clumsily to the floor.

Minutes later the TV snapped on downstairs and he heard the deep, unmistakable crack of a pop-top beer. Suddenly Mike had never felt so parched in his life, and for a lingering moment his mind reverted to the preacher's story of a man locked in a dry, unsearchable desert. He felt like that now, like a sordid creature abandoned to his own insatiable thirst—only where was his fulfillment? His salvation? Where was *his* damned pump?

"*Cheers,*" he whispered, then opened his fifth and took another swig. Soon the last bit of sunlight went seeping from the shutters, and Mike Lunsmann found himself in darkness.

CHAPTER 30

It was dark now, and the boy was scared.

He'd heard Pa come in from outside, and though he hadn't wanted to leave Mama alone she'd patted his head and told him to run along. It wasn't the first time she'd told him that and he knew what his mother meant when she said it. So he'd come here and was now sitting in the oily blackness of the closet, eyes clenched tight as he listened to the noises from downstairs—yelling and crying and sometimes the crash of something hard against the walls. Chase was crying too, and in that moment swore to himself that someday he'd hurt his Pa for all the bad things he'd ever done to them. He promised himself that, on all the baseball cards in all the world.

He heard footsteps, first up the stairs and finally entering the room itself, the door slamming roughly behind them. Chase remained silent, the blood running cold in his veins until at last he heard the soft groan of the mattress, followed minutes later by a deep series of snores that seemed to rattle the walls. Moving through the darkness, Chase edged closer to the louvered closet doors and tentatively eased back the slats.

He let out a breath.

Outside his father lay collapsed across the bed, a careless ragdoll bathed in the light of the setting sun; he moaned raggedly, shifting against the sheets as sweat shone like a heavy grease through his short crew-cut hair.

Chase waited, struggling to keep his mind from the blaring silence at the bottom of the stairs. He moved slowly, his breath held fast in his lungs as he reached out with one trembling hand and eased back the closet door. His father grunted once and stirred on the bed.

Now get out, he told himself. *Just get out and run run fast as you can, as far as your legs will carry you...*

He started out, quietly making his way in small steps to the bedroom door. Once more his father shuffled restlessly against the sheets and Chase stopped, the tears brimming now like fountains in his eyes. He reached out, his breath coming low and hot as he twisted gently at the knob. As he did so, the boy became aware of a soft hissing noise at his back—it was, he thought, the sound of eggs scrambling on a stove—and slowly he turned, eyes settling on the dumb old candlethingy his Pa kept in the window.

Chase froze, staring numbly as the room was flooded by a sudden gentle glow, washing over him in deep blue waves; without knowing it, a low whine had formed at the base of his throat. Still the light grew brighter, casting long shadows down the wall and shrouding him in a warm all-over glow which seemed to radiate from everywhere at once.

He opened his mouth to scream, only the scream wouldn't come and instead he shut his eyes and began to cry and when he opened them next he was standing outside on the balcony—what his mother called a widow's walk—and the light was gone, now no more than three dimly lit candles in an upstairs room. He walked over, and looking inside noticed his father still sprawled drunkenly across the bed. Except...except that room and the world it represented had assumed a strange narrow-looking tilt.

He turned away, gazing over the endless fields below, and though they were as green as any he'd ever seen there was also something...*different* about them. He was still wondering what it might be when he was startled by the dark figure of a man at the far end of the balcony, his shadow stretched long by the lamp of the late evening sun. He wore a long black coat and a wide-brimmed hat with greasy hair spilled from underneath, stopping somewhere near the middle of his back. Despite his appearance, there was some intrinsic gentleness about the man—some *kindness*—that told Chase he was safer here than back in that narrow world with his father.

The man looked at him, his too-thin lips curved in the beginnings of a smile.

"Looks like a full moon tonight," he said, pointing to the stars. For a moment he stared across the sky, past the few scattered clouds and into the perfect circle that had risen and now shone ominously through the deep blush of twilight. He asked, "You're Chase, right?"

"That's right," Chase answered. "How'd you know?"

The stranger cast an amused look. "You don't remember me, do you? Chase, I've known you since the day you were born—sooner than that, really. Remember that time you got Rocky Mountain spotted fever and had to spend a week in the hospital?"

Chase nodded solemnly.

"Sure," he said. "Mama says they thought I was gonna die, all because of one lousy tick."

"That's right, they did. And did you know I was there that whole time, right by your side? But then you were sleeping through most of that, so I would assume you don't. Your daddy…he sure was tore up about you."

Chase glanced down at his feet, almost ashamed, and for a moment the man was quiet.

"Come here," he said, and together they moved to the nearest window, staring inside as a narrow Saul Jessup snoozed away in his narrow world. "Believe it or not, your father is a very special man, Chase. Did you know that? If anything were to happen to you, why, he'd be very upset. It would crush him."

"*Right*," Chase said. "I guess that's why he treats me the way he does."

A slight smile creased the man's face. "Oh, don't blame him," he said, "that's only because he doesn't understand how to show his own love. But that's what it is, no bones about it. *Love*. And just that one little smidgen of it has made him stubborn, more stubborn than we'd have ever thought. But then we've dealt with stubbornness before, many times, and we know just what to do to make him come around, to make him a…*willing vessel*. Then, when he's finally ready, we'll call him out. And it'll be all because of you, Chase."

Chase looked up at the man—with his long black hair and ghastly pallid face, a fiery sort of glee burning in his eyes—and for the first time felt a pang of fear. "What do you mean?"

"We expected more from your father, Chase…and one way or another, we'll get it." The stranger turned then, an awful grin creeping over his lips. "*See*," he said, "*we have to put a fire under his ass…*"

And staring back, Chase recognized that eerie grin as one he'd seen only once before—and that stretched across his father's drunken face. He turned to run and felt a firm hand latch on his back, and when at last the grip was too tight and Chase called out, there was no one there to hear him. A sudden rush of pleasure went coursing through the dark man's being, through his endless blackened spirit and a body nowhere near as human as it looked.

He would have fun with this one, he decided.

It had been a long time since he'd had fun.

A long time since he'd felt so *alive…*

Chapter 31

"**D**oug, I thought you said ten *o'clock*..."

"Shut up, Gary. Okay? She's gonna call when they're ready, so chill the fuck out."

Gary grumbled something and tried taking another sip from his cup, but couldn't make it happen. After a final attempt he offered the cup to Doug, who wasted no time putting it down.

Pushing back his frustration, Doug took a seat on a nearby stump and tapped away at his phone. He noticed a call a few days earlier from a number he didn't recognize, and without thinking hit SEND. Three rings later a gentleman at least twice as tipsy as himself came on the line and, following a somewhat blurred exchange, Doug discovered the call had come from a payphone in some bar he'd never heard of nor cared to visit; it didn't take long for an image of his father to come dancing into his head, followed by a frazzled sort of melancholy that sent his feet in search of another drink.

He'd stumbled in that direction when his phone rang, and snapping it up he heard Nicky's voice on the other end. Yes, Sissy's parents were in bed. Yes, come over now. They would be waiting in the backyard. Doug hung up, had started two steps toward the house when he felt his perception collapse in a sudden ruthless tailspin, stopping him dead in his tracks. He hovered there a moment, positive reality had been caught up in some mystical burnout—spinning perpetually but never going anywhere—and waiting for the feeling to pass. It never did.

Boy, was he tore up.

But none of that mattered, not tonight, and was quickly forgotten as Doug snatched up his cup and continued toward the house.

▲ ▲ ▲

"So what do you think?"

"I don't know, Doug. Not gonna lie, I'm feeling pretty buzzed here." Brent stood back, posturing as he paused to light a cigarette and blow smoke to the stars. "I guess driving's not really something I feel like doing right about now."

"C'mon Brent, it's just down the street, you know?"

Brent looked away. As it happened, his eyes fell on the girl whose ass he'd had his hands glued to a little earlier. He curled a lip in her direction before turning back to Doug and saying, "Hey, look, why don't you ask around a bit? Ask Jesse, or Larry Gaskins. Or that guy Matt, ask him. You said yourself it's not that far, they'll probably give you a lift."

They looked at each other, and in that moment Doug knew the score was settled. Of course it was; he'd pretty much figured this would happen. Why else had he put it off? But it was no use; the Great Brent had spoken. Doug didn't like it, it wasn't fair, but there it was, and there was nothing under heaven he could do about it. *Go on, Brent. Go on and plow the girl, 'cause that's all you're thinking about anyway. Never mind me.*

"Sorry, man."

Doug said all right, said fine, but when he walked away there was a certain stiffness to his walk that he couldn't ignore. He grabbed another cup of PJ, chugging down some swallows before finding Gary and tugging at his shirt: "C'mon."

"Where are we going?"

"C'mon, Gary."

He dragged Gary past the house, through the yard to the long, darkened acre of the impromptu parking lot. Ignoring Gary's usual spat of dumbass questions, Doug scoured the line of vehicles, his eyes stopping on a clustered mash-up of bicycles near the front. He walked over, dropping his hands over a pair of handlebars.

"Go on, what are you waiting for?" he said. "Grab one, Gary, let's go."

Gary didn't move. "I don't know Doug…"

"Listen, we're staying the night here, right?" he said. "Well, probably these people are too. So it's not like they're leaving. And like I said—we'll be *right* back, they won't even know the bikes are gone. I just want to see Nicky for one hour."

"No way," Gary objected. "Who knows how long it would take just to ride these junked-up things over there, we can't stay an hour. Besides, you're drunk. Twenty minutes tops."

"All right, twenty minutes."

Gary hesitated. "I don't know…"

Doug sensed the first touch of fire crowding on his face. "Gary, it's no big deal, man. Just hop on and let's go…"

Gary shook his head. "No. No way, Doug. Look at you, you're wasted."

Doug glared back, face filled with something Gary had never noticed there before, his eyes bloodshot and hair tousled and his face a darker shade of red—in that second, Doug Lunsmann looked *crazy*. A funny nervousness crept into Gary's stomach.

"Fine," Doug said. He grabbed a bike, popped the kickstand, sat on the seat. "Go on back to the house then, Gary. Go on and talk to some more geriatrics, see if you can get that woman with her Klingon face to touch your leg. I'm leaving."

There was a moment of silence as the two boys gazed at one another, each silently questioning what role the other would eventually come to play in their lives, if any. Doug shrugged and shook his head, had started to wheel away when he heard the gentle creak of a kickstand, the sound of two tires crunching over gravel, and turned to see Gary Northrup gliding forward from the too-wide seat of a cruiser bike.

"Wait up, Doug!" he called after him. "Just wait the hell up for me you crazy bastard!"

Chapter 32

Saul tossed his latest can into the garbage and grabbed another from the fridge.

He'd finished the first case an hour before and now was drunk and could feel that old slick emotion worming its slow way to his heart. Soon—he wasn't sure when, but he'd know when the time came; he always did—he'd gather what little was left of himself and lumber it up the stairs. *It's that time of the month*, he thought with a smile, and even a case of Pabst couldn't cool the excitement he felt burning inside.

It would be good tonight, he thought. There was something in the air, some little spark that told him how merciless life had been to him, and to his son, and what an integral part he now played in making sure life dealt just as viciously with others. Take any wild animal, for instance, and let it roam free, unburdened by death, and eventually the entire ecosystem is threatened. The real world is no different, and that's why you needed men such as himself—*equalizers* to help hedge in the lowlifes and control the population, and to stimulate karma's uncanny bent for natural selection. Man, after all, is the most feral beast of nature's kingdom, and left to himself would pave an open freeway straight to hell.

Being an equalizer, he knew, was not so much a job as a calling—and one Saul shouldered reverently. There was no denying the white-knuckled thrill of destiny which coursed through his veins whenever he did his thing, and he knew it was God alone who had appointed him to do it. Who else could perform such wondrous acts? What other Force had handpicked the recipients and then delivered them to Saul to be judged, as he himself had been judged?

It was because of Chase, he knew, that he'd been chosen. Saul would never forgive himself for what happened to his son, even if he'd never known exactly what that was. He'd had a million bright ideas on the subject, each more horrid than the last, and yet none had proved particularly appealing. His son was dead, that much he knew—even Mariah had known that—and he was dead because Saul Jessup had been too busy being a lush to be a father. That unknown planet through the upstairs window was a reminder of the fact, as it had been for the past twenty years, and as affirmation of this Saul found he could enter it only after humbling himself in the very shame that had lost him his son—that is, through his own damnable thirst for escaping this world. And so it was that all who came to him did so through this same door, to suffer in their bodies as he had suffered in his soul.

Yes, he'd witnessed the cruelty of this world first hand. First he'd played victim to it and now would be the one to dole it out. He'd crafted the head-stone—FORGIVENESS IS NOT ENOUGH—to remind him of that, of his sole purpose on this earth, and now every month when he was called to do his work he would go there and do it out of reverence for the son he'd lost.

Saul stared grimly into the walls, rolling over the memories in his head. He'd been looking forward to tonight, to taking a break from this old body and crawling into something a little more comfortable. He raised the beer to his mouth, and when it was empty he stepped into the kitchen and a slant of moonlight washed through the curtain, catching him squarely on the chest. Something shifted inside him, and the can dropped to the floor. This sensation had become a familiar one in the past twenty years, and heeding its call as any obedient soldier of God would, Saul Jessup turned on his heels and started up the stairs.

Chapter 33

The thrill of it carried them, pushing the boys forward like padawan banshees from the bowels of hell. That lasted maybe ten minutes, until at last Doug's stomach felt like a blender of rotten eggs and Gary needed more air than his soft body could supply. So they cooled their jets and took a breath, and a mile later spotted the Chevron station up ahead.

Then the station passed and the bright lights faded and civilization slowly crumbled to trees. Porch lights blinked shut, only to be replaced with the neon flash of animal's eyes, the occasional swarm of lightning bugs. A deafening clatter of frogs filled the air. A sign appeared, tucked away beyond a reach of loblolly pines: WELCOME TO LANCER COUNTY.

"Doug, you said three miles," Gary groaned. "I don't even see *houses* anymore, how much farther?"

"Not much farther," Doug told him, hoping it was the truth.

A quarter mile later they'd turned a curve when they spotted the glow of headlights up ahead. "*Car!*" Gary called, and together they veered to the shoulder as the lights drew closer, breaking around the bend. Doug raised his arm, hoping to shield the glare but losing his grip instead, handlebars twisting and sending him crashing to the gravel at the side of the road.

"Doug! Get up!"

But already the car was upon them, headlamps blaring down as Doug pulled himself up and, in a flash of inspiration, loudly compared the driver to a rectum and held up one not-so-ferocious-looking middle finger. Then another feeling, a sudden nausea as the car whizzed past and Doug caught the logo on the driver's-side door, blue on white. Last of all he made out the lightbars on top the roof and by now his mouth was dry and his hands were gripped into fists.

He glanced over, saw Gary straddling the seat of his bike up ahead.

"Doug, get uuu-up!" he called. *"Friggin' coppos!"*

They watched as the cruiser rolled carelessly down the pavement, a silent figure in the darkness. Doug waited, waited, waited, not moving until suddenly the brake lights burned red and all the air was pushed from his lungs. Watching scenes from a movie, he only stared as the car whipped viciously and spun around, tires squealing softly as the cruiser roared to life.

Then came the lights.

Doug leapt to his feet, hauling up the Roadmaster after him and quickly closing the gap between Gary and himself. The air whizzed past his face, singing a sweet melody until at last Gary had fallen behind in that terrible world at his back and Doug heard the endless revving of the cruiser's engine; soon he was touched by the first flash of colored light, casting an ominous glare across the trees.

And that was enough. Without thinking he hopped from his bike, jumping the small ditch between the road and the trees with an agility he would've previously thought impossible. He pushed on faster, faster through the pines, not stopping, a fresh batch of terror washing up his legs at the sudden crunch of footsteps from behind. Still he kept forward, pushing on until soon the flashing lights had faded and the footsteps were gone and now the forest was dark, filled only with the desperate roar of the frogs.

Creep-creeeaaap. Creep-creeeaaap. Creep-creeeaaaaappp.

Minutes later he slowed to catch his breath, and was still stumbling along through the darkness when he spotted a break in the poplars up ahead, the bright drape of stars just beyond. He drew closer, still struggling for breath, until at last the forest ended and Doug took his first step onto bright red sand.

His eyes fell lazily on the shape of a house in the distance, and three flames burning gently, like hearth light, from inside. There was something odd about that light, he decided, something he couldn't quite put a finger on. His memory squirmed, some cold finger of despair working gently up his spine and bringing on a shiver as he silently studied the house; staring,

Doug couldn't help but wonder at its solemn beauty against the moon, at its oddly welcoming warmth and promise of rest for wearied souls, and as he did so all those former feelings slipped away and an ethereal calm settled over his mind.

He started in that direction…

Chapter 34

Mike heard footsteps.

He jerked at the sound, his arm almost striking the empty bottle of Jack and sending it off into the wall; had that happened, he couldn't imagine Jessup's reaction at finding a drunken man in a sling at the back of his bedroom closet.

Whatever it would be, Mike didn't want to find out.

He crept forward, and through the slats saw Jessup stumbling wearily across the room, his face showing that same glazed-over look Mike had witnessed in his own mirror too many times before. Only there was something else—something more than just the gross inebriation—as if Jessup were being drawn, fished out by some unknowable desire...

As he watched, the room blossomed with a sudden explosion of light, coloring the walls in an eerie blue that called up images of the deepest ocean. Mike flinched, nails digging spastically into his palm as he fumbled for that handy-dandy mental cube from hours before, eager to cram; presently that box was nowhere to be found, however, and instead he only stared as Jessup's withered frame approached the window and was swallowed by the softly shimmering light. His skin glowed, brimming with a sudden translucence that showed he truly was a man of flesh and blood; had he been afforded the time, Mike could've counted the number of veins trailing the old geezer's body, each squirming worm-like against the backdrop of that horrible neon glow. He watched with wonder as Jessup faded slowly through the mist, his body bending incongruously as it was snapped from the floor and into the brilliant radiance beyond.

And then was gone.

The light faltered once and began to shrink, collapsing quietly in on itself. Soon, Mike knew, it would appear as three burning flames in an upstairs room, no different from any of the other myriad candles one could witness in windows across the nation.

He opened the door and stepped out.

CHAPTER 35

Saul eased onto the balcony, a familiar fire thrilling his veins as his sallow skin grew tight over his bones, as the arthritis faded and sobriety settled like a veil over his mind. His hearing was back, his sight superb. The first stirrings of an erection rumbled in his jeans.

He stepped left to the next window and ducked inside, grabbing up his usual fixed-blade Buck and Ruger twenty-two. These had been his standards for the past two years, and he cherished each for the work they did: capable weapons of the warfare he had been chosen to wage. With his trusty rifle strapped over one shoulder and the knife tucked safely at his belt, Saul returned to the window and stepped outside.

The moon shone like a bleached beach ball as he paced on the ledge, his young heart racing. Glancing over he noticed his kiddos from the month before, still dangling from the oak, their bodies flayed and what remained looking more like something that belonged in the tail-end of a meat truck than carousing the halls of a high school. At the end of the night, once their replacements had arrived, these would be pulled down and tossed to the chickens; by this time next month, their carcasses would be indistinguishable from any of the other collapsed skeletons scattered over the grounds. Until then they gleamed softly in the night, almost shining, and after a final savoring gaze Saul turned and—

His lips peeled back in a knowing grin.

The grin only grew wider as he stepped forward and got a better look at his prey—he was young, Saul noticed, and the young ones were always fun. The drinking was still new to them, and when that first bullet passed through one end and out the other, he'd known some to break into delirious rows of laughter. This one was a walker, and the walkers he gave a little more time. Oftentimes he liked peering deep into their eyes before pulling the trigger, searching maybe for traces of the son he'd lost so long ago, or maybe just turning thoughts of what dirty deed these peckerheads had done to deserve the likes of him. Not that it mattered, of course.

It all ended the same.

Saul licked his lips and raised the rifle. His heart was jumping, a high and steady rhythm. He smiled darkly, anticipating the sudden thrill of ecstasy which was better than any woman, better than what any woman could provide. His finger tightened on the trigger and—

"Drop it, Saul. Nice and easy."

▲ ▲ ▲

Mike steadied his grip, struggling to adjust to these new conditions he'd stepped into. It wasn't like the other times, he realized—that is, he wasn't wasted.

In fact, he was completely sober.

Only there was some other feeling, as well, an exhilaration he'd never felt before; his skin felt tight and his clothes felt loose, his shattered arm healed. Even his eyes seemed sharper, without the fuzz, and were now zeroed in on the man with the crew-cut hair and the big floppy ears. He trained the pistol on Jessup's head.

"You heard me, Saul! I said drop it!"

Jessup turned, and as he did so Mike eased out of the sling and tossed it from the ledge; it fluttered once in a wind that wasn't there and drifted to the earth.

"Make one move," Mike warned, "and I'll blow that smirk right off your face."

Jessup stepped back, holding out the gun in one hand.

"Easy, now," he said, stepping closer. "Not so sure you want to do that, stranger. Why don't we just talk this—"

Mike fired.

The blast echoed like a cannonball over the fields; Jessup's rifle was flung from his hands, hitting the balcony floor. Mike focused his aim, ready for an impulsive assault; but Jessup merely stared back, that sly grin still pasted to his oversized chin.

"Nice shot, cowboy. For your own sake, I hope—"

"Shut your mouth. Now, down on your knees."

"Oh, so that's how you want it? Sorry, boss man, but I don't swing that way—"

Mike fired again, blowing a quarter-sized hole into Jessup's palm. His eyes darkened and a low whistling rose in his throat, exploding in a tight roar of fury.

Mike yelled, "On your knees!"

Jessup dropped to his knees.

"You know," Mike said, "I should've known it was you, Saul. Some wasted old couch-comber with nothing better to do than sit around and let his mind go to cabbage. Tell me, how many have you killed so far? Do you even know? And how long have you been at this anyway? Long time, I'll bet. Since Chase died, am I right?"

Jessup's face became a strange grimace of disgust. His head tilted, first to the right, then the left, a curious gleam worming softly into his eyes. "Who are you, stranger?"

"Let's just say I'm the one that got away, Saul. And now I've come back to bite you in the ass. Maybe I'll hang you from that tree over there, how about that? But not before I rip the skin from your bones, you sick bastard."

Saul was nodding profusely. "You think I'm scared a you? With that little knuckle-launcher?" He laughed. "Take a look around, Texas. Where do you think you are? This is *my* world, shit-heel."

"Is that right? Tell me this then, Saul—whattaya think would happen if I put this damn lampstand out for good, huh? What would that mean? 'Cause you and me, we can stay locked in this hellhole forever far as I'm concerned." Mike took a step toward the window. "You wanna hang out with me, Saul? You wanna be my friend?"

His fingers inched toward the candles, creeping closer and closer until something caught his eye and Mike glanced over, staring into the pane of glass to his left. What he saw there turned his blood to ice in his veins, and suddenly Mike understood why it was he felt the way he did.

Chapter 36

Doug pushed forward, eyes trained on those oddly calming lights up ahead. Soon he could make out the fluttering forms of chickens, some pecking idly across the yard, others jumping wildly and nipping at shadows hung from a sprawling oak at the side of the house. Coming closer he noticed two figures on the upstairs balcony, their slim shadows back-lit by the soothing glow of candlelight. He picked up his pace, struggling closer toward the towering columns of the porch when a sudden blast of gunfire tore across the night.

Doug froze, and for not the first time in his life wished he could somehow close his eyes and simply vanish, be whisked away to some better place; but that wasn't happening, not tonight, and instead a terrible gray feeling stole into his heart. The feeling was darkened by the noise of another blast, this time followed by howling, and suddenly Doug found himself running.

He headed for the small copse of trees to the right of the house and ducked inside. He reached for his cell phone, had dialed Nicky's number when—

We're sorry but your call cannot be completed—

He gripped the phone in both hands, as if hoping to squeeze out a miracle. When that didn't happen he turned back to the house, watching as the figures danced back and forth on the ledge. Then came the third shot and he'd almost convinced himself to flee, to just turn and run and never look back. Only there was something about that man with his scruffy-curled hair and landing-strip sideburns that gave him pause, something that reminded Doug in some strange way of himself...

Mike stared in horror at the reflection before him, and for a moment could not believe his eyes. Thick muttonchops were slathered down the sides of his face; his hair was bushy, curling at the ears, his face too thin, and gazing at it Mike's mind moved back to all the years he'd worn this unlikely mask as his own. He was a somebody in those worlds, an up-and-comer, a man of promise, and churning up in him now those feelings felt dubious and foreign.

In those worlds, he'd known it all.

He'd only been staring a moment when he turned and saw Jessup moving in, a large fixed-blade knife in one hand. The blade buried itself in Mike's leg, and when his gun shivered once and spat, he knew the shot was wide. He toppled to one knee, was about to pop off another when Jessup's foot passed in a whizzing arc before his face, knocking the pistol from his hand.

In the next second he was on his back and Saul dug in, pounding fist after fist into Mike's face and throwing wild haymakers that rocked his skull and sent spools of blood from his nose. He was stronger than Mike would've guessed, their youth thrown in the balance and Mike found wanting. Saul ripped the knife from his leg, though not at the angle it had went in, and Mike called out with such agony the voice seemed unnatural even to himself; a second later he felt the sharp point pushing in on his throat.

"I ought to slay your ass right now," Jessup breathed. He jammed the knife deeper, and a spark of blood appeared, attaching itself to the blade.

Then the blade was gone and Mike felt a hand rummaging through his pockets. Then that was gone too, and when he looked next Jessup was flipping through a wallet.

"Officer Michael Lunsmann," he proclaimed. "Hammond Po-lice Department. Well, fancy that—a real-life lawman right here in my little slice of paradise. You know, I've had peons like you sniffing up my leg for years, but you're the first that's ever made it through."

He turned the wallet in his hands, flipping back and forth until something caught his eye and Saul stopped. He glanced at Mike—then back to the wallet—to Mike again. His face scrunched up.

"Well, I'll be damned. Is that you, McFatAss? Didn't recognize you without all that blubber on your face. Tractor my ass—I shoulda seen you coming." For a moment his eyes went serious, considering—just a flash, and then it was gone. "Oh, well. Don't matter. See, 'cause like I told you before—this is my rodeo, sheriff. *My* rules. And guess what? According to my rules your face is spaghetti, pal, you're done for. How's that sound?"

Mike opened his mouth, closed it. There were a thousand tiny insects burrowing into his leg, and each had a taste for human flesh. Visions flashed through his mind, too many to count, and more than the pain he found himself frozen by *fear*: unable to move, cowering at the image of being slowly butchered and sacrificed to whatever sick god this maniac might serve.

Jessup strolled forward, gathering up the gun he'd knocked from Mike's hand and then walking to his own. He lifted the rifle, examined it. "You chipped my walnut stock," he said petulantly, then lowered the barrel and fired, leaving a splintered scar in the board inches from Mike's head. Saul whistled the close call and then made his way past Mike and over to the far window, draping one leg inside. "Now you sit tight while I go bag me a young'un, hear? Your she-nanigans done put me behind, Mike, now who knows where the little pecker-head's run off to?" A cool little grin. "I'll find him though…I always find 'em."

"Killing them," Mike sputtered, "that'll never bring your son back, never bring back your wife. Don't you understand that, Saul?"

Jessup's face went hard, assuming a stony-eyed glare that made his skull seem somehow thicker than it actually was, like a helmet. In his eyes Mike could still detect the faded scrawl of age, a depth forged by the slow hammer of time…only there was something else there as well. Something cold and calculating and with no room for any warmth, no love, no fuzzy feelings of compassion but only that crafty snake-wisdom gleaming darkly within.

"You know what it's like to lose a son?" he asked. "Do you, Mike? To know that you have everything to do with why he's not alive right now, to carry that kind of thing around with you?" Mike thought of Dougie, thought of how he'd had the chance to be a father once and how he'd blown it. Just as his own father had blown it with him. *A series of examples*, Mike thought, not understanding the phrase. "I'll never forgive myself for that," Saul said, "be-cause see that would be asking too much. I don't deserve forgiveness—and neither do all the other deadbeats of the world. I'll teach 'em about loss just like I was taught myself, and when I'm done they'll know what it means to have regret. To have scars that never heal."

"Sure, Saul. Woe to the fragile human condition. Fuck 'em all, am I right?"

Jessup smiled grimly. "That's right, sheriff. You wear your badge, and I'll wear mine."

And with that he was gone, ducking once more through the open window. He returned a moment later, a coil of rope draped in one hand. Took his first steps onto the balcony but by then it was too late and he was met by the solid weight of Mike's body, victim of a running tackle that sent the two of them reeling backwards. They crashed to the floor and Jessup scrambled, struggling to free himself from the tangle of rope—and now it was Mike's turn to lay it down, swinging hard and catching him across the nose. The next one landed just over the eye, followed by another left hook, and by the time Jessup had shaken the rope his face shone like a cracked vase against the moon. He reached down and Mike saw a sudden sheen of light and thrust himself forward, staying the knife before it could go forth and rend its dirty damage.

They struggled, tipping back and forth across the ledge until suddenly Mike felt a warm finger digging, twisting into the wound in his leg. He leaned forward, clamping his teeth hard on Jessup's nose; there was a tiny squishy-crunching sound, and as if by magic the finger vanished from Mike's leg and the knife hit the deck.

At that moment he noticed the rifle Saul had left leaning on the balustrade. Both men scrambled forward, no more than two shadows rushing in the night, two mammals running a race only one could ever win, a race where second place was as good as last, and last place left you dead. Then Mike had it, the stock cool in his hands as he snapped it up and—

Sudden fire went scorching through his chest.

Mike reeled backwards, the rifle dropping like an anvil from his hands. He met the balustrade and it gave way, spilling him in a sudden freefall over the edge. Seconds, minutes, hours later he landed with a crunch, chickens clucking wildly as they scrambled through the dirt. Above them Saul Jessup emerged on the balcony ledge, one hand still gripping the forty-five that went in the holster on Mike's shoulder. A cold smile wrapped his face.

"Feel that?" he called. "See, that's the evil being purged from your body. *Exorcised.*"

Mike hardly heard him. His legs were numb, there was a ball of glass rolling around in his chest, and every time he took a breath the ball got a little bigger. His breathing had scaled back to gasps, and even these were too short for comfort. Everything seemed wrapped in a fog.

At the top of the ledge, Jessup tucked away the pistol and lifted the Ruger in his hands. There was a thin popping sound, and Mike felt a twinge of pressure in his right leg. Another pop and this one entered his stomach, lighting him on fire; Mike writhed, twisting and turning and only at the last second noticing a familiar object buried in the sand only yards away...

"Don't fight it, sheriff," Saul called. "In ancient days when disease swept through a village, sure there was death and tears and all sorts of fear...but when it was over there was great celebration, see, because really it was a *cleansing* influence. *Purification.* They knew that."

Mike stole another glance, struggling to jog loose whatever thing this was he'd lost in his mind. Then the tiny roar of motors in his ears, rushing toward him in the night, the flash of a four-wheeler, and at last it came to him: *his Glock.* Of course, his Glock, the gun he'd lost so long ago, knocked from his hands by T.J. Chadwick and his speeding Banshee. Still here, somehow it was still here and if he could only pull himself over and...

"Now we've got all fancy with ourselves, thinking there's no place for suffering in our world! We've given up on misery, but misery hasn't given up on us! We do everything we can to get away from her—run to all the pleasures the world has to offer—and behind every one there she hides, waiting to come out and make herself known..."

Mike inched forward, the blood and sand and sweat all mixing down his face as he raised one arm, flopping it deliriously to the ground over his head.

Not even close.

Then another pop, and this time the fire was in his hand. He drew it back and from somewhere far away noticed his finger—the small one—had been replaced by a bloody stump pumping thick crude toward the sky. The pain hit him like a punch, swelling up inside. Mike blinked, unable to move as he sensed the life slipping like a cool wind from his body and—

And suddenly the figure emerged, appearing from the shadows at the side of the house. There was something in his hands, and no sooner had Mike realized what it was than three blasts roared across the night. Three blasts, but it was the first that entered Jessup's skull and sent him spinning on the ledge, turning his body a lithe one hundred eighty degrees. Finally his legs crumbled, limply giving way as he breached the balustrade and tumbled over the side; he fell awkwardly, splashing to the earth in a clumsy head-dive that cracked his neck as it fed violently into the dirt. His snake-eyes faded, lips parting in a final sigh to the world as his body settled in the dust, a contortionist performing a trick gone terribly wrong; then only silence.

Mike looked to the figure stumbling toward him across the sand.

Shadows played over his face, mixing with the fog of Mike's own pain until at last the features shone clear and Mike sensed the tears rolling from his eyes.

"Son…"

Doug stared back, his young face wrapped in an expression void of all sense and understanding…but then he'd heard the two men, had heard every word, and deep down knew that it was true.

"Dad? Is that…is that you?"

Mike only nodded, still struggling for breath. And while he'd wondered at first, he knew there was no need in anyone telling him how Dougie had gotten here; if he'd found nothing else over the past three months, he'd at least discovered that—the one thing that made this train run.

Besides, he could smell it on his breath.

"But *how?*" Doug asked, studying the thick muttonchops down the sides of his face, the slender waist buried beneath a too-big jacket. "Dad, I don't understand—"

"*It's not important,*" Mike managed, and something in the words sent Doug's eyes working once more, this time over the great splotches of blood on his father's chest, the finger that wasn't there on his hand. A streak of panic stole into his face, cracking it into a thousand pieces, and as the pieces fell he dropped his head and began pleading with his father, begging him to *please don't die, please please don't die.* But not even Doug in his drunken state could be taken by such fantasy, and so they only held each other and wept, forgiving trespasses and uttering the regrets that had been running on a circuit ever since that first schism had spilt them apart...though by now neither could remember precisely what that schism was.

When it was done, Mike explained as best he could what had to happen, and how it had to happen. If he was right, not only would it arrive his son safely back home—just as Mike had returned from his previous trip—but would ensure that nothing like this ever happened again, at least not here. There was some question as to what would happen to Mike himself but, considering his current condition, that bit of worry didn't seem worthy of his time.

When he'd finished, Doug stared down with renewed respect at the man who would one day become his father. And though he could see that older man buried somewhere deep in this one's eyes, he couldn't help but think that maybe his father would be waiting for him after all, waiting back in the world Doug had stumbled out of and was hopefully heading back to. Only this time that man would be worthy of his time, worthy of all the sacred, trivial things Doug had taken from him the hour he decided Mike Lunsmann was a liability, a vaguely familiar face with no discernable purpose in his life.

"*Here,*" Mike blubbered. "*Use this...*"

He reached down into the pocket sown into the lining of his jacket, revealing the brown paper bag. He lifted what was inside, the plastic bottle miraculously still intact, and as Doug took it in his arms the Everclear glistened sharply against the moon, seeming to glow.

Doug glanced up and saw three yellow flames, like hearth light, still burning in the upstairs window. Without wanting to, slowly his eyes slid to Saul Jessup, now no more than a rag-doll body collapsed in the sand. At last he looked to his father, though in this light the man seemed more like an older brother...or a best friend.

"*Go,*" his father told him. "*Go, Doug...*"

They embraced, and when he rose Doug, too, was covered in blood and the first touch of sobriety had moved into his face. He grabbed the Glock and ran past thick Doric columns to the front porch, climbing the steps and bursting through the door. For a moment he paused, observing the strange, trashy elegance of the living room to his left, the furniture moldering and remarkably out of style. Then it was up the stairs, and topping the rise Doug saw golden light spilling from a room down the hall. Suddenly there seemed to be a thousand sinister things waiting for him down that hall, what sorts of things he didn't know—things with teeth, probably.

He crept forward, his father's gun gripped tight in one hand and the plastic bottle in the other. Entering the room moments later, his eyes swept past an old four-poster bed and then over to the window; he stood frozen, only staring as the candles burned bright against a moonlit sky and danced shadows across the walls. Past the flames he noticed the ruddy expanse of earth before him, the land spotted with crumbled cars and the bones of men who no longer breathed. Finally his gaze shifted to the lampstand itself, the ornate metalwork gleaming softly and covered in silent monsters with some secret to tell and a strange language long since dead to the world.

He stepped closer, not understanding his own dark emotions but knowing that his understanding was not what mattered. What mattered was doing what his father told him.

Another step, and now he could feel the subtle warmth of it crawling up his face.

He twisted the cap and the smell of Everclear floated up, filling his nose. One more step and now the bottle was raised and the window erupted in flames. He backed slowly out of the room and the swell of flames followed, trailing him like an obedient dog on a leash. No sooner had the inferno started, however, than he felt a peculiar tingling at the center of his stomach, a sensation which only grew worse as he continued down the hall.

He tracked down the stairs, transforming the stairwell into a cascading wall of smoke and flames. He was pushing through the living room when suddenly the tingling became too much, engulfing his chest, and Doug doubled over, fumbling the bottle to the floor. Billows of smoke surrounded him, clouding his vision; Doug began to choke and then jumped to his feet, pushing blindly through the flames and out the door and collapsing on the safety of the porch.

He staggered down the steps and into the yard, past those large Doric columns until finally the figure of his father appeared in the distance. For a moment their eyes met, reality slowing to a crawl as one loving gaze passed between them, father and son, two strangers soon to be separated by the impenetrable gulf of time. They'd had fifteen years to forge whatever relationship there was to be had between them, and all at once that time was up and only memory could serve them now. A lazy smile parted on Doug's face, but before it was full he blinked once and suddenly his world was wrapped in a darkness thicker than death.

Chapter 37

He woke in the backseat of a car he'd never seen before.

He sat up, the sun breaching the horizon and spilling gold across the seats and making his world brand new. Only after that first familiar hint of cherry did Doug realize the car was Brent's after all, and that the only thing unrecognizable to him was the night that lay behind.

He climbed out and stood awhile staring over the grounds of Abilene Plantation, its covered-in-trash yard and empty stages and cup-littered porch looking less like a good time than the aftermath of a hurricane. More than a few had braved the elements, their sleeping bodies draped over picnic tables or else splayed on blankets across the grass, and for some reason the sight of them sent a shiver straight up Doug Lunsmann's spine.

His head felt like an earthquake, and lighting a menthol he stood for a long time watching the smoke spin circles toward the sky and wondering what he'd been up to the night before, what sort of hell he'd raised and how high the flames had flown. He turned and saw the dwindled pack of bicycles—ten-speeds and sportsters and Panama Jacks—and at last that small portion of the night came creeping back, the dread of it moving like an advancing army on his mind. But had he really taken that ride? Had he really been that *dumb?*

Yes, he had. And now his only fear was that he'd been dumber than this.

He stood awhile debating, running it over and over in his head. But it was no use. That black curtain had only shifted positions, ending now somewhere down the road on the way to Nicky and the promise of true sexual birth. He was still trying to coax forth the other end of that ride when he turned to see

Gary Northrup in a bitter march toward the car, his incessant chatter preceding him across the yard.

"Where the hell have you *been?*" he called. "You asshole, do you have any idea how long I spent looking for you in those woods last night? A long friggin' time, that's how long. And where were *you?* Huh, Doug? I swear, if that cop hadn't…"

Only then a peculiar look came over Gary's face. His eyes bulged and went dim. He walked over, stopping a few feet from where Doug stood puffing his cigarette.

"Doug…you okay, man?"

Following Gary's gaze, Doug glanced down but what he saw seemed incomprehensible, as if he'd been the butt of some practical joke during the night. Only some part of himself knew that wasn't true, wasn't true at all, and instead it was all he could do to stay on his feet as his eyes slipped down the front of his shirt. He touched his face and felt it there too, caked like a second skin. And though the color was a rusty brown and he might've tried to convince himself it wasn't what it seemed—that he'd spent the night wallowing in a puddle of mud, perhaps—he knew exactly what it was. Knew that his Dark Appetite had again gotten the best of him and he'd had a little too much to drink. That because of some mysterious glitch in his mind he'd actually blacked out—yes, him, Doug Lunsmann—and that he was now covered in the crusty remains of what could only be *blood.*

Not his own.

Gary took another step, the fear creeping gently and settling in his eyes. "Doug…what the hell happened to you last night?"

Only there were no answers to that question, none at all, Doug's mind as clueless on the subject as he was on hostage negotiations or the construction of a Harrier jet. And though some clues might fall his way over the long years to come, in the end that night would simply go down as ONE OF THOSE THINGS, soon to be forgotten in the surging onrush of time.

As his son and Gary Northrup hashed out their differences beneath the tranquil warmth of a morning sun, across town Mike watched that same sun—albeit through a slightly different lens—as it mastered the horizon and splayed itself over the reddened acres of earth. It was a miracle, that sunrise, and while he was grateful for having lived long enough to see it, Mike knew it would be his last—that his precious road of fate ended here—and his mind registered this fact with a dull conviction that left him hollow and cold.

Not twenty yards away, the Jessup house had been reduced to a charred pile of rubble, small flags of smoke still waving proudly from its remains. The transformation had been swift: a blaze that lifted high, lighting up the night, and then gradually collapsed in a crash of flames and smoke and ash. Half-buried in the rubble was all that remained of Saul Jessup, an old man trapped in a younger man's skin, and looking at him now Mike felt nothing at all. Far off to his right he spotted the more grisly remains of T.J. Chadwick and his three friends, their figures swinging gently in the breeze, but again his emotions betrayed him; he may as well have been looking at the carnage left behind by some unknowable force of nature. There were a thousand tears to be shed, sure, but not even one of those could ever change the way things were.

Looking closer, Mike noticed a hazy version of the gravestone still planted near the oak. The stone was cast away from him so he couldn't read the epitaph, but then why bother? Those four little words had been inscribed on the wall of his heart and even should he so desire, Mike doubted they could ever be wiped away. Instead, staring at the crude stone brought up images of his own son, and the parting half-grin he'd given before finally being snatched from this world and back where he belonged, back into a world where he was still just an awkward teenager fast on his way to becoming a man.

His son was safe, that much Mike knew—safe and alive—and though his ragged contribution to Doug Lunsmann's life may be over, he was forever grateful for the good times they'd shared. Those memories would live on, even if he wouldn't, and for him that was enough. In a world where less was better than nothing at all and laughter played second fiddle to pain, it was enough, and given the chance he'd do it all again, bumps and bruises and all. Hell, it was worth it. *Life* was worth it.

The sun beat a brutal pressure on his face, pulling sweat from his brow. With slow and deliberate movements, Mike lifted a cigarette from the pack in his pocket. If there'd been another bottle tucked away down there he would've taken that out, too—and for once, he was glad there wasn't. A few feet away a chicken fluttered past him, kicking up dust.

And as his cigarette streamed a ribbon of smoke to the sky and the earth spun its reckless course through space, a long-forgotten song from childhood came drifting into Mike's head. He listened with glassy-eyed wonder, a great swell of memories clamoring up the hill of its sublime light until at last his mouth opened and a long wind forty-three years in the making came rushing up the cavern of his throat, dissipating in the eternal summer glare.

Then it was gone, and Mike Lunsmann's world faded to white.

Chapter 38

Kathleen Covington slid the last of the boxes into place, completing an almost perfect square near one corner of the basement. She stared at the small collection with a hesitant, slightly perturbed glare, as if perhaps Mike himself would pop out of the largest box, cigarette dangling from his lip, a bottle of something in one hand. They'd share their usual dance, him stepping forward, her stepping back, the two never quite touching. He might try for a kiss, depending on the weight of the bottle. Then she'd stuff him back inside and return to the family she'd always wanted and he'd return to the darkness from whence he came.

Only that didn't happen, and it never would. Because Mike was dead.

It had been two months since she'd last sat down at his kitchen table and indulged a cigarette of her own, and since that time he'd managed to find himself one stumper of a hiding place—so good, in fact, that she no longer believed Mike even knew he was there. His rental car—the battered Buick she'd last seen him with—had been discovered near the end of an old logging road, not far from the site of that terrible house fire she'd read about in the papers. Remembering the guarded way Mike had talked about it, Kathleen couldn't help but wonder if his absence had anything to do with the so-called vacation he'd mentioned to her that afternoon. Whether it did or whether it didn't, none of it much mattered, because he was gone and she couldn't bring herself to believe he was ever coming back.

Once the shock had faded and she'd grown accustomed to this fact, Kathleen had set about the task of shutting the doors on whatever rooms in which his fragrance still lingered in her heart. Perhaps sometime in the future she'd open these doors once more, relics to be scorned and praised, but for now they would remain closed.

As if to put the final touches on this sordid trade-off of the heart, Kathleen walked over and placed one hand on the boxes: a kiss through the fingertips, a wave through the soul. These boxes were all that remained of Michael Lunsmann's life, and taking them in had been her final peace offering to a man she'd once loved. Bart said she was keeping faith, that there was nothing wrong with that. That it was a good idea, you know, on account of Doug. Maybe he was right. She hoped he was.

But she didn't believe it.

If only to test her own conviction, she reached out, turning back the flaps of the nearest box. Could these dead bones walk? she wondered. Could these boxes symbolize anything more than what they were—leftovers of a man now departed? She looked inside, waiting for some little light to flicker and tell her yes, that it was so, and instead found herself staring at a stack of notebooks she hadn't noticed before. She lifted the first from the box, getting lost in the faded, zebra-colored design of its cover; there was another just like it underneath. Curious, she opened to the first page and began to read: *Dearest Kat…*

PART FIVE

CHAPTER 39

It had been a long time since Doug Lunsmann had thought about his father. It was not something he was in the habit of doing. The man was dead, after all, had been that way for some time, and so what point was there in thinking about a dead man? None, none at all.

Only it wasn't the fact of his father's death that made him so uncomfortable; it was the sense of *unfinished business* which lingered like a specter over his mind whenever images of his father crept in. More often than not the images were those of Mike Lunsmann collapsed on a hospital bed, his arm pierced and his mind gone, a survivor of whatever mischief his late night in a bottle had brought about. It was the last Doug had ever seen of his father, and though there'd been no body to prove it, he'd known the man was dead the instant he heard the Buick had been discovered empty in some forgotten wood of Lancer County.

So yes, he supposed you could say there'd been no closure in that relationship. Not much in the way of warmth either. Not there towards the end, at least. He'd kicked himself around for a few years about that—and for a long time had liked the way that boot felt on his ass. Then one day he'd gotten a grip and let that shit go and never looked back. He'd entered college and come out the other end with a level head and found a nice-paying job working for the state and an ample apartment in a nice part of town. There was a woman in the next room—a hottie—and he loved her like nothing else. Life was good. So why had his father shown up like this so late at night when things were going so well—and ruined it?

"Doug? I thought you were coming to bed?" Her warm arms slipping nimbly around his shoulders, one hand gliding down his shirt. She kissed him drowsily on the side of his head. "C'mon, babe…"

"I'll be there in a minute," he told her.

"Another drink?"

He looked down at the small glass in one hand. He hadn't even realized it was there.

"Just a nightcap is all. Want one?"

She made a sound. "Better not. I haven't been feeling so good. Think I'm getting sick."

"Even better," he said, "one of these will knock you right out. Why don't—"

"Please, no."

He stared at her reflection in the window. "All right, suit yourself. Go on and get some sleep then. I'm sure you'll feel better in the morning."

She sighed, ruffled his hair and kissed him again on the head.

When she was gone, he finished his glass and poured another. He hadn't drank this way since college, but for some reason it had been easy lately, easy to get lost in that numb cocoon only a few hard knocks could provide. He was drowning out something—he sensed that much—only he didn't know what it was. Or was he just telling himself he didn't know? And why had he *really* offered Katie that drink? Was it really as casual a question as he'd thought, or had there been some deeper reason for it? Some *purpose?*

These thoughts and more as he sat staring into the window over the sink. Framed inside the glass he saw the malformed image of his own reflection, a thing growing ever stranger as time wore on. His hair was longer than ever— too long for his tastes, actually—but also thinning, and he feared that soon he would start balding. A light beard covered the bottom half of his face. His eyes were dead. He lifted the glass to his mouth and let the bourbon slip down, cool and smooth, and in the window the stranger did the same, as if in mockery, his eyes burrowing into Doug's with such untoward vehemence that Doug imagined one arm reaching from the pane and throttling him in his chair. And for one fleeting moment, he wished the fantasy were true. *Please,* he thought, *please let it be true.*

Only that was just the booze talking, wasn't it? That was just his silly emotions tossing mud out the monkey cage of his own mind. Just one man's struggle to deal with the numbing knowledge that he'd brought life into this world, one future father's attempt to stifle the terror that drenched him like a cold rain on this his dark night of the soul.

He took another belt and the world took another step back. Another, and now he could breathe. One last dip and he was almost there. Then he was drunk and the stranger scowled back balefully from the glass, glowering with a vacuity usually reserved for creeps and invalids. For a time Doug held his gaze, wondering what bizarre things lay ahead for this creature in the glass—oh, what terrible wonderful things—before turning to screw the cap on his empty bottle and pushing it to the bottom of the trash. Then it was dark and he was in bed, counting the small hours until morning came to take him away, thrusting him back into a clockwork world.

Later, as Doug Lunsmann's mind slipped from the bedroom and into that other world of dreams, a car rumbled to life outside and started slowly down the street. Behind the wheel sat a man who remembered what better times were like and knew enough than to believe they were ever coming back. His eyes clicked back and forth in his head, two islands perpetually black and untouched by love and not quite of this world, stranded in flesh so pallid as to be translucent. Long hair sprouted from his skull, trailing a slick sheet to his ass.

He drove on through the city, going wherever it was the roads carried him next. The city had changed a lot over the last hundred years, but the game…well, that hadn't changed at all. Actually, it had gotten easier. And it had gotten that way because of one simple fact, something he'd learned early on this planet—namely, that if nothing else humans are a bloated race of malcontents: frail, fickle creatures unworthy of even the lowest grace. They are the silkworms of the universe, spinning their magnificent fabrics of iniquity, boasting in their futility, more than happy to exist in the doldrums as long as they are permitted to believe they had no choice in the matter, and were forced there by another's hand. Yes, he'd seen this city grow from a pis-shole in the mud to the grand marquee it was now, and the only thing that'd changed about the people here was the fashion of the hour—a little less hair on their chins and a little more fat on their bellies and better smells to cover their own stink. Yet their desires remained the same, as dark and hollow and uncomplicated as ever.

His lips parted in a smile which looked unnatural on his face, and when at last the smile had faded his voice opened on a song as ancient as the earth itself. By the time it was through, he'd traveled to the ends of this county and into the next, wheels rolling effortlessly over the pavement as he searched for some warm place to make his own, for a bit of peace in a realm of insufferable hurt, for some common man or woman with an open door and a willing heart.

And, just maybe, a little room to spare.

About the Author

Hamelin Bird is a devoted reader of speculative fiction and has researched his supernatural detective fiction through overnight ride-alongs with local police. He lives and works in North Carolina.

www.hamelinbird.com

CPSIA information can be obtained
at www.ICGtesting.com
Printed in the USA
LVHW032121260221
680048LV00006B/1399